AMY KEEN

Fisher King Publishing

Acknowledgments

I never got my head around writing one of these sections the first time, let alone being able to do it for a second.

A huge thank you to all the wonderful, supportive and motivating people in my life. Your input and kindness has helped me bring this story to life and I love you for it. You know who you are.

Most importantly, thank you so much to everyone who has invested their time in reading Embers and has followed Scarlett and Jake to this point. I hope you love this book and the next stage of their journey as much as I enjoyed creating it. You are making my dreams come true for which I will be forever grateful.

For everyone with a dream

"Just knowing it exists, I know that I must try."

The Siren's Call - D. Hayes

PROLOGUE

I grew more painfully aware of how much deeper we were going which meant I was losing track of how to get out. The air further down was damper and the putrid scent of the death housed in the rooms all around us was lingering, haunting the maze like a horde of ghosts.

ESCAPE

Please stop. Please stop. I don't want to die.

In childhood, I thought courage was holding back tears when I was in pain, or looking under my bed before I went to sleep at night. Now, after everything, I knew courage could take many forms. Right now, it was having the confidence and self-assurance to look up at an alien sky and feel only the overwhelming surge of possibility, not fear. Yeah, I wasn't finding that so easy.

The landing gear hit the tarmac with a thud so low and deep it reverberated through my core. I felt the air in my lungs compress; I was pinned against the leather seat while the plane braked, its hulk groaning and creaking with resistance. That sensation; I had experienced it before, it was an unwelcome nod to the time I was paralyzed, pinned into position by something invisible. Fear had been as dangerous then as the drugs they had plied me with; it seeped into your organs and disabled you, one vessel at a time, and if you didn't stop it you were lost to it. I refused then and this damned plane was no match for that situation. I blinked slowly in time with low breaths through the g-force feeling. Please stop. Please don't hurtle me into the terminal. I want to live. I glanced to my right and Mr. Glasses-Keeps-Himself-To-Himself was still reading; his bifocals perched peculiarly low on his hooked nose – clearly mine was a solitary fear.

My mind chose that exact moment to dredge up that fateful time seven months before. I hadn't known it then, or hadn't wanted to acknowledge it, but that was when I really knew everything had changed. Funny that; it wasn't the near-death experience, the almost constant police detail that inched daily by our house in the weeks that followed; but that moment on the bridge, the vision when I saw his desire, no, compulsion – that was when I knew I needed to leave, at least for a while.

Jake had begged me to wait for him, but I was answering some silent call from my soul to do it, to show courage when really the easiest thing in the world and the thing I wanted most was to hide in whatever the adult equivalent of curling up under a comforter was.

Just the day before I had been in something like that kind of safe-haven; on his bed, my arms draped over him, being lulled into submission by his very being. His smell, the sound of his heartbeat gently pulsing under his shirt. I had been ignoring the low rumbling sound within my head that caused my vision to throb and pulse, I resisted the urge to tap into it and open my mind. I didn't trust it or the way it gnawed at my consciousness and made the air in my nostrils metallic and musty. I knew I was fighting something away, rejecting some other sight or sound meant for me, but I didn't want to lose the now, not on my last night with him. It would come back. It always did; the start was an irreversible chain reaction of events that couldn't be halted. If a vision was coming for me, it would seek me out like an expert hunter, hiding in the shadows and stalking my movements until it found a weak spot, a lull in my concentration or energy. Then it would strike. It hadn't arrived that night, or on the plane, but it was still there in that corner of my mind now reserved for my more unusual skills and it throbbed like a second heartbeat growing louder all the while.

I shook my head from the sensory headlock and focused on Jake.

Three weeks was a long time to go without him, the constant he had become and that mouth, how would I be OK without that mouth? Those kisses.

I recalled his wicked smile as he had squeezed my body against his. We had been lying in silence for what felt like hours, both ignoring the elephant in the room because I was due to leave the next day and then there would be twenty-one days where we would go without each other. Twenty-one days where I couldn't touch or hold him, kiss him, smell him. I smiled wistfully, remembering the two T-shirts I sneaked from his closet and into my bag last week; stowaway clothes to carry his scent with me until I got the real thing back. We had barely been apart in nine months; it was hard to let anyone else into our little bubble. Who the hell else would ever understand something like that?

"Are you sure you can't come tomorrow. Please?" I had pleaded with him relentlessly. My playful tone failed to hide the sadness in my voice. Get over it, it's three weeks. That is exactly what Taylor said, and Lydia. They were right, just three weeks.

"I wish I could baby," he had whispered into my hair. I never tired of hearing him call me that. It sounded so pure. "But, I need to finalize the crap with the lawyers then we can really put all that..." He hesitated and I knew he was curbing the urge to curse. I wouldn't have blamed him. I felt that way every time I thought about it. "Crap. Behind us. Then, we will be together in Europe and we will have weeks to do what we want, when we want." He had shifted my chin up to his mouth and kissed me, meaning it. It made me burn like always. There was something about his skin, his hormones entangled with mine, which made it impossible for me not to touch him or want to be near him. I could already barely remember my life without him in it and while life before him was undoubtedly safer, more normal, I knew now it was hollow, a half-life.

It was his idea to get away. After the incidents with his father, the asylum, we found solace just in each other and the kind of obsessive bond that we seemed already to be developing just got stronger. Only we were there, only we knew what really happened and we vowed to keep it that way. Obviously it was apparent that his dad was troubled and mixed up in something dark but the only evidence we let them find suggested little more than an isolated case of madness and abduction. If they knew more they didn't let on, probably too much paperwork or the worst possibility... they knew everything and had their own motives. We tried not to think about it. Everything else we had under lock and key. Safe.

Trying to throw Mom off the scent was the hardest, but we kept our story so tight, so together, for so long that she had no choice but to believe us; though moments passed when there would be a word, a look, just something that suggested she knew deep down there was more. I think she was just afraid to ask, to face the possibility, as I was, that everything you ever feared could be real and the horrors that existed in nightmares might actually be right down the street. We stuck with what we hoped would sound most plausible, praying that the fear would hold her back from pressing us into some kind of nervous confessional; Jake's dad had some kind of breakdown and I was in the wrong place, at the wrong time. Simple, believable lies which I wished I could somehow force my brain to believe and erase the fact that it wasn't over and every moment was borrowed, stolen from their plans. I hadn't been able to forget that vision; it clung to the side of my memory with fierce talons of pure fear. The bridge, the eyes, feeling his determination to hunt me. It was terrifyingly real and never far from the fore of my mind. There were moments I could almost feel his breath on my face.

The plane finally stopped and so ensued the lunacy of every passenger trying to be the first one off whether they were near an exit or not. Muffled groans and the rattle of multiple seat belts unbuckling filled the sweaty, recycled air. I needed to get out, be somewhere else for a few minutes. I closed my eyes.

Jake had looked so spectacular last night. My final few minutes with him were seemingly inconsequential, but he looked as amazing as I had ever seen him. He had sauntered to the counter, all bed hair and ripped sweatpants. I frowned when he reached the kitchen so soon; I had wanted to watch him more, the way he moved seemed hypnotic to me, but his apartment was tiny and it was never more than about twenty paces to the furthest point. The small home had been a swift, impulsive acquisition. The big house had too many memories and having that many rooms only served to increase his feelings of isolation, so he wasted no time and within three weeks of his father's death he had put down the deposit on the little one bed place over the bookshop I found myself in on the first day we really talked, before the first vision. Our synergy seemed to know no bounds and I felt on some level that my obsession with books factored into his decision, like he felt he needed another reason to draw me out to spend time with him. This was of course ridiculous.

I had become so at home there, that small, barely furnished place. I loved nothing more than watching him move around his own space, the way his back flexed and stretched as he poured his juice then closed the refrigerator.

"Will you be OK? Really?" He hadn't taken those piercing eyes off me and my insides were instantly ignited. He had made no secret about his displeasure that I chose to go ahead of him and I knew he didn't understand it.

"I will be fine. I feel like I have to push myself. It would be so easy after everything for me to let it consume me, be fearful of everyone and everything. But this is standard Jake. So many people do this. It's traveling and it will be fun." I had been lying and not that well. "And... it will give you time to miss me."

"OK. I know what you're saying, it just feels wrong. It's my job to keep you safe and I don't like the idea of you being so far away." He flicked his eyes away from me and if I didn't know him better I would have sworn I saw a flush in his cheeks. "Plus everyone I speak to keeps reminding me how cultured, well-read and charming European guys are." He stopped but I could sense he hadn't said it all.

"Are you kidding me?" The idea he could feel insecure was awful and his pain cut through me, but my subconscious danced excitedly in the background, delighted by his overt display of concern.

"Jake Mayer. I should be the one worrying. You, left here with a cool new bachelor pad and a cheerleading squad's worth of girls desperate to hop into my place. That's something to worry about!" I smiled and his sadness eased as he rolled his eyes. He didn't believe how unbelievably hot he was to me and well, actually every woman with a pulse. He pulled me into him and kissed me like it was going to be three years.

"I love you. Call me as soon as you land." He had playfully shunted my resistant frame towards the door and I headed down to my car fighting with every fiber of my being to avoid turning around. His shape was illuminated in the apartment window but I kept it in my periphery as seeing that face again would undoubtedly have tipped me over the edge. I was barely keeping it together. You chose this, I chastised myself.

Eyes open. Mr.-Glasses-Keeps-Himself-To-Himself stood hunched below the overhead lockers trying to secure his spot in line to exit the plane. The queue finally opened up and to my surprise he gestured for me to get ahead of him. I smiled at him and awkwardly brushed against him as I tried to negotiate the personal space challenge presented by airline travel. Lesson one, do not ass brush yourself against a man who clearly is uncomfortable with proximity let alone contact. He looked like he might throw up. I tried not to be offended.

It then dawned on me that having a spot in the queue was just a tease; you may have left your seat but there was easily twenty more gross cabin-air minutes to suffer while people leveraged their clearly non carry-on luggage from the lockers all red-faced and flustered at the watchful eyes of the other two hundred and odd impatient passengers. Why was I traveling again? Ah yes, the save yourself from crippling fear, learn to be courageous and avoid the secret society hunting you down thing. Great plan. Just close your eyes Scarlett, think of other things.

Mom was singing in the kitchen when I got back from Jake's and a wave of white-hot panic flooded my body as I watched her. Was I brave enough to leave? Why was I so insistent on proving that I could do it? No one really knew what had happened but they all had their own version and it was exhausting. So we made our plans quickly, leaving no room for second-guessing or hesitation. I had some money my grandmother had left me for my eighteenth just days before the move to Salem and Jake; well he had money coming from the house and his father's estate so it seemed right.

Sometimes it was better just to live; those were my words, hadn't I meant them? Seeing her there, happy, I felt so guilty that I was leaving. The move hadn't exactly turned out as planned and neither her nor my dad could get their head around how close it all came to me... well, falling foul of those monsters. If they knew the truth I'd never be allowed out again, let alone allowed to travel to Europe alone at first and then with my stomach twistingly beautiful boyfriend.

Mom tapped on the doorframe, Phish Food in hand and we sat, laughed, cried a little and hugged until we both fell asleep wrapped in my comforter. I felt her shuffle out from my grip and head to her room but my mind was numb from sleep and I didn't try to stop her. I accepted her kiss on my cheek and rolled over to what remained of my last night in a familiar bed for what could be six months if the money lasted.

Finally, real air. It was warmer than at home and I was immediately swept up in the contagious excitement of Paris. Best laid plans to learn French were sidelined for lazy afternoons with Jake and final exams so I completed my stereotype by grasping my immaculate, previously untouched phrasebook in my hand as I wrestled for my place in the cab line.

"Ouch." My huge bag slid ungracefully from my shoulder and fell with a thud to the floor. A foot moved shiftily away to avoid its impact and its owner glared at me. A short, rounded man dressed in expensive clothes huffed in displeasure very audibly.

"Pardon," I offered. Yes, knew that one. He glared before commencing a thoroughly reddening barrage of abuse in my direction in French. I didn't catch a single word but I knew none of it was complimentary. I stared back hoping to break his run but to no avail. He gesticulated furiously towards his expensive shoes and prodded at my bag with a nicotine-stained finger. I was about to reach breaking point and the redness translated into tears of embarrassment which pooled at speed in my eyelids, when an arm extended from the side of me and a body followed; building a defense between me and Yellow Fingers.

An even more furious exchange ensued and by now the rest of the cab queue was enthralled in this soap-style drama unfolding over a dropped bag, which, incidentally, did not touch the man's shoes. The defense barrier body held up a casual hand inches from the angry man's face as a stop sign to the conversation and the rage was palpable. By now three or four people had stepped around to catch the cab he could have been in and when the next one finally arrived he slumped into the back seat and waited for the security of the closed door to angrily show the mystery body the finger. A ripple of laughter and mild applause spread through the waiting crowd and all I could think of was how much I wanted the ground to swallow me up. I had been in Paris five minutes and I was already causing a drama. At least it was not witch style drama; I knew first hand that kind got much messier.

Mystery body span around to reveal a dark haired man, young, twenty–seven, maybe twenty-eight, with deep set brown eyes and a full length black ensemble. A scooped T-shirt separated by a black leather belt woven through the loops of tight-fitting black jeans. I blushed. I didn't want the attention of this foreign crowd. He smiled a victorious grin and I managed to mutter a thank you.

"You're welcome Scarlett." My name fell so effortlessly and casually from his lips with the lilt of an accent I couldn't place. A year ago I would have shrugged such misplaced familiarity off but it brought a wave of unease over me.

"How did you...?" His eyes were boring a hole into my

dipped head. I lifted my face to finish but he stopped me before I could speak.

"Your luggage tag," he pointed to the garish cupcake-shaped tag Brooke had sent me when she found out about my trip and right there in full capital, Sharpie glory was my name. I exhaled. I needed to get a grip. I still hadn't thanked him and my unease was swiftly replaced by embarrassment and guilt.

"Oh. Thank you, for err, saving me." Now please move out of my way. I flashed a smile and looked up. His face fell a little and he nodded in acceptance and swept his arms aside highlighting the way to my now waiting cab. Had I said that out loud? I brushed by him with more travel-induced personal space invasion and that fuzzy sensation in my head that had been bugging me for weeks erupted into a borderline migraine crescendo. It felt like my brains were literally vibrating in my skull and the sound of static evolved into a break in my vision. I paused for a minute and my symptoms lingered. He stared intently but said nothing else and I forced myself to sidestep away towards the cab and as if by magic the sound dimmed to a residual hum and my eyesight clicked back into focus.

"Rue de Dunkerque, s'il vous plait." I fell into the curve of the seat and threw the waiting queue one last glance. Mystery body was leaning on the iron railings, staring right at me. I held his gaze for a moment, as a challenge, but my stomach twisted with unease again and I looked away. Strangers didn't sit well with me since all that crap with Jake's dad. I think the hardest bit was they were all so normal looking. I wish they had a tell, something that made them stand out, but that was it... they all blended in and they were probably everywhere.

Hostel traveling was always going to be a bit of a stretch for me. I wasn't renowned for my ability to compromise on comfort. Needless to say my search for a hostel that fit both my budget and my extensive list of requirements was challenging. I smiled remembering Jake and I sat at his computer, me between his legs on the chair as I wrote off hostel after hostel. "You're going to have to say yes to one of them Scarlett." He was laughing at me and it prompted a play fight. We ended up toppling off the chair and rolling around in hysteria until I was crying. Part laughter, part grief for my stubbornness and part of the trip I insisted on doing alone. Now here I was. The smile I found in that memory faded as I pushed my key card into the lock on my door.

The room was basic, no shock there. But I had to concede it was much better than I had imagined. Images of Leonardo DiCaprio arriving at his hostel in that movie *The Beach* were my closest point of reference and I was happy to report that it was nowhere near that gross. I delighted in the fact I appeared to have the twin room to myself and hoped it would stay that way for the entire week I was there. I didn't relish the thought of small talk and second guessing strangers. This trip was more about proving a point than making new friends.

The international tone on my phone, which thank the lord my dad had said he would cover the bills for, made me feel so far away. Long, drawn out rings dragged on and on. Then, like magic all the weight, anxiety and heated airport drama fell away in an instant with the sound of that voice. His effect on me never waned; it stirred me inside the same way it had the very first time he spoke to me. He was my tonic for all things.

"Hey baby. You're there. I was starting to worry." I checked my watch, now on Parisian time and it was 9.00pm. I had somehow managed to waste two hours since I landed and it was 3.00pm at home. Home. Funny how I was so adamant that place would never be that for me, but now it was where he was and that made everything OK.

"I'm sorry. It took me longer to get to the hostel and sorted than I thought." My heart could barely take the distance. I ached for him everywhere and imagined his kiss across my neck. The memory drew my hand to my hairline and I touched it, wishing.

"Well as long as you're safe. It's weird in the apartment without you. I don't like it." There was a real sadness in his voice. He was lonely. Though it wasn't official, we had pretty much been living together for three months. I went home to replenish my clothes stock, study and keep Mom company on the rare nights she was home. Her guilt about working so much was the driving force behind her consent. The exhibition she launched over Halloween was the biggest success in the museum's history and once the rumor mill started about my abduction, even the locals came a bit more.

It also went unsaid but understood that he had more than proved he could watch out for me.

"I know. It's weird here too, but not so bad. Everything will be better when you get here though." I sighed. I knew I needed to sound happier, make him feel relaxed about my being here alone so I regaled him with my airport drama.

"You should have seen the guy's face Jake. He was furious and spouting all these words in French. I think at least seventy per cent of them were expletives. He was so pissed." I couldn't stifle my giggle at the memory and it lifted his mood too I could tell.

"Anyway, I better go. I think Dad's phone support has limits and I have another nineteen nights without you to make it through." He exhaled slowly and I was lost in thoughts of lying next to him on crumpled sheets. His dark hair, no longer tousled upwards, falling to one side. He looked unbelievably other-worldly when he slept. No one human should be that good looking.

"OK baby." He felt it too. "I love you. No hot Parisian boys, OK?" I heard the half smile but I knew it came from somewhere real. The hot jock that could have had anyone chose me and for reasons I will never fathom thought I could do better. The very idea. I didn't know when he would realize he had all of me, but I had been known to pray he didn't work out how average I was. At least not before I managed to marry him. Holy crap, even I knew I was insane but somehow it wasn't scary at all, which should have set the red alert alarm bells off further. I chastised myself. I never envisaged that at eighteen I would or even could feel so completely in awe and in need of someone to the point I could entertain forever. When it came to Jake Mayer, forever seemed frighteningly too little time and anyway, I'd be nineteen in a few months, so that's more normal... my subconscious goaded me.

"There's only you. Only ever you." He said goodnight to me and hung up. I was left pondering. It took me a while to realize what the feeling I was having could be. I was absolutely starving. It was now 9.30pm and I hadn't eaten since being on the plane; which I didn't think even counted. I locked my bag away in the locker and headed out armed with my trusty phrasebook, and about seventy Euros; I made a mental note to change more tomorrow, and my phone. Just in case.

Thursday night and Paris was alive with activity. Restaurants were full to capacity and the July air was warm enough for people to sit outside. Fashionable couples lit cigarettes and sat in plumes of swirling smoke while chattering in furiously fast French. I caught a few words when the noise was broken by an English or American accent. I snatched some conversation from the warm air and battle to ignore the gnawing ache of homesickness, ashamed of my inability to embrace the adventure. I was only about a block away from the hostel when I saw it, that echo of home, and it was the only option. Stepping inside I felt ashamed of my behavior. I was in one of the most beautiful cities in the world, famed for incredible cuisine and great wines and I was sitting under the golden arches about to tuck into Le Medium Big Mac with fries meal. The shame.

Shame aside it was good and I felt like I was allowed on my first night, to seek some solace in comfort food, and made a note to myself that I must not eat like this the whole time or I'll be ten pounds heavier by the time Jake arrives, not good.

Back in the Parisian air, I felt brave, wandering the streets, being a confident European traveler. This felt good, I could do this. I found a little bar and ordered myself a coke and pulled out the phrasebook and tried to commit some key words to memory. For the first time a surge of excitement rushed through me and that courage for embracing possibility finally seemed realistic.

Back at the hostel I pulled on one of Jake's shirts and pulled it up over my nose so I was immersed in him and allowed myself to sleep. Tomorrow meant... possibilities and if I could drown out the constant barrage of sensations and sounds in my mind then I may even be able to relax.

FIGURE

I spent two days eating more cheeses than I even knew existed. Coupled with amazing bread and pastries the whole not eating myself stupid thing was not really working out. But I was as happy as I could be without Jake here and we were texting constantly so it wasn't so lonely.

Three hundred pictures already. I was a fully-fledged tourist and next on my list was the Louvre and it did not disappoint; I was blown away. Seeing the art I had read about and seen on The History Channel was incredible and very moving. The museum was a lot like the airport; surrounded by people, I still hadn't been able to shake the sense of isolation but the new me was determined to enjoy the experience.

I forced myself to unwind. I sat on one of the benches inside the museum and focused on a painting on the wall before lowering my shoulders that had been hunched since my arrival, unclenching my fists and filling my lungs with a full breath. It was the first time I managed to really let go. Once I dropped my self-consciousness I suddenly felt alive and Paris started to look and feel a lot more like the pictures and movies I had seen; suddenly inviting, warm and awaiting real exploration.

More than forty-eight hours after my arrival I found the impetus to unpack my bag entirely. I reluctantly pulled the last of my jeans out of the bottom of the bag and as I placed them down on the shelf they unraveled to reveal a small black box, which fell to the floor with a thud. Held shut with a pale blue ribbon; I picked the mystery package up and removed the bow with excitement. Inside, a silver bracelet with charms sat on a tiny black pillow. An S, a J, a miniature Eiffel Tower and a heart. Inside the lid was a note.

Dear Scarlett,

Just a little something to see you through until I can be there with you. I am no good at this and I know I don't do enough to show you how I feel. We had such a weird start and I will never be able to say how sorry I am about what that monster did to you. I think about it every day and I will spend every moment trying to make it better. But, from now on I promise I will be there to look after you. Whatever happens, please know how much I love you. You amaze me every day with your courage and strength and I can't wait to be with you.

Whatever happens, I will always be here.

I love you. J xxxx

I thumbed the tiny, beautiful symbols in my hand and raised them to my mouth to put a kiss on each. I grabbed my phone, conscious that he thought I had found it and not even acknowledged his kindness.

The bracelet is perfect, like you. Has it been three weeks yet? Miss you xxxx

It was evening time so I knew he would get it and my mouth curved into a smile as I imagined him and that face pottering around the apartment, occasionally pulling a hand through that hair. His response was almost immediate and it warmed me, he was missing me too it seemed.

Glad you like it. I know it's a bit corny, but I wanted to give you something you could keep. Counting the days. J x

I love it and it's not corny. Hurry up and get here. xxx

God I wanted him with me. Why had no one warned me about this? I had read about it, love. I had heard my mom talk about her first love, and meeting my dad and I knew it was a trick to think that yours was always the very purest, most sincere love. But, what if it really was? I found it desperately hard to believe that there was another soul on earth that could find joy in another person the way I could with him. I could lose hours on the smallest details, sitting without action, just looking. I wasn't sure that I would ever totally be able to articulate it but that was the part that made it even more likely that I was right. If from twenty-six letters that have born some of the most beautiful words and prose in history, there wasn't a combination that could accurately describe how I felt with satisfactory accuracy, then maybe that made it different. It was in every way, more.

Still roommate-less, I had managed to spread my things out everywhere. I heard my mom's voice in my head and couldn't help but laugh thinking of how crazy her OCD would be if she walked in. I bent down and grabbed my sandals and two discarded T-shirts and in lifting my head I felt suddenly dizzy. At first I thought it was a head rush, but it didn't stop. The dizziness turned into a surge of tremors, nausea sent bile into my throat as the threat of a fresh vision rose unrelentingly to the fore of my mind.

My hands grasped at the cheap starched sheets as I slid heavily to the floor. A bag fell, the way mine had at the airport. I couldn't see who owned it, but there were papers everywhere and whoever it was didn't want people to see what was on them. Fingers greedily searched for the debris and stuffed it back into the bag. I didn't get anything else. Suddenly it was over and I found myself slumped on the floor and alone. Instinctively I reached for my phone; but something stopped me. I couldn't let Jake or Mom know, they would probably stage an intervention. I had to handle this. It wasn't as if I didn't know this could happen. It was more just that it didn't matter how many I had; they always took it out of me. The feeling was always so invasive and the aftermath left me violated.

This was only my ninth. I considered myself lucky that the frequency seemed to slow somewhat once I was out of reach of Dr. Sutcliffe and Jake's father. I made a promise to record them after the second and I had kept up to date ever since. Catalogued in a notebook; a library of dark fairytales which generally lived in the space under my bed; along with the rest of my secrets, but I had reluctantly brought it with me in the realization that I was very unlikely to endure this trip without having another one and I didn't want to forget them, I had to keep track. It wasn't lost on me that it might also come in useful should, well, should anything happen to me. At least it would act as some kind of hideous field study guide for anyone interested in ending tyranny for people with powers the world over.

I showered to wash the residue of the vision from my skin and stood under the powerful cascade, renewing myself and trying to get back to reality. Grabbing my camera, I headed down to the Internet cafe, which stood directly opposite the entrance to the hostel. I needed to keep up appearances so posting a few tourist pictures online would keep everyone happy that I was enjoying myself and doing well. I selected a few and even included some cheesy, self-taken pictures of me with the Louvre in the background and another of me in the tidy, post-apocalyptic bag emptying session in my room. I flicked casually through the files; recalling the memories as I watched my adventure play out in a slide show.

My heart stopped as my subconscious, which had been dropping hints for about twenty minutes, finally managed to break through and communicate with my eyes. There, and there, and there. A dark figure, the same person in at least twenty shots. Never clear, never in the fore, but always there. My heart pounded and the knot in my stomach, which was never absent, only ever dormant, twisted and tightened fiercely. I looked around me; how could I be feeling such anxiety, terror even, when the rest of the customers sipped their coffee and tapped enthusiastically on their keyboards? Stupid really. Why did I ever think I would be able to make believe, play at normal? Of course there would be more. Of course they wouldn't stop. I was a fool for thinking it. I looked outside and the street, now bathed in darkness, was empty, no shadowy figure there. I scooped up my things and tossed my Euros onto the table. It was only about a hundred yards back to the safety of my hostel but it felt like it took me years to cross the void of the street. My breathing was hurried and by the time I collapsed onto my bed I was crying silently. Large salty tears rolled down my flushed face and I twisted the charms of my bracelet furiously in a bid to draw some comfort from the fact Jake's hands had also been there.

Despairing, I picked up the phone; I had to hear his voice. As I scrolled through my contacts I was disturbed; my heart quickened again as the door lock clicked, someone was coming in. I bolted up from my near fetal position and pulled my knees to my chest as the door moved slowly open.

A small, dark-haired girl peered around. She was no taller than five feet and her hair was cut into a fashionable crop. I had always wanted that haircut but had been too chicken to do it. Her face was strained and her lips pressed into a hard line until her eyes met mine. She lit up.

"Hiiii," she screeched. She yanked her luggage in behind her; a rather enviable holdall on wheels, which beat my battered rucksack hands down. "Ugghh," she sighed as she struggled with her bag to make it to the middle of the room. She thrust a petite hand with immaculately painted black nails into my face. "I'm Ava. Nice to meet you." She reminded me a little of Lydia on that first day, all excited and ready to talk my ear off. I guessed she was about twenty-five but didn't ask.

"Scarlett, hi." I tried to match her enthusiasm but it had been a weird day and I was still distracted by the photos. She wasted no time in opening the wardrobe and throwing armfuls of clothes in at a time, nothing folded or hung. Looked like I had found a kindred spirit.

"So, Scarlett." She sounded like she was from everywhere, her accent was a collage of sounds from all corners of the globe and her willingness to talk so freely with me gave me the impression she was used to this. Most likely a seasoned traveler that could spot a newbie a mile off.

"How long are you here in Paris for?" She was still busy scooping armfuls of clothes onto the shelves; God knows how long she was planning to stay.

"I am here for at least a month. I am waiting for my boyfriend. He is coming in just over two weeks and then who knows. We will probably stay a while together then we thought maybe Spain or Italy. What about you?" Her eyes were wider, attentive. She was processing the detail.

She hopped onto the end of my bed and crossed her legs, her fingers tapping on her knees. "Well, not sure. I am here for probably two weeks. I am traveling all over at the moment." I knew it. "So, I am here to visit with my brother – he lives here – and then I am going to go wherever I feel like it." She was the kind of person I was pretending to be. She was a free spirit, committed to experiencing life and comfortable with no fixed abode. I was nothing like that. Some of the clothes she had thrown in to the closet unfurled and cascaded back onto the floor. She uttered some foreign words and sighed as she ignored the pile and moved back to her open bag.

"That's cool." Jesus, I sound like a child. Think of normal, proper questions Scarlett, I urged myself. "Where are you from?" I was intrigued, as I still couldn't place her accent.

"Kind of everywhere. My father is…" She stumbled. "Was from Lebanon and my mother was French so I grew up here and there and a few places in between. Hence the weird accent." The light in her eyes dimmed momentarily; there was a sadness there.

"Oh OK. I'm from Washington, well I was. I live in Massachusetts now." She nodded and smiled but I sensed whatever was making her feel sad was lingering. She hopped off the bed and started rifling through the significant amount of clothing she had just distributed in the wardrobe. "I'm meeting my brother for some food. Would you like to join us?" My subconscious screamed no, it didn't want to go back outside, but I couldn't help thinking it would be nice to have some people to talk to, to feel sociable. I had only had my own company for a couple of days and I was boring myself already. My fingers found the 'J' on my bracelet and rubbed it for comfort as I battled with my mind to reach a decision.

"Really? I mean, I would love to if you are sure? I don't want to get in the way of your reunion or anything."

She span around, draped in a purple tunic, and gazed at herself in the mirror on the back of the door. "Honestly, you would be very welcome. I know what it's like when you spend too much time on your own." She turned to me and raised her eyebrows. Girl code for 'is this the right choice of clothing' and I nodded – looked good to me. I changed too so as not to look so deathly casual and miserable and pulled my hair down in honor of Jake.

We walked for about three blocks. "We always meet in the same place, same time when I arrive. It's kind of a tradition." She smiled and bounced excitedly into the doorway of a small, traditional looking restaurant. A restaurant for local people. The smell was intoxicating. Garlic, chilies, fresh bread and strong coffee all danced in the air, making room for one another as I inhaled each one. I realized I had hardly eaten today and my stomach growled in anticipation. Wooden chairs painted deep red were littered around small tables with plain tablecloths below dimmed lights which hung down from the ceiling. It exuded a warm, comforting glow.

"He's not here yet." She searched the crowd, their heads nodding and bobbing as they supped, clinked, chewed and gesticulated their way through their meals. "This way." She signaled with her head and grabbed my hand simultaneously. She led me to a four-seater table at the very back of the restaurant nearest the bar where a small, white-haired man was busy pouring wine.

We sat down, me opposite her, and I twiddled my fingers. "You hungry?" she asked me. I nodded; the noise was almost deafening. So many voices and alien sounds. She raised a confident hand and with effortless fluidity requested something from the wine guy. Within seconds a basket of steaming mini bread rolls arrived in a little wicker basket with a plate of cheeses. She leaned up and placed a gentle kiss on each of his cheeks and he smiled before wandering back to his wine.

"Here. This will keep you going. He is known for being late I am afraid." My mouth was already stuffed with bread and I reached for a glass of the water, which had also just arrived, to help move it on so I could engage in conversation.

"Thanks. Didn't realize how hungry I was. This whole traveling thing has really thrown me off. I either eat constantly or not at all. I guess I am not so good at living without a routine." I flashed a nervous smile. How weird to be sat in a small French restaurant with someone I met ten minutes ago. I wished Jake were with me. I needed to feel the reassuring comfort of his hand in mine and his warmth next to me. I glanced at the empty seat, overwhelmed by longing.

"Yeah. It can be odd when you are not used to it. But the real test comes when you need to slip back into normal life. It is amazing how quick you forget how to be normal and run on a schedule." She smiled and held my gaze. "Hence why I have never gone back."

I tried to get my head around the idea of living nowhere and I simply couldn't imagine never having somewhere to call home.

"How do you, you know, live? I mean you must need money and you wear nice clothes. How does it all work?" My naivety was shaming and my cheeks reddened as I realized how monumentally out of place I was in this exotic and grown up world.

She let out a small laugh. "Well. I work for a few weeks at a time wherever I land. Mostly bars and restaurants like this one. In fact I worked here for three months last year." OK, that makes the kisses make more sense. "And… sometimes I do modeling, like at colleges and whatever for still life classes. Basically whatever is around at the time." She eyed me cautiously to see how I would react.

"As in nude modeling?" She started to giggle and I shook my head at the notion. I couldn't even entertain it.

"Yeah, but it is very tasteful and really quite liberating. I do tend to stick to bars if possible, the tips help top up my funds." Conversation flowed naturally, I liked her and I had forgotten temporarily about the tears and the anxiety before she had careered into the room. I craved this kind of normality.

I didn't catch the door opening in my peripheral vision, I was too engrossed in our latest topic; books, finally something I understood. The first I knew about his arrival was Ava's expression. She suddenly burst into a toothy grin and her eyes lit up. In the dim light the man who had moved alongside me to embrace her was a blur. They were a tangle of dark hair and arms gripping tightly. Hurried words in fluent French passed over me and I felt awkward like an intruder.

"Come, sit, I want you to meet Scarlett." Ava beckoned for her brother to sit next to her. The blur shuffled with his back to me and he shrugged off a black jacket. As he spun my stomach churned and I was hit with an alarming sense of familiarity. I knew him. How? Who?

He swept a hand over his forehead to sweep his dark hair out of his eyes and it clicked. The eyes, the black clothes. Mystery airport guy.

A smirk rose from his mouth and reached his eyes; he didn't say anything. Ava interjected. "Scarlett, this is Elias, my brother. We call him Eli for short." She hadn't clocked the grin on his face or the freak out on mine. How weird to see him here.

"Ahhh Scarlett. Nice to see you again, especially without the huge angry guy on your case." He extended a hand; his wrists were obscured by all manner of bracelets. Black beads, twine, leather braids. He was still all in black and I was shifting uncomfortably in my seat.

Ava looked confused. "Wait... you guys, know each other?" She flashed Elias a glance and looked back to me. We both went to speak at the same time. He held up his hands and gestured for me to regale her with the tale.

"Yes. Well, no." I couldn't look up, paralyzed by his intense staring and the weirdness of the situation. "He, your bro... Elias kind of saved me from an angry guy at the airport when I arrived." He was nodding in agreement and Ava playfully slapped him.

"Aw. My brother, the hero." She mock fawned over him like he was Superman. "Wow. That is crazy. See Scarlett, the more you travel the smaller the world feels huh." I nodded and smiled. Elias still had his gaze fixed on me. He was watching me so intently I couldn't work out what he was thinking. Ava broke off his stare with a barrage of questions and I took solace in the shield of the menu.

Dinner was weird at first, but the mood lightened and they told me anecdotes from their childhood. They were close, you could sense it and I got the impression they were the only ones left. Everyone else; parents, childhood friends were past tense.

An hour in and I felt less weird about Elias; I had to accept that coincidences could happen and not everyone was, well, like Jake's dad. Turned out Elias was nice. Quite flirty, which I found uncomfortable, and I caught Ava shooting him a few warning glances, but it was nothing I couldn't handle.

"That was incredible." Ava unceremoniously discarded her cutlery, which hit her empty plate with a clatter. Elias was still eating and I was forking my food around the plate. "Eli, have you told Scarlett about your work, bet she would love to hear." She stood up and I felt myself squirm, where was she going? His eyes followed her nervously; the weird air between us seemed mutual at that moment. "Bathroom. Be back soon." And with that she sloped off.

"So, your work. What do you do here in Paris?" I was trying to make the effort. He twirled his fork on the plate and looked up at me through a web of thick black hair, which just reached the end of his nose with his head dipped.

"I'm a photographer. Freelance. Lots of magazine commissions mainly but whatever I can get to be honest." His accent was more French than Ava's and it was kind of soothing. I had gotten lost in the sound for a moment and snapped back as his fork hit the plate.

"Oh... a photographer, that's cool. Why Paris?" I shunted my half-eaten plate of food away. Damn bread and cheese starter.

"Why not Paris?" he asked. His tone was a little indignant, he felt judged in some way.

"Oh I didn't mean anything by it; just Ava travels so much I wondered why you chose to stay here, in one place I mean." It was back, the stare. His eyes locked on me and without addressing my point he changed the subject.

"Why are you here Scarlett?" Where was Ava, Jesus, how long did it take? I thought about the question hard. Why was I? I was running, escaping. No, I was finding myself, searching. I didn't really know.

"I suppose I am here for the experience. I had a crappy year so decided to defer college and head to Europe to enjoy myself. I was lucky enough to have some money gifted to me in my grandma's will so I chose to use it seeing the world." Too much perhaps? I couldn't tell if he was fascinated by what I was saying or looking through me in his own thoughts. It was the latter.

"Where is your boyfriend?" I hadn't said I had one yet. "Why would you come all alone?" He slid a hand across the table and placed it on mine. "You are very brave to come alone." His words sent a chill surging through me and the part of my hand he touched burned, not like when Jake touched it but differently. I didn't like it. I slipped my hand out from his and chose my words carefully. I didn't understand him.

"I needed to get some experiences of my own, just a few. He, his name is..."

"Jake," he said at exactly the same moment. My eyes narrowed and I looked back at him. "How the hell do you..." Ava slumped wearily back into her seat and just like that the conversation stopped. He hadn't looked away yet and neither had I. We were locked in a visual stand-off and I could not work out what it was he expected of me.

"I err. Think I am going to head back. Thank you for

letting me join you." I reached into my jeans pocket and pulled out thirty Euros and put it on the table in front of Ava. Elias looked down, like I had hurt him in some way, and a seed of fury sprang alive in my gut. Who was he? Why the hell did he want to know so much about me? And how the hell did he know about Jake? I wasn't staying to find out tonight. I would get back, away from him, get some sleep and maybe find another hostel tomorrow. Get my distance back.

Elias didn't say another word, in fact his confident glare had faded entirely and he ran his fingers through his hair with a hint of despair.

"Oh. OK." Ava seemed a little put out. "So, I'll see you in a little while? You sure you're OK to get back alone?" Hmm, let me think, would I rather be here with your weird brother who seems a little too partial to eye contact and knowing things about me he shouldn't or go back to a room with a lock. The latter please. Darkness swelled in my stomach and I knew these feelings were seldom for nothing.

"Yeah. Please. Stay and catch up with your brother. I don't want to hijack your entire evening. Bye guys." I smiled, carefully maintaining eye contact only with Ava and turned to leave. I knew he was looking, I could feel him but I didn't turn.

The air hit me like a brick, the temperature having dropped since we went inside. I pulled my jacket around me and picked up my pace. I wanted to be walking to see Jake. To end the night curled up in his arms, feeling safe and loved. I glanced at my phone, two text messages.

Hi baby. Hope you're having fun (not too much ;)) Let me know you are ok. J xxx

You OK? Getting worried. J xxx

I tapped as quickly as my fingers would let me and spilled out about Ava and dinner. I didn't mention Elias and I couldn't decide why. I didn't want him to worry. Yes, that was it.

Once inside the sanctuary of the room I climbed into my pajamas and curled up under the blankets. I was unsettled by the coincidence, his questions. My eyes were heavy. I needed to relax, and sleep. I took a glance at the picture on the side table; Jake and me in the woods. Mom had taken it just a few weeks after, everything, but in spite of what we had been through we looked so happy. He had that effect on me; he had many effects on me.

When light started to shoot through the gaps in the cheap curtains I was woken from a restless night. I had slept but my head was filled with dreams. I kept seeing Elias's face and he was mouthing words to me that I couldn't make out.

Ava was asleep in her bed, the evidence of which was a limp hand that dangled lifelessly from tangled sheets. I checked my phone, 8.00am. I grabbed my clothes and got ready in silence. Ava stirred but didn't wake and I managed to leave the room without her noticing. I liked her, but I felt I needed to keep her at arm's length, just find my own way and generally stay away from her brother who I was fascinated, but also completely freaked out by.

The streets were already alive. Why was it so busy? Then I realized, for the normal folk it was Monday, which meant commutes, meetings, school runs and general normality. I headed across a park to a small coffee shop and patisserie I had found as part of a previous exploration the other day and took a seat in the window. I liked to watch people go about their business. There was something oddly comforting about the mundane nature of every day just happening in front of you as well as a certain joy associated with having no particular thing to do.

I sipped at a hot chocolate with the works and cut up my pain au chocolat into pieces before popping one in my mouth. Amazing. I was allowing myself a rare moment of relaxation. They normally only occurred when I was with Jake. Out of his reach I tended to feel strangely naked and vulnerable.

I flicked through magazines, my phrase book and watched Monday morning, but my mind was torn. I was half thinking about Jake and what I would do to him when he arrived and half thinking about the mystery man, Elias. I shook off the thought, I didn't need to waste time with the who and the what, I was supposed to be having some life affirming experiences. So, with that in mind I paid up and set off. My list of places to see was endless but I saw one suggestion in the guidebook which sang to me; Shakespeare and Company Bookstore. I was giddy with joy. Any place that had hosted Ernest Hemingway and James Joyce was a hit with me. I took to the streets with my map and inhaled as much as my lungs would let me. Experience it all Mom had said, soak it up.

I hated the subway at home and would never use it if I could avoid it but Europeans really know their transport. I caught a metro to the nearest stop and felt positively accomplished. I had made it across Paris, on my own, and I was about to feast my eyes on one of the best bookstores in the country. This was a good day.

I took the subway steps two at a time as if racing to reach the sunlight that streamed in from the street above. I absorbed the increase in sound and smells as I headed up and reaching the top my stride was broken by more hustle and bustle. Rush hour seemed to last longer in Paris.

I worked my way through the crowds and twisted and turned through some smaller streets, following my map to get me to my store. I turned right down a small street and suddenly there was an impact and I found myself flat out on the sidewalk. A hand reached down and pulled me up.

"We must stop bumping into each other Scarlett. Literally. Are you OK?" Elias pulled me to my feet, his face awash with a wry smile as he put down his bag on the sidewalk. Adrenalin flooded my veins and my legs threatened to give. Why him?

"You." It was an accusation. "How are you so... everywhere?" My mouth was a stern line and my eyebrows furrowed at his joviality. His smile faded and a look of concern spread over his face, his expression more akin to mine now.

"I'm sorry. I didn't mean to startle you." His hands were still on my arms and I glared at the contact, forcing him to drop them sullenly. "Look. I think we got off on the wrong foot. Maybe you'll let me buy you coffee and I can explain." He looked at me hopeful, flirty, a weird glint in his eyes and for a moment the anxiety and anger in my stomach waned. How could you even entertain butterflies? My sub-conscious scolded me and rightly so. Imagine if Jake was stood here, some mystery girl inviting him for coffee. Just the thought made me nauseous. I missed him.

"Look. I don't think that is necessary. I just want to go about my day. Please leave me alone." I wiped off the dust from my jacket and sidestepped him. He spun around and his arm grabbed mine but he didn't get a chance to speak. In moving forward he kicked his bag over and a huge pile of papers fell out. The vision. His expression froze. He bent down with an unparalleled urgency and stuffed them back into his bag. A breeze caught the remaining few and I trapped one that threatened to escape under my shoe. Reaching for it, I looked into his eyes.

"Scarlett, please. It isn't what you think." It hit me like a subway train. This was it. I batted his eager hand away and scratched the paper up from the floor. I turned it over slowly, deep breaths heaving in my anxious chest. This wasn't a piece of paper. It was a photo. Of me.

My mouth went slack as I processed the image. Me

walking outside the Louvre, taken from a distance but zoomed in. He was watching me. The black space in my stomach knotted with such ferocity I felt like I might faint. I steadied myself on the adjacent building. He still hadn't spoken. A dry heave wracked my throat as I put it all together; he was the figure. The one in my photos.

A voice I barely recognized rose from within my throat and forced its way into the space between us. "I don't know who the hell you are. Or what you want but I want you to stay the hell away from me." I thrust the image, now creased from my enraged grip, into his hand. His face wasn't in the slightest bit apologetic; if anything, he looked hostile.

I turned to walk away, though every fiber of me screamed run. Without looking behind me I sensed him close to my back and he shoved me into the dark narrow doorway to my left. I was scared and I was seconds from trying to contact Jake, the way I had before. It seemed if I could do it only in moments of extreme stress then this should definitely count.

When he spoke air hissed through his teeth, he was seething with rage and I was totally confused. Confused and completely terrified. "Just. Listen. To. Me." He had my hands pinned to the wall at my sides and his breath was alien on my face. Only Jake belonged this close to me. I didn't make a sound. I couldn't scream, or move.

"Scarlett. I am not going to hurt you. Please, just listen. I know it looks bad, but whatever you're thinking it isn't that. I'm not one of them." He released his grip and took a step back but his eyes stayed fixed on mine.

So many thoughts raced through my mind. Who does he think I think he is? Why was he following me? Elias didn't move. With his arms folded over his chest he leaned against the wall.

"What the hell is going on Elias?" I was pacing back and forth in the tiny space. His touch was softer this time as he grasped my hand in his.

"I know all of this is hard to take in." No kidding. "I can tell you everything, but please let's go somewhere and talk. Not here." He was still holding my hand. I shrugged free.

"OK. You have ten minutes and if I don't like what you say and don't buy it, I will scream to high heaven and believe me I will make sure the police hunt you down." A feint smile passed over his face and he muttered something that sounded like, "They said you'd be like this"; more riddles.

"You got it. Your terms. I just want my chance to explain." He stepped out onto the street where people carried on; blissfully unaware of what was happening to me. Not that I knew what that was. I knew I could run, but in spite of the darkness I felt and the incomprehensible fear, part of me had to know.

We walked in silence to the nearest bar. Him leading, me following in a stupor behind, my feet dragging under the weight of my fear. I wanted Jake so badly right now it was hard to breathe.

Elias came back to the table with two glasses of what I

assumed was some classy French brandy. I'd never had brandy in my life but now seemed reasonable. I swallowed it in one and felt the burn in my throat. Followed swiftly by guilt; I'm not supposed to drink. Is it even legal here? No one even batted an eyelid so I guessed they weren't concerned.

He exhaled sharply and rubbed his face with his hands as he prepared to talk. "OK. Now, before I start you have to promise to hear it all. Before you decide anything." My hands were twisting around each other, palms sweating and my breath had become erratic. I was really struggling to contain the alarming levels of terror. I hadn't felt this nervous since, well, since the last time.

"Right now. I am seconds away from leaving. Start talking." I didn't recognize myself. I was never normally this aggressive but all I could think was I won't lose myself again. I won't leave Jake.

"No. No. I'm ready to talk. Just listen." With that he reached into his jacket pocket and pulled out a small envelope. He raised an eyebrow at me and slowly slid it over the table until it was in front of me. It had a number three written on the front. No, no way. My vision went fuzzy and I started to slip. I saw his hand reaching for me and then, black.

GUARDIAN

"Scarlett. Do you hear me? Open your eyes." Elias was standing over me, panic etched on his face. His hands stroked hair from my face and my eyes flickered on like light bulbs after a power outage. Everything was so bright.

"I hear you. I'm fine." Embarrassed, I shunted myself back up to sitting and rubbed my head. An egg-sized lump was forming under my hairline and it throbbed like a new heartbeat.

"Scarlett. You passed out. Here, drink this." Please, no more brandy. Elias thrust a glass of water chinking with ice cubes into my hand and I suddenly became aware of all the eyes on me. They probably thought I was some drunken idiot. If only that were actually what was happening.

"Drink. Now." Oh, bossy stranger with too much information about my life. He was without doubt one of the most confusing encounters I had ever had. Then my memory surged back into action and I recalled what had made me faint in the first place. The envelope.

I sat back in my seat, sipping intermittently on the water. I felt it travel down my burning throat into my stomach; it was churning like an ocean in the perfect storm.

The warmth of embarrassment was lingering but he was politely trying not to notice. I needed to know, but I didn't want to. What ever happened to normality? Washington seemed so long ago I could barely recall. All that I was there was altered permanently. Yet, even in my darkest moments I couldn't bring myself to wish for it back, as me then, who I was, was me without Jake and that just wasn't enough anymore.

"You sure you're OK. You still want to know?" Elias' face was bleak, pained. The responsibility of whatever it was he was carrying on his shoulders was an obvious burden.

"Can we just get on with it? First, I wanna know what the hell this is?" I pointed at the small envelope still waiting, taunting me from the table. The eyes of the rest of the bar were now back looking at papers, or the TV suspended over the optics. At least I wasn't the center of attention anymore. One less thing to worry about.

"I think, of everything I am going to tell you, that is the one thing you already know. But, OK, we can start with that if it makes it easier."

"Elias. Stop with the cryptics. I can't handle this and I don't even know what *it* is that you keep referring to. Please talk straight and do it quickly." I felt like I might combust with anxiety. He didn't look so relaxed anymore either. My volatility had surprised him. You and me both, I thought.

"This is yours. I was supposed to leave it somewhere for you to find but I hadn't figured out where or when yet. Then all this happened." He waved his hand in my direction. "And. Well, my hand was kind of forced."

"Forget the envelope for one second. I can guess what it is. I have no idea why you would have it as I burnt it to a cinder last year but that aside. Who are you? Is Elias even your name? And what did you mean when you said you weren't one of them?" That was a lot of questions even for me.

He blew a long, drawn out breath through his lips and casually brushed his hair off his face. The unread words in the envelope called to me. Tugging at my curiosity so hard it was difficult to remember to breathe.

"Yes. Of course it's my real name." He was being dismissive.

"Well forgive me for feeling slightly, I don't know... suspicious, wary. Call it what you want but I am entitled to feel totally weirded out right now." My voice was raised again and a few of the patrons' eyes returned to our table.

"OK. Let me speak. You said you'd let me talk. So let me." He lifted his head. He had galvanized himself for this; you could see it in his eyes. Those dark eyes; sadder now than at the airport.

"You are... a member of The Occularis. Right?" I nodded

and glanced around to check no one was listening to this conversation between two mad people. "Well I… am kind of like you. As in, I have powers of my own, but different. There are loads of us; people with different... gifts. The Collective. We, like them, are all over and we kind of watch out for each other. We meet and share and help each other." He spun a Euro on the table and I was tempted to slap it down onto the wood. I needed to focus on this.

"Well. I know lots of people, just like you and about a year ago there was a lot of unease, unrest. They were all very anxious and they started talking about something big coming and a struggle. They were talking about what was coming, what was going to happen to you."

I was listening to every syllable, placing it slowly, working it through. I didn't speak but I gestured for him to carry on. Where the hell was this going?

"Anyway. I sat down with one of my friends. He has visions, just like you. He explained it to me. He said that the prophecy was coming. That's you. Like all the stuff I know you have read about yourself. They were worried for you. Scared you wouldn't make it. You are their fairytale. You are the bedtime story they tell their kids Scarlett."

"What do you mean their fairytale?" Didn't feel much like a fairytale for me.

"Every society, community, has its myths and legends. No exceptions. The history of The Occularis is all focused on you. You are the one who they have always believed would bring them down." They. The word spun in my mind. He meant the Venari. My head hurt.

"For centuries The Occularis have been waiting for this girl with flame red hair to come and save them. You. When word spread as more of them got visions of what was going to happen to you, they all tried to see the outcome but it was impossible. You were still so new, had so much free will that they couldn't be sure you would make the right choices. The ones that would lead you on to fulfill your role. But you did. You survived."

"So... after you did it. Survived. They knew the legend was true, that you exist and you will come and save them."

"I didn't understand all that stuff when I read it last year and this hasn't really helped me. How the hell am I supposed to bring them down? And I still don't get where you come in with all the creepy photos." I passed the conversation back to him like it burned my mouth. I didn't understand. Part of me didn't even want to. I had managed a blissful few months with Jake and now I was back to square one with drama and letters and, them.

"I can't tell you how. Even the legend doesn't say how, just that it's you and you are the only one." He paused and a wicked smirk crossed his face. "No pressure." For the first time in what felt like an eternity, we both managed a smile. The brandy had taken the chill from my blood. It was a pretty funny notion; Scarlett Roth, superhero. My face muscles strained into the unfamiliar shape and the darkness faded for a brief moment.

"OK. Next question. Why have you been following me and does Ava know?"

"That's two questions." He was stating it and had no intention of carrying on until I pushed him.

"Don't be pedantic." I scowled and the frustration crept back into my hissed words.

"OK. OK. There was a Council, a meeting held. About you. Here." He looked around him. In this bar?

"Here?" I tried to confirm the detail. This bar didn't look like the kind of place for such a meeting. I looked around and tried to imagine hundreds of people mumbling about visions and persecution with the morning news on in the background. The subject matter seemed a bit incongruous with the setting. Though it appeared I knew very little about anything anymore. "No. Paris." He rolled his eyes.

"Go on." I softened, recognizing the look in his eyes of total exhaustion and exasperation.

"They, the others like you and well, all the other factions of The Collective for that matter, agreed you needed to be protected."

"And that's where you come in I presume." I involuntarily started to laugh. A small giggle rose in my throat and burst out of my mouth. I raised a hand to my mouth as if to shove it back in. It was nervous laughter but also kind of relevant. This guy, the guy with all the bracelets, was the one supposed to keep me safe. Give me strength.

"Wow. Thanks for finding it so funny. Good to feel appreciated." His words couldn't hide that he felt wounded. "You know, I didn't have to and I have already shaken off some guy, probably one of them." He rolled up his sleeve and showed me his forearm. It was littered with angry purple and blue bruises. You could make out the handprint of the assailant. It was big.

"He was on to you. And what's worse, by some ridiculous misfortune you have got my little sister all tangled up in your mess. So, do me a favor? Give me a break would you?" My smile was long gone. This was exactly what I hadn't wanted, more people dragged into my mess. He was right; I didn't understand the gravity of the situation.

"I am sorry. I didn't mean to laugh. It's all just a bit much. I think if I don't laugh I'll just dissolve into the fear of all this. Elias, I am terrified. This world, this responsibility… I didn't ask for it and I don't understand it." My head lolled into my arms on the table and tears burned in my eyes.

"I am sorry too. This isn't your fault. I offered to be your guardian. Help you in any way I could and I will. I stand by it. Ava doesn't know about what I can do and she doesn't know about you either. It is a weird coincidence, that is all." God. I needed Jake with me.

"You never told me what you can do. What your power is." I hadn't posed it as a question. I wanted him to want to tell me.

"I can hear things. Clearly. Kind of seek specific

47

conversations out over considerable distance. I am a bit like a personal GPS. I can find people when they talk. It's hard to explain but that's how I knew where you were when you were sightseeing." He seemed relieved to have it out there. We sat, united by our oddness and smiled.

"So what? You can just listen to anybody, anywhere?" I liked the idea of his, it sounded a little more controllable. This was like an upgrade on what Betty, well later Annie had been able to do. I got the impression from Annie herself and from Alice, that hers was more limited. Elias obviously had the 2.0 version.

"No. Sadly not. I need a connection, not necessarily a physical one. It can be information, like with you I knew you were here and I had the envelope. Sometimes it is an object that belongs to them or just being near someone who has seen or spoken to them will do it. It isn't an exact science. But I appreciate it doesn't ever just take me over like yours and I have to say I am grateful for that." Finally we were on an even keel. He understood me and I him.

The conversation lulled. Elias nodded toward the bar and headed off for more drinks. I sat under the weight of all this information, trying, to no avail, to make sense of it. To work out how less than a year ago I was just a bookish girl in a Washington high school. Now, here I was with a relative stranger, discussing my role in saving an entire community of people. This was crazy and too much.

Then a lead weight of reality hit me as my eyes met with

the small envelope on the table. It still didn't make sense. How was it here? I picked it up; tracing the corners with my fingertips and a surge of buried memories flooded my nostrils. The smell of cleaning fluid, dusty library books and the leather of the car seat as I was driven to safety. The curiosity burned my hands and my body pulsed with terror, or was it anticipation? I didn't know. I ripped the paper open and pulled out the final note. The words I had vowed not to read. One thing that hit me instantly, there weren't many.

After all the hype, the conflict of whether or not I should let these words spell out my future the way the others had; I felt cheated that somehow I tried to leave this behind me but here it was.

I was reluctant and I was procrastinating. The warm glow of the brandy was a distant memory and the muted sounds of multiple conversations were merging into an undesirable hum in my ears. Elias sloped back into his seat. He had slowed when he realized what I was doing, like he thought he was walking in on a private moment. He said nothing; instead he pulled out his phone and busied himself looking self-conscious.

Scarlett, forgive me. You have suffered unthinkable horrors. That much I know. But, these are not secrets for me to keep from you. These are clues to your life and I cannot withhold them from you. Take what you know, trust only those whom you feel you can, your instincts are getting stronger, trust them. Use what you know and find him. Quickly. E.J. Alice

Amazing. Another riddle, in a foreign country and no clues. I shifted the note across to Elias, who was still pretending to be busy with his phone in one hand and his third brandy in the other; he was swilling it around, fast. The ice chinking against the thick glass suddenly seemed deafening.

"Elias. Look at this. Does this mean anything to you?"

"Elias. Put that crap down and look would you." My angry alter ego reared her head again and he was snapped back to reality so fast he looked like he had whiplash. Eyes wide with shock.

"OK Jeez. You're not the only one whose had a crappy day you know." He snatched the paper from my trembling hands and I watched as his eyes darted back and forth, taking in each confusing word.

"Scarlett. I'm sorry. I have no idea. But, I probably know who does." Pausing for breath he looked contemplative. He picked up his phone.

"Hi. Yes, she has it. She wants to know what it means." He was avoiding my gaze, his eyes fixed on the paper. My eyes searched for clues in his voice, his expression.

"No. She plans to stay for a couple of weeks." He shunted the slip of paper back to me. Eyes still locked on some imaginary person over my shoulder. His voice was hushed and suddenly I was the intruder, the person feeling out of place. I felt the same pang of helplessness I had felt when I first found the letters. My life was playing out for me again but it was less a case of not being behind the wheel, more that

I wasn't even along for the ride. I was like a hitchhiker in someone else's life these days, barely able to make it to the most basic of destinations without the hand of the gods, or in this case 'those that have gone before me' forecasting all manner of adverse weather and severe delays.

"Yeah. Sure. See you Saturday. And... Thanks." Finally back with me Elias shifted in his seat.

"Well?" I was beyond tired of the dramatic pauses and tension. I just wanted the answers. In theory.

"That was my friend. Pierre, the one, you know, he has the visions like you. He was the one with the letter. He is very in with The Occularis community around here." He produced a cigarette from his pocket and balanced its tip between his lips as he spoke, his words slightly muffled by the action. "Walk with me." He gestured to the door and strode off ahead. The paper lay discarded on the table, now strewn with glasses. I grabbed it and shoved it begrudgingly into my pocket where it lay heavier than it should against my hip.

The sun was high in the sky and the tables that spilled out into the streets from endless cafes and restaurants were throbbing with life. It was gone noon. Elias and I had been sitting for hours. He drew long, pensive breaths on his cigarette. That first whiff of a lit cigarette, the one that is more match than nicotine, was always an alluring smell to me, despite the fact I despised the act and the smell that followed intensely. I fought my desire to gasp in that bit of the air. His hair was shining in the sun and he had to squint to lead me across to the park over the road. Traffic whirred and hummed and the smoke was replaced by a fog of diesel fumes in the air, which hung low and seemed to veil my face in waves of suffocating heat.

We walked for more than five minutes, him slightly ahead, me lagging, thoughtful and full of anxiety at the back like a child waiting to be reprimanded. He stubbed out the butt under his pointed black boots; surely he was roasting in all that black in this heat? "Saturday," was all he offered.

"Saturday," I repeated. He kept walking and for reasons that weren't clear he hadn't even looked at me since he came off the phone. He finally stopped when we reached the railings that surrounded a small boat pond. Generations sat with lovingly crafted vessels and tended to them before setting them to sail. Squeals of delight hung in the air and the simplicity of it all was enough to almost make the lump return to my throat, though it seemed it was always so close these days. Normality was constantly torturing me with its proximity; serving me hourly with reminders that all of that was lost to me now. Every gaze held slightly longer than a second, every shadow in the corner of my eye and every shiver or chill and I am right back there. It was exhausting.

"That is when he is coming."

"Who?"

"Pierre. You are going to have to think quicker if you want to fulfill this role of yours." Elbows rested on the railings, he produced another cigarette. I promptly grabbed it and snapped it. His eye contact returned as a disbelieving, disapproving glare.

"What the hell?" He was seriously pissed and he kicked the railing with force. A couple of the kids looked up, jolted by the clatter of his sole against the metal and their parents hurried their glances away from the all-black wearing stranger.

"You literally just had one and it's bad for you." I mirrored his pose, my elbows touched his, prompting a flashback to the airport proximity. He concealed a barely there smile.

"You sound like my... Ava. You sound like Ava." He shook off the taste of the word that never made it and rubbed his temples with the palms of tense hands.

"Sorry. I know you are feeling the stress too. I didn't mean..." I placed a hand on his forearm and his eyes found their way up to my face. "You were saying?" The warmth of another person's skin was nice, missed.

"Pierre had the letter. He was the one who gave it to me and I think he can help us figure out some of this crap. But he isn't here until Saturday and he doesn't want to do it over the phone. So, we need to sit tight until the weekend and then I'll take you to him."

"We need to sit tight? You don't need to do this, this job Elias. I don't need to be watched over, despite what you think. I can take care of myself." I folded my arms in a futile display of frustration and he smirked.

"Yeah. Well I made a commitment and I don't want it hanging over my head for the rest of my life if something happens. Besides, what are you so worried about?" He was already five steps ahead and I hurried to keep pace.

"I'm not worried. It just feels weird. I mean I hardly know you and if this was the other..."

"The other way around. So, that's what you're worried about, about him."

"He has a name. And yes, I am. I don't care what you think about that but Jake is everything to me and the idea of hurting him in any way is too much to bear. He has been through enough to be with me and if I'm not careful he is going to realize that this, all this baggage that comes with me," I said pointing at him, "isn't actually worth it." I intercepted a rogue tear that escaped and turned away to hide my shame from his judgment and obvious lack of empathy.

"Who don't you trust Scarlett?" He pulled me round to him, his gaze fixed on me. "Me or you?" He had both my elbows in his grip and his face was inches from mine so I felt his breath, a cocktail of smoke and brandy, pass over me.

"My God." I wrenched my arms free. "That's what you think? That I don't want to be around you because I don't trust myself. Please. My concern here is that he won't understand, why would he? I go away and within a week I have some male bodyguard and a whole new world of crap to contend with." I slumped, cross–legged, onto the grass at the side of the path. Elias sighed and fell onto his knees next to me. He was unbelievable; sure, the issue here was the surge of overwhelming temptation.

"Look. I'm sorry. I didn't mean to be a jerk. I know you are just looking out for him. Let's start over. I want to help you. I want to protect you but that is it. I am not some weirdo who is randomly following you around Paris; I am trying to keep you safe. Please let me keep my promise. Hopefully, then, we can work this whole mess out together." He offered me a hand and I reached for it. Pulling me up to stand he laughed. "And that way, when you're famous, I might at least get a credit." Eyes scrunched in a smile he dropped his hand from my arm. We understood each other now.

"Hmm... Not interested in fame thanks all the same." Jeez it was hot. I wished I had worn something more summery and I mentally trailed through my clothes in the hostel, I needed to get back there. "Oh my God. Ava." I had forgotten all about her. While I was sure she of all people could look after herself, it seemed wrong that I had left without a trace this morning. Elias seemed totally unfazed.

"What about her? She is a big girl, Scarlett, and much more used to going it alone than you." He didn't try to conceal his tone, he was mocking me again, my ability to manage being alone and he was right. I couldn't even find it in me to be pissed about it, because he was so right it was painful. Without Jake I was half a person, I felt lost and alone and the facade of trying to look normal and like I was dealing with everything was as big as the burden of the everything.

"OK. I get it. I need looking after. I just meant she is probably wondering where the hell we are." He had found time to covertly light another cigarette and I inhaled that first scent from the air around me. He closed his eyes with each drag like it was repairing him and I could empathize with that need for something as I had an addiction of my own, but it would be days before I got the chance to have my fix.

"So, what happens now?" Really... what would happen? Was I supposed to let him walk ten steps behind me at all times until Jake came, and then what? Casually explain that once again I have him embroiled in a manhunt where the prey was yours truly and his very being near me meant he was a target too. Awesome. Such a fantastic grounding for a normal, healthy relationship.

"We wait. We need Pierre to work out the next steps. I only got as far as making contact with you; everything else is to be decided. So, we wait and once we get the chance to make a plan we take it from there. With your permission, I would like to be, well, around you so I can do my job and then we will assess it all after Saturday. That cool with you?" My heart pounded; was this betrayal if I didn't tell Jake? Who was I protecting by keeping it to myself? You. My subconscious was very clear, and judgmental.

"Yeah, that's fine," I sighed. I knew I had to tell him but this was exactly what I hadn't wanted, him worrying and dropping everything. Though suddenly, the thought that I could have him here was overwhelming and inside my jacket pocket my phone held all the possibility to make that happen. Selfish. You are putting him in danger. I released my grip. I needed time to think about all of this and work out what Jake needed to know. I wouldn't lie, but I may have to omit, to keep him safe. At all costs, he must be safe.

Ava had been off exploring, and, true to what Elias had said, wasn't even the slightest bit bothered about what we were doing. They had gone off to dinner and after much hushed conversation I had finally convinced Elias that if I stayed locked in my room I would be OK. I hoped. I tidied my things, stared out of my window and did a lot of longing. Paris hummed and twinkled outside trying to bewitch me and lure me out onto its spellbinding streets, but despite the weight of my promise, which lay heavy in the pit of my stomach, I knew it was worth it.

My phone vibrated across the glass top of the side table and my heart leapt. I knotted my hair into a loose ponytail as I skipped across the room. I sat down on the bed and its cheap mattress threatened to swallow me whole. Jake had tied up everything with the solicitors and he was coming as soon as he could, maybe even as soon as next week. Tears burned in my eyes but they were confusing tears of relief, joy, the craving of him and the safety he would bring to me in this strange, foreign place. I wiped them away and collapsed onto the bed. I imagined him with me, arms wrapped tightly around me, his face in my hair like always, and my breathing was normal for the first time all day. The very knowledge he was coming was enough to settle me and all I could think about was feeling his skin on mine, that familiar burn which threatened to make me combust every time. The room seemed immediately more airy and comfortable as I released every inch of tension that had been resident in my muscles for days, relishing the opportunity to lie in peace with no Ava and especially no Elias; whatever his purpose and despite the fact I believed his intentions towards me were entirely honorable, he put me on edge and Jake would sense that in a minute. I buried the feeling that trouble was brewing and refused to acknowledge it fully; this was my moment to enjoy the thought of him and I banished the darkness in my gut for another day.

WAIT

It had been four days and I was still riding high on the idea of Jake coming out here early, though he hadn't confirmed when. Ava and Elias had done a great job of occupying me and we had taken in the sights, streets less traveled and I had tasted more incredible cuisine than I ever knew existed. There wasn't even the slightest pang of a craving for another burger and I felt like an adult; sophisticatedly savoring the delights of another culture with what the French would refer to as a certain level of joie de vivre. I absorbed the Parisian air; walks over bridges littered with street artists and music playing out from café bars and recognized that these were the experiences I had been told about. No matter how much darkness there may be in the world, this all happened regardless; the light and life continued for the most part obliviously and that was some strange comfort.

Tomorrow was the day of reckoning; Pierre was flying

home from a work trip to Norway or some other part of deepest Scandinavia where he had been photographing models for a fashion line. It seemed everyone here had fashionable, creative jobs and put the call of real life in the rat race to bed for good, which held some great appeal for me too. If only I had some kind of appropriate skill. Elias was twitchy all day. I waited for Ava to leave us alone to get drinks before bringing it up.

"What are you so worried about?" I pressed him as his constant table tapping and cigarette breaks were drawing attention to him and I was sure Ava was observing us more closely these past couple of days.

"Oh, I don't know. My involvement in some medieval style power struggle. Something like that." He was flippant but there was no hint of amusement in his dark eyes. They were filled with fear and the reflection of his glass swilling round in his hands was the only indication he was here with me as he spoke. We were in a small American themed bar, a token gesture to make me feel more at home. It was Ava's idea and she appreciated the clichéd décor of Harley-Davidson badges and vintage Pepsi signs much more than me. Friday night had brought out the real drinkers and I felt like a child gate-crashing a grown-up party with my soda among the noise and heat which gave the air a scent of sweat and newly applied aftershave on bodies ready to really let go.

"I thought you said Pierre would help… and that I needed to relax and let you protect me. I have to be honest, your expression right now leads me to believe I should neither relax nor trust you to jump to my aid." I slid him ten euros. "You look more likely to jump off a bridge. Take that and go get yourself another drink. I expect you to be a little more positive when you get back." I smiled through my concern and hoped it was a momentary lapse; I really needed him to keep a clear head as I couldn't be trusted to. I made a silent plea, a prayer that Pierre would have all the answers and that suddenly this whole thing would make more sense and be less complicated once he shared his wisdom. I tried to have faith in that, but it was tough.

Ava was over by the bar, flirting and fake laughing with two guys, one of whom had his hand practically up her dress at the back, not that she seemed to mind. She fluttered her lashes at them and those eyes, those dark eyes that Elias shared with her and they were powerless, handing over money for expensive cocktails that all ended in 'ini' and came in a range of neon colors, each more toxic than the last. I wanted to go but didn't feel like I could leave her here as prey to a bar full of drunken men. She leant over to put her hand on the back of the stool of the first man, a tall blond guy sporting a three-size too small white shirt and teeth so white they made my eyes hurt; her hand slipped and he extended an arm to pull her up. She was laughing uncontrollably and the two men were speaking silently, confident that she was an easy target. I couldn't watch anymore. I marched over and stood my back to them trying to get her to focus on me.

"Ava. I think it's time to go." She snorted with laughter; way more drunk than I had thought.

"Noooooo. You go. Darren and Hayden will look out for me won't you boys?" She flashed them an exaggerated wink and they piped up in unison. "Yeah, sure we will."

"See. I finnnne." By this point Elias had joined me and wasted no time in threading her coat onto her arms before dragging her away. She slurred some expletives and complaints but her eyes were heavy and the fight didn't last long. We practically carried her outside and Elias steered us left. The temperature was cooler and Ava acted as a welcome shield from the evening air.

"Errm. The hostel is the other way Elias." I had stopped in my tracks and Ava took it as a cue to loll against me limp like deadweight.

"We are not going to the hostel. I am taking her to my place. I can take you back to the hostel after if you want, but I don't want her there in this state and to be honest you probably don't either. I'm willing to bet she pukes later and I can't really put that on you. She is my little sister after all." He glanced at the rag doll on my shoulder that used to be Ava and half smiled.

I considered it and in reality, I was happier with this plan.

We walked what felt like miles, weaving through people only starting their nights out and Ava was getting heavier and heavier. We stopped suddenly at a nondescript door. It had no number, no bell and no keyhole, just a futuristic pad. Elias placed his index finger through a small cat flap type hole above the keypad and a small light flashed green before the door clicked and he shoulder barged it open. We were in a concrete foyer; the monochrome scheme was obviously his thing. We passed three or four doors before reaching an elevator at the end. We went in and hit the tenth floor. The doors opened to reveal a smaller hallway with just two doors, one to the left and one to the right. We went left and Elias repeated the finger swipe thing before we were granted access to his apartment.

Once inside he unhooked Ava from my now dead arms and carried her off to what I presumed was a bedroom. The living space sprawled out in front of me; in comparison to my hostel room it was positively palatial. The kitchen to my left was all beaten steel and glass. Mismatched lights hung at varying heights over the counter, which had beer bottles and a small ceramic ashtray grouped together, the smell of stale cigarettes still clung to the air. It had that industrial chic thing going on and I liked it. The living room took up the rest of the space. Exposed brickwork had been painted white and housed four huge frames in a row; close up of lips, the steel of the Eiffel Tower, some graffiti and an eye all in silver, thin edged frames. His work. A black leather sofa ran the length of the wall and a glass coffee table sat on a gray rug, littered with negatives, prints and some rather heavy looking, expensive books; coffee table books. There was a small TV, which looked old-fashioned and out of place perched on a low-level steel filing cabinet in the corner alongside the end wall that was, I guessed, one huge window blinkered by heavy gray curtains. Why no color?

I walked over to the curtains and glanced behind me before quickly tugging them apart. Holy Crap. What. A. View. The arty photographer done good. My eyes feasted on the sparkling, bejeweled map of Paris below but there was only one thing I could concentrate on. Its bluish glow lit-up the dimming sky and it was like magic. There in spectacular, illuminated glory was the Eiffel Tower. I had seen it a few times in the last week and had become quite blasé, but the vista was dominated by that one thing; I couldn't look away. It was right there, this was the view, the one people paid for on postcards and dreamt of before visiting this city. How the hell did he afford this? My awe was interrupted when he appeared next to me.

"Nice, huh? They call it the million dollar view." I heard the smile in his voice. He moved round and wandered back to the kitchen. His hair glowed bluish, black under the fluorescents. "Drink?" He was already popping the cap of a beer.

"No, thanks. I better be getting back." I stepped away following a final look, desperate to commit it to memory. He nodded before swilling back his beer and putting the bottle down next to the others. Spurred on by the sight of the ashtray he balanced another cigarette on his lips and moved off towards the room where Ava was.

"Let me make sure she is OK, then I'll take you back." He disappeared from view and I took another few tentative steps. I liked his apartment; it had a nice feel despite its industrial influences. A muffled voice came from the bedroom.

"She is fine. We can go." With that he appeared in the door, without a T-shirt and I felt myself blush a little. My eyes darted around desperate to fix on something that wasn't his bare flesh. They managed to note his skin was more olive than I had noticed before; perhaps all the black clothing drained his face. I awkwardly tried to fumble for my phone and pretend I hadn't noticed the line of dark hair from his belly button down to the elasticated top of his boxers, also black. Oblivious to my embarrassment, he pulled the T-shirt down and scooped up his jacket one arm in as he opened the door and beckoned for me to follow him.

The elevator was more tense this time, without our drunken companion and we struggled for words, so we were silent, but it felt like there were thousands of unsaid thoughts clogging the air, robbing it of oxygen and I was delighted to almost fall out of the doors when they opened, relieved to have air, space.

He smoked, we walked and we still said nothing. I sensed this might be us, the only kind of relationship we would ever have, one forged by accident, awkward and too riddled with challenges. Our odd entanglement made a normal friendship seem unrealistic; my sense of guilt and his sense of obligation.

Elias insisted that his role meant he must walk me into the room, check it was safe before he would allow me to enter and stay there alone. I protested, to no avail, and we trudged the stairs together weary beyond our years.

He opened the door and the room in darkness was silent. He paused and fixed those confusing eyes on mine, face close again like in the park and breath still smelling of cigarettes and alcohol. I shifted to go inside and he outstretched an arm to stop me; not aggressively, more affectionately.

"You could have stayed with me you know. I would feel better keeping you safe where I could see you." His hand brushed my face. No, Jake did that; no-one else's hand belonged there. I shifted my face away and contemplated the situation. I liked him but not enough, not like that to even allow this conversation to play out the way I thought it might. He was drunk, more than I realized and I was willing to bet he would be mortified in the morning. I still hadn't said anything.

"Elias. Look, you've had a lot to drink. Just go home, sleep it off and look after Ava. I will see you both tomorrow." His arm was still in my path. His eyes narrowed.

"I could come in for a bit if that would make you feel safer?" His mouth spread into a suggestive grin and I was losing patience.

"Elias. I am going in, now and alone. Go home." He moved his hand back to my face and I wriggled free.

"Scarlett." His face was moving in to mine, eyes already

closed. Before I could think a figure burst from the dark of the room and swung the door wide open, almost tearing it off its hinges; it hit the wall inside with a thud.

My heart was racing from the shock, the sound and the sudden movement. The figure, my eyes still too confused to focus as adrenaline ran through my veins, pushed Elias to the wall next to my door.

"She. Said. She. Was. Fine." The words were distorted with rage and hissed through clenched teeth but, that voice, the sound; my eyes flickered back into action with my pounding heart in tow.   Jake's hands were pinning Elias' to the wall, he couldn't move and his face was just confusion. Elias looked at me and then looked back at Jake.

"Well. If it isn't the boyfriend. You don't know the half of it. If you had done your job and not left her alone I wouldn't even need to be here." His words were still slurred but the impact had no doubt sobered him a little bit.

Jake released him and threw a punch so hard Elias fell instantly to the floor and a stream of pure red blood snaked down over his gaping mouth onto his black shirt. He sniffled it away and swiped the moisture off with the back of his forearm as he stumbled upwards to standing.

"Well. At least you can punch. You might not be a total lost cause." He smirked again as he took in the sight of the blood on his sleeve and then brought his eyes back to me. Jake followed suit and I stood, silenced and in shock. Every part of me wanted to grab Jake that moment and kiss, touch, breathe him in but I was mad. Beyond mad.

"Elias. Go. Now. I will speak to you tomorrow." I pointed back to the elevators, my hand suspended until he showed signs of moving. Unsurprisingly, he didn't argue. He snorted a disgusted laugh before shaking his head and padding back down the hall like a wounded puppy.

Suddenly softened by the smell and presence of him here I turned to find him, but he was gone. I stepped into the room, now flooded with light and he wasn't there. I heard a sharp intake of breath and the faucet running in the bathroom and walked through to find him washing his bloodied knuckles. I was still mad, but so in love with this version of him; the protector, my protector.

I slid up to his back and wrapped my arms around his waist; overwhelmed by the feeling of him under my hands, it felt like it had been a lifetime. He shrugged me away and my lungs froze.

"Who is he Scarlett?" His voice was broken, timid. All the rage of the moments before had dissipated and he was now just my Jake, frightened and confused, like me. The, the horror. Did he think? How could he even think that?

My stomach clenched and I found myself bowed, retching fruitlessly into the toilet, my knuckles white as they clenched the cool porcelain. There was no hand to comfort me, no other words, just silence and the shape of him still hunched at the sink beside me.

"You really think? After everything we have been through

that I would come to Europe and hook up with some guy?" I pulled myself up and rested my back against the bath. His eyes were on me now, finally. Tears streamed uncontrollably down my face as I stood to meet him. My body touching his and my anger replaced by such unimaginable pain that something I did could hurt him or that he would feel it was even possible. My hands found his face and his skin was slightly rough under my hands; the bracelet caught the light and broke my gaze for a split second.

His eyes were dipped and he looked broken. "Jake." He didn't move, his breathing was labored and fraught with something I couldn't define.

"Jake. Look at me." He brought his eyes to meet mine and I held his face harder in my grip. "This is not whatever you think it is. Elias…" His eyes rolled and his body contracted at the very mention of his name.

"He was just drunk tonight. He is on our side, we need him." Jake looked at me confused.

"What do you mean we need him?" Now he looked worried and I was sure he sensed where this was going.

"It is a long story and not one I am even sure I understand, but he has been keeping an eye out for me and I want to tell you all of it, every second but please, please." Tears formed in my eyes again. "Please just be here, just us and not talk about it tonight. Can you promise you trust me and I will tell you everything tomorrow?"

His face remained blank and I felt so vulnerable in that

moment. Did he know he could break me with a single look, a word? I felt the shift, he softened and I finally exhaled as his hands searched my torso, his lips pressed on me and his breathing was heavy now, but with longing and love. I felt the return of the life, that spark he ignited in me and my legs felt soft beneath me.

Jake's arms carried me to the bed and he placed me down, brushed my hair from my face and planted a trail of kisses along my jaw, the impulses shot through me and I was on fire. He was here and he still loved me.

"God Scarlett." His words were more breath than sound but hearing my name leave his lips in this way was almost too much. I needed him. "I've missed you. So. Much." His grip on me was so firm like he was frightened I might fall away from him forever. When would he realize?

"Jake. I…" His tongue passed over my lips and into my mouth, stealing the words from me he already knew and he tasted them as he kissed me furiously. His chest, that skin, my skin, it was all back in place and having him with me made everything perfect. The world outside was irrelevant and even the view which had so captivated me earlier disappeared into nothing, buried deep in the part of my mind I no longer needed in that moment, that part that wasn't him.

When morning's light won its war with the cheap curtains and flooded the room, I found myself under his arm. He was still asleep and whistling slightly as he breathed in. His chest moved with grace and I was taking all of him in. When his eyes opened he caught me staring at him and smiled. It was all I could do not to dissolve in his gaze.

"Morning baby." He peeled himself off me and stretched into his shape. "Right. I am going to get showered. Then, I am taking you for breakfast and you can tell me everything about your mystery man." He smirked and hopped off the bed, my eyes followed him until the door closed and I was alone on the bed.

"He's not my man." My voice was raised. "You are." The door opened a crack and his face appeared amidst a whirl of steam from the running shower.

"You got that right. Now... get up and get in here. We have Parisian baked goods to sample." He disappeared into the steam and left the door open as my invitation. I grinned and ran in after him.

I watched him take the first bite. He closed his eyes in silent appreciation and I leant over to brush the flakes of fallen pastry from his mouth. He grabbed my hand and kissed it before squeezing it reassuringly and handing it back to me.

"So... hit me with it. Something is obviously going on." He had lost the joyful expression I had been enjoying all morning. And all night. I broke the news, the complex tale of my 'role' rearing its unwanted head again and how Elias was my protector and Ava had no idea. I told of my horror in seeing the copy of the letter and slid the real thing over the table to him so he could see for himself. Then, I finally made it to today and how we had to find Elias and Pierre, to work out what the hell we did next.

"Well, that is certainly a lot of information." He stirred his coffee and looked back up at me. His face broke into a smile. "One week. I don't see you for one week and you are already embroiled in some serious drama." His hand grabbed mine under the table for just a moment, a sign of solidarity. Hepulled my chin back to face him from the window where I had taken my embarrassment and the nagging fear that he might run.

"Baby. Don't. Stop thinking that I am going to go. I can see it in your eyes and I don't know how to make you believe me. Whatever is coming, we will be ready and most importantly together." I squeezed his hand back and was engulfed in a wave of love for him. Pierre, Elias, we had to get moving.

Judging by his voice on the phone Elias wasn't feeling so hot after last night. A mix of shame and wounded pride disguised his voice. We agreed to meet in an hour, at his place where Pierre was already waiting.

It was an incredible day and if Jake and I had been a normal couple it would have been so idyllic and romantic strolling arm in arm through the streets of Paris. Instead, here we were, walking to meet another stranger who had some kind of pivotal role in my future safety.

Elias buzzed us in. When the elevator opened he was already leaning against the door frame. Something was different. He was wearing a white shirt, still with the black jeans but it was a change for him. Oh, then there were the angry, purple bruises forking out from the bridge of his nose, perfect half circles mirrored on each side. Jake strode ahead of me and I panicked for a moment thinking it was round two but he extended a hand. Elias thought for a moment and then met it with a shake.

"Elias. I think we got off on the wrong foot yesterday and I am sorry. Scarlett explained and I am grateful that you have been keeping an eye out for her." Elias nodded and the apology appeared to be accepted. Jake paused, Elias' hand still in his own. "But." His voice was hushed but I could still hear and it was intentional. "If you ever try anything with her again I swear to God I will do more than bust your nose." With that Jake released his grip and beckoned me over. Slightly embarrassed I smiled half-heartedly at Elias and he stood for a moment, dumbstruck.

"Jake. I err… I get it. I was out of line. Sorry." He waited for approval and they shared a nod of mutual understanding. I felt like a chess piece. Though Jake's knight in shining armor routine was still doing it for me and I was dizzied by the attention.

Inside the apartment a tall, thin guy, probably the same age as Elias, stood up from the sofa. He was the exact opposite to Elias, all sculpted blond hair casually but purposefully arranged in scruffy, fallen spikes. He had on a pair of jeans, skin tight like Elias' but instead of black they were cherry red and fed into a pair of tan leather brogues, separated only by the slightest glimpse of some striped socks. His ensemble was crowned with a skintight white button-down shirt, purple tie and a brown corduroy blazer. I assumed this must be Pierre as I didn't think we were expecting anyone else, but I wasn't really prepared for this new age schoolteacher look. Well, what did other people who could see the future look like? I didn't have that much of a frame of reference.

"Scarlett, this is Pierre. Pierre, Scarlett and her boyfriend, Jake." Pierre stepped forward and shook my hand, then Jake's.

"Scarlett. It is totally amazing to meet you. I feel like I know you." I was embarrassed and felt a bit like an exhibit in Mom's museum.

"Hi." Jake had his hand on my lower back and the warmth of his touch radiated comfort through my T-shirt. We sat, it all felt really stilted and unnatural to be here. Elias brought coffee and lit another cigarette, happy I think to not be the one with the knowledge in this particular scenario.

"So, Pierre. I don't wish to be rude but I think now is the time to tell me what you know."

He nodded. "The letter. Do you have it on you?" I dipped my hand into my purse and found the paper, now worn and curling at the edges from multiple viewings. He took it so carefully; the way Mom took out artifacts for her work, keeping contact to a minimum.

"OK. It's as I thought. We need to find Edward Jacques. Soon." He passed it back to me. "How do you know what the initials stand for?" Odd how I was so out of the loop, in my own life.

"I didn't know for sure who we would need until I saw this. But E.J. could only ever be him. He is a famous sociologist and has a keen personal interest in our, let's say, particular predicament."

"Is he like us?" I didn't wish it on anyone, but being in the company of other freaks made me feel a little better. A pang of guilt thumped the breath out of me as I thought about the dark world I had inadvertently brought Jake into; though with his father it was likely to have been inevitable. I hoped, at least then the blame wasn't all on me.

"No. He isn't one of us, but he is one of the few normal people who knows about them and what they do. They, the Venari, killed his daughter in the eighties. He has been working to out them ever since, collecting evidence, notes, links between them and disappearances. But, as you know, they are pretty damn good at keeping secrets."

"That's awful." I could only begin to imagine what he had been through trying to bring the truth out. People didn't want to see it, they couldn't believe it. The Venari were frighteningly well practiced at blending in, as we knew only too well.

"Well, if he knows and has information what are we still doing here? We need to go." Jake was desperately trying to feel like he could add something. He didn't realize how much he was doing just by being with me.

Pierre shook his head as he sipped his coffee. "No, sadly it isn't that simple. He is famously reclusive. Many Occularis members have tried to get in front of him, hoping for help, answers, information, but he won't see them." He placed his cup down tentatively and looked up at me.

"Though, now we have you." His eyes were fixed on me and his mind was calculating. He has me? Back to the position of pawn. "This does change things somewhat. If he has even half as much research as I think he does, he must know of you, your purpose. If he will see anyone it will be you."

"OK. So, do you know where to find him?" I sensed this needed to be sooner rather than later. I turned to see Elias; he still hadn't said a word.

"Yes. I think we need to go today, while it is light." What new horrors could the dark possibly bring after all I had seen and found out? Jake pulled me closer to him and kissed my shoulder. He whispered through my hair. "You don't need to do anything you don't want to. There is always another way." No matter how much I wanted to, I couldn't believe that there was. The other letters were right, they led me down a dangerous path but Alice knew what was coming and she definitely had my best interests at heart. I had to have faith in the fact I could do whatever it was that I needed to. I survived last time. I could barely believe what I was thinking, what I was about to do.

"OK. Tell me what you want me to do." Pierre was

scrolling through his phone contacts at speed. He looked pensive and I was searching for some reassurance that he thought this would all be OK.

"I need to go home first, but we can meet back here in say an hour and a half and I will take you then. It isn't too far." He shot a glance at Elias who had been busy chain smoking in the corner. He was slumped against the wall, his head back and eyes closed, blowing swirling plumes of smoke. "Elias. Can you stay with Scarlett until I get back?" I felt Jake's body tense at the idea he alone couldn't protect me and I thrust my hand onto his leg. No, don't think that I pleaded silently.

Elias slowly came to life, eyes blinking like it were the first time and he nodded. Why so silent? His sudden introspective behavior alarmed me and I hoped it was nothing more than his wounded pride.

"I'd like to go and change before we do this. Elias, Jake and I will go back to the hostel and meet you back here."

"I really think…" I knew what Elias was going to say but Jake glared at him and Elias' eyes dropped. "Look, I get it. You don't trust me, but two heads are better than one and right now, we have no idea what we are dealing with. Or more to the point we do and we need to be mindful of that. We all want the same thing."

"And what's that?" Jake's tone was hostile and suddenly the progress between them at the door dissipated.

Elias searched for my response but I didn't want to give Jake any reason to feel like I wasn't totally on his side.

"Keeping her safe Jake. Look, I get it, she's yours. I just want to do what I said I would. You can go on ahead; I'll hang out at a distance, just in case." Elias was already pulling on his coat and Jake's grip on my hand was so tight.

"OK." Jake conceded, but he wasn't happy and he was marking his territory with contact. Elias observed our proximity and I read it in his face that he was getting the message.

Pierre hadn't said a word, he was gathering his things and as he shifted towards the door he turned casually and smiled at me in a way which could only be interpreted as pity, before closing the door softly, leaving me with the two chest thumping Neanderthals.

"OK. Let's go." Jake stepped off and led me by the hand while Elias put his next cigarette into his mouth and inhaled his calm.

Elias was out of sight maybe two or three hundred yards back and it felt impossible to me that in this glorious sunshine as people idly walked and drank and took snapshots, that there could be something so awful lurking in plain view.

Jake and I held each other tight as we walked down the hall. Without a word he pressed his arm across me to halt my pace and signaled for me to be quiet. My heart raced. Then I saw it. The door was open, wood splintered where it had been separated from its lock, with considerable force. Jake pushed me back to the wall. "Call Elias, now. Get him up here." But before I could act Elias appeared breathless at the top of the stairwell. He had been listening. I would have been mad but at that moment I was just grateful. He ran ahead of me, all three of us silent, and stood alongside Jake who was up against the door frame listening. Nothing. Whoever it was seemed to have gone. The two of them walked in together and I tiptoed cautiously along the hall, my legs weak with fear and my pulse racing. It had started.

"Gone," Jake said. I followed them in confident that the coast was clear to find them crunching over broken glass. The mirror from the wall lay shattered over the floor among shards of shredded bed sheets and clothes. The curtains were ripped off their rails and lay in a heap on the floor among discarded drawers and Ava's open suitcase. Ava.

I looked at Elias and I didn't even need to say anything. He sat down on the bed, his head fell into his hands and he was quiet. Before I could speak I realized, he wasn't crying. He was listening. That's what he had been doing before, at the apartment, listening to someone.

"What can you hear?" He raised a finger to silence me and I backed up. Jake looked at me, confusion etched across his face. He mouthed 'What?' at me. I shook my head signaling that I couldn't tell him now and he threw his hands into the air in exasperation.

Elias fell onto his back and sighed. "She is fine. I can hear her talking. Sounds like she is talking to a guy, no one has her." I smiled and let out the breath I didn't know I had been holding. She was OK. Thank God.

Their voices were hushed as they explained to the old guy on the desk what had happened. He looked happy to be behind his Perspex shield. They were getting pretty animated and competing for their say. Jake marched over to me. "They have offered you both another room and your money back but I told him you aren't staying here." Elias appeared over Jake's shoulder.

"You're all going to stay at my house, until we know what the hell is going on. You'll be safer there." I looked at Jake, expected a fight but he nodded and just like that, they were a united front.

"Our things?" The image of mine and Ava's belongings tossed all over was ingrained on my memory. It was a message, just to let us know they were watching. This, scariest of all, meant they still were.

"They have sent someone up already to clean it up and everything is being sent over to mine later. I already grabbed your passports so everything else can wait." Elias was very matter of fact and Jake looked more impressed than put out. I had no idea when he managed to do that.

We had to make a move, we were meeting Pierre in half an hour so Elias set off ahead and we followed this time. We waited a good five minutes before we strode out into the Parisian sunshine like we didn't have a care in the world.

I saw Pierre long before we got to him. He had changed his cherry red chinos for some mustard ones and the blazer was now black; presumably this was his serious, meet-ascholar ensemble. His face was distorted with distraction and then the fading light took the sheen from his blond hair. In fact, he looked altogether less positive than he had just an hour or so before and though I tried to ignore it, the observation caused the knot in my stomach to tighten further and I wondered if one day it would get so tight, the anxiety so much that I might just implode and disappear. No, I turned to look at Jake striding alongside me, managing to look confident and collected in spite of everything and my fear shrank. I didn't want to disappear no matter how dark and complicated things might become; that face, even in shadow was my light, my salvation. He squeezed my hand tight as if he was listening to my internal monologue and lifted my tense fist to his mouth, where his reddened lips parted so slightly and with such tenderness that I immediately warmed.

Elias was already with Pierre, his eyes brooding and secretive. They exchanged some hushed words while we remained just out of earshot. Having spotted us Pierre nodded at Jake and turned around, his pace fast and strides urgent.

We passed through the evening chaos and yet more blissfully unaware tourists. Pierre hailed a cab and we all piled in, he took the front seat and muttered an address as we all sat in silence and I tried to distract my over eager mind by watching the continuous tick of the fare. Three Euros, four, five. It made it to twelve and Pierre stuffed a twenty Euro note into the driver's chubby hand with one hand while the other opened the door.

I hadn't been watching the journey so I had failed to notice that we had left the movement of the city for a more suburban setting. A large house, obscured behind tall iron gates that were once green but now neglected, looked faded and sad as huge slithers of paint peeled off and clung by a thread to the metalwork. The taxi pulled away and left us, four anxious bodies with a burden of unknown responsibility.

Much of the twisted and turned iron of the gates – once no doubt someone's masterpiece and a sign of the magnificence beyond – was marked with deep cuts where autumn colored rust showed through. The gates failed to meet, one warped by impact of some kind kicked outwards towards us and the latch failed to find its other half. Pierre pushed tentatively and the bent metal moved backwards with a piercing screech as the rusted hinges ground against one another. The noise had startled us all and I looked up involuntarily towards the house where a shadow moved behind a tired wooden shutter.

"I saw someone." Three pairs of eyes met mine and followed my pointed finger to the ground floor window, in which the shutters had been snapped to a close. Somebody didnt want visitors.

"Come." Previously soft Pierre was more tense and direct now as he ushered us in front of him towards the house. It was beautiful, once. Three floors with miniature metal balconies at each window. The path to the large blue front door was barely visible under years of moss and mulch, remnants of last winter clung to the ground, decomposing like the house that rested on it. The door's glass panels were crudely blanked out with rough cut timber nailed to the frame and it wasn't clear if he was trying to keep people out or himself in. The doorbell hung limply on a wire, pulled from its place, and the doorknocker had long since been removed, leaving an outline faded by sunlight.

I could sense everyone's feelings were the same as my own; this was a very sad and lonely house. The love and care which it would have once been privy to was lost amid years of darkness and neglect; this man had shut out the world and, by the looks of the closed shutters inside each window, the light too.

"Well. Go on." I nudged Pierre who stood closest to the door. He sighed and outstretched a hand but paused nervously, his tense knuckles poised inches from the wood. I stood behind, flanked either side by Jake and Elias whose trading of warning glances and silent threats was not as subtle as they thought. I grabbed Jake's hand and fed my fingers through his. His palms were sweaty and he held me tightly, anxiously.

Pierre knocked loudly with three consecutive thuds. There was only silence beyond the door and no sign of the shadow figure in the windows anymore. He turned to the three of us, his eyes seeking encouragement or suggestion. I shrugged and Elias was too busy picking at the nails he had spent the taxi ride biting.

Jake dropped my hand and shunted Pierre out of the way.

Facing the door head on he wrapped loudly with his fist clenched and the wood groaned and rattled beneath his hand. It remained silent for what felt like minutes and Jake had raised his fist again ready for another go when he was startled by a rattle of chains and the grating of metal as the unlocking of multiple locks played out on the other side. We took a collective step back, Jake threw his arms protectively across my middle and Elias and Pierre mirrored him until I was concealed behind a wall of anxious testosterone poised for confrontation.

A pause punctuated the air after the locks were undone and we all held our breath not really sure why we felt so on edge – we were meant to be coming for help.

The door creaked open no more than about three inches and a pair of manic, wide eyes filled the dark void from within. The pupils facing us contracted at the shock of the evening light and our eyes stared back.

From my left Pierre cleared his throat and took a step toward the door. The eyes moved back defensively and Pierre reached out a hand as a symbol of our peaceful intention. They came back accompanied by a slither of pale, unshaven face sporadically peppered with white bristles.

"What do you want?" he barked, but his voice wasn't strong enough to strike fear, only pity. Jake stepped forward to join Pierre and took a sharp intake of breath as if he planned to lead this inquisition but Pierre silenced him with a glare. I reached for his hand and pulled him back to me. I knew he was too subjective to handle this, he would never be able to separate his emotions to draw out the kind of information we needed.

"Mr. Jacques, please." Pierre held out a hand to shake but the eyes remained fixed and still. "We need to speak with you. It is of extreme importance." His hand hung in the air, an awkward symbol of the struggle ahead. He relented and let it fall sadly to his side.

"I have no need for nonsense. You are in the wrong place." His French accent was buried beneath excellent English and a huge sadness. The face disappeared and the door shifted at speed back to the frame. Jake rushed forward and wedged his boot in the gap; he cried out in pain at the weight of the door against his foot.

"No. This is exactly where we need to be. So please don't make me force my way in." Jake's tone was unnervingly serious, he meant it and I felt the threat of this opportunity dissolving become real. I thrust a short, sharp jab of my fist into his back, just below his ribs, which made his body recoil, but his foot remained wedged in the frame. He was so stubborn.

I stepped forward, desperately trying to swallow the darkness and fear. My heart was beating so loud I looked to Elias sure he could hear it, but he remained paralyzed by something between fear and distraction, nails clenched between a tense jaw.

"Sir. Please." I didn't even try to hide the pleading in my

voice. "My name is Scarlett Roth. I need to..." I was cut off by the door swinging open to reveal the rest of the tired face to which those eyes belonged. I recognized the look he gave me; I had seen it before at the door of the guesthouse in Boston. His pale lips parted as his mouth fell slack with some unrecognizable emotion. No one moved.

"Please. Help me." I begged. And before I could stop it, every shred of fear cascaded from me in huge sobs as my legs buckled and I fell to the floor. Hands, bleached with lack of sun and colored with age spots, were the first to reach me. Edward Jacques had emerged from the shadows and knelt at my level.

"I wondered if you'd find me. If I let you in I will make no guarantee, none at all about giving you what you need." He backed up, most likely in acceptance of the fact that he wouldn't be able to help in anything so physical. His faded clothes hung shapelessly from his angular, hunched frame. He looked like a man whose very life essence had been stolen. Perhaps it had been.

Jake and Elias came to my aid in unison, but Elias backed off immediately when Jake's eyes reached him – it was a warning.

"Come on baby. I got you." His arms enveloped me and he half carried my trembling body through the frame. Pierre hung back and followed last as we stepped into a hallway that opened out in all directions, the focus of which was a large staircase. A huge grandfather clock stood next to an arch into what looked like a study or library. A thick layer of dust clung to every surface and seemed to hover in the air. Jacques shuffled into the study beckoning for us to follow and we gathered around a desk piled ten deep in books and papers. The worn, floral carpet was barely visible under the cover of documents. Newspaper clippings were pinned at all angles to the walls, even pasted over the shutters, which offered the guarantee of darkness. He worked by the light of two lamps, one on the desk, the other balanced precariously on a high shelf which housed more huge books that looked like scrapbooks; their spines contorted under the weight of clippings and scraps forced into the pages.

"Please. Sit." He said it without a hint of irony and we looked at each other bemused before perching uncomfortably on unreliable stacks of books. "Let's make this quick please. I have work to be doing. How is it that you think I can help you." It was as if he didn't really think he could help at all. I looked at Elias, Jake and Pierre and my unspoken request to let me lead this was heeded. Their heads bowed and they were silent.

"Sir." I didn't know where to start.

"Edward. Call me Edward." He closed the book open in front of him with the kind of urgency with which a schoolkid hides a test paper. He looked everywhere but at me.

"Edward. I believe you know who or rather what I am and the reason I am here." My fingertips rifled through lint and the button from my jacket saved but never reattached in my pocket, until I found it, the envelope. I pulled the slip of paper out and passed it to his waiting hand. None of this was a surprise. A sigh filtered through his thin lips and he gently tugged the paper from me.

"I see." He offered nothing else and his eyes looked down. He was conceding, preparing to delve into painful memories and most likely terrifying truths.

"You see." I confirmed. "OK. I burned this, well not this one but some other version of this because I didn't want to know what it said. Now it seems this message was important enough that emergency drafts were made and I find myself here against all my better judgment. So, please. If you know something, anything that can help me, I need you to tell me now." I dipped my head to find his gaze and he stared back, his own eyes glassy with emotion and a realization that he was resigned to retelling his own pain and maybe mine.

"My daughter, Rosalyn, was like you. She saw things she didn't want to and for a long time I believed what they told me, that she was a very sick girl who needed professional help. It made sense, I was an absent father so consumed by my work, securing research grants, writing papers and traveling to give lectures that we barely knew each other." Jacques paused; he raised a clenched fist to his mouth as if to force down some rampant sadness, which threatened to escape his throat. He cleared it with a cough and subtly grazed a handkerchief across his silently weeping eyes.

"When it was too late, when she had gone, a hysterical

American woman turned up on my doorstep shouting about how she knew the truth and that she knew Rosalyn had not been sick." Elias had started pacing, his hands were inward and sore and he needed a new outlet for all his nervous energy.

"Alice?" I was saying it more to confirm the facts in my overworked mind.

"Yes. Ms. Markham. She was very insistent. Despite restraining orders, plural, she maintained her campaign and six months after Rosalyn died, at their hands, I finally sat down with her. Mostly just to put an end to it. I was drained and had lost my only child. I just wanted peace." The weight, the sadness was incomparable to anything I had seen or felt and that was saying something.

He pulled out an immaculate gold pocket watch in complete contrast to the shabbiness of his clothing and his home. He flicked it open and handed it to me; it contained a picture of a girl with perfect porcelain skin, she had long dark wavy hair and the bluest eyes; this was Rosalyn. I smiled and placed the watch on the book next to him. I glanced behind me, Elias was still pacing, Jake was fixed on me. Pierre stood staring at the mountain of books on the shelves of the back wall, his fingers gracefully tracing the spines as he tried to gather information about what exactly Jacques did have on them.

My weary eyes turned back to the empty man before me; he was staring at Rosalyn's picture and the sadness in his eyes changed somehow, it became a fierce resolve and the atmosphere and his breathing shifted enough to make Pierre and Elias look over expectantly. Jake shuffled on his perch causing a cascade of books from the adjoining pile to tumble to the floor where they simply blended in. Jacques shook his head to stop Jake, who was red-faced and already hunched to gather them up, from bothering.

"She had fled here after she realized they were after her. To Paris. My part was incidental. She followed all suspicious disappearances and deaths, keeping a huge scrapbook and finding out what she could. Obviously they weren't all that way; some were the usual, ordinary. She knew the signs to look for I suppose." He pointed to a stack of filed books bursting with rough-edged paper cuttings that sat on the wall shelves. Alice's books.

"Through sheer bad luck my local notoriety, through the university and beyond turned Rosalyn's death into a bit of a media circus. They wasted no time in reporting on our challenging relationship, my poor parenting. So, inevitably, she made it onto Alice's radar."

"Rosalyn's mother?" I surprised myself and him with the question and a feeling I couldn't quite place told me I knew more than I realized. It was a niggle, a strange weight to add to the others.

"Died. When Rosalyn was three. She was murdered when she interrupted an intruder trying to rob us, here. I was, as ever, away with work. Rosalyn was asleep and went unnoticed so she survived." What a foundation for growing up. This was such an easy one for them. They wouldn't have had to try hard to make a case for Rosalyn to be mentally challenged after her life experiences. Seemingly unperturbed by my questions he continued to flesh out the puzzle.

"Anyway. When we finally spoke, she, Alice, told me she knew that I thought she was mad but that she could prove she wasn't and she needed someone like me, an intellectual she said, to look at the information she had collected and take notice. It was a very tense time. She would always turn up shrouded in darkness, her face covered and she refused to sit near windows. It was her who started this." He gestured to the shuttered windows that now alluded to total darkness outside as thin black stripes of night sky forced through the wooden slats that weren't already obscured by paper.

Jake sighed and rubbed his reddened eyes. "Can we please, please get to it?" I was taken aback by his rudeness and I made no secret of it.

"Jake!" I scolded him and he retreated.

"Sorry. I'm just tired I guess." He avoided my gaze and shook his head to shift the redness in his cheeks.

"No, no. I understand. These things have a tendency to require a sense of urgency." Jacques spun his chair round to the room for the first time and all three of them looked up like a teacher had just walked into a class.

"She talked me through what she could do, what had happened to her and thousands of others. I refused to believe it at first, but doing what I do I also knew the strange ways people could behave and what she was suggesting fitted a pattern and one that I had to recognize Rosalyn was part of." He pushed himself up and pulled down three huge scrapbooks from the shelves next to Pierre who had stood aside, captivated. "I had thought Rosalyn's... turns... were a sign of distress, a physical, if not delayed reaction to the stress of her mother's death, my failure to manage raising her alone."

"So you realized. The Venari." I shuddered at the sound of that word on my lips. "They're real."

He nodded. "I started helping her, looking into other cases and it became an obsession. Then one day she was gone." His eyes were heavy again.

"She never came back. But a courier came, maybe three weeks after I last saw her, with a safety deposit box key and that's where you come in." I turned my body round, every pore alert with anticipation.

"I presumed, like with everything else, she knew what was coming. She left me one book, not like the others, just notes and thoughts. A kind of journal about her own visions. All of them about you. She said you would come, that she had pointed you here and when the time came I was to share with you all that we had learned to help you end it. And here you are." He let out a long, troubled breath and his head fell into his frail hands.

"So all this..." I acknowledged the piles of work, "is what will help me to end it?" As if my eyes had only been partially open before, I suddenly acknowledged more shelves, piles of documents and news cuttings. I wouldn't have any idea where to start.

"In theory, yes." He closed the book that lay open in front of him and turned back to me.

"In. Theory?" I forced his eyes to meet mine as the new, more dominant me reared her head again. "What do you mean in theory?" I repeated.

"I just." He paused and you could almost hear his brain processing. "I am concerned that all of this, that all it will do is make you more of a target. Haven't you ever considered just, I don't know, running away?"

"Mr. Jacques. For someone who has spent years researching these people you don't seem to know a great deal." His eyes spoke of his offence at my words. "Forgive me, but if you know anything about them you know that they do not give up. They have found me before and they will again. I need to know, fast, what it is that you have here so I can work out what I am supposed to do with it." He nodded silently, defeated and already weary of the task before him.

"Miss Roth, you are very persistent. She said you would be and I think it's necessary. To delve into something this dark you need to be prepared for a fight. I just hope..." His voice trailed off and an unspoken wave of acknowledgement washed over all the bodies in the room. I could die. No one wanted to say it but we all knew it was their end goal, to wipe me out for good.

It was my job to undo the spell of that thought and I sparked back into action, unable to process it, unwilling to. I was staying with Jake. "OK… so where do we start?" I clapped my hands together in mock enthusiasm and Jacques jolted. I realized then I would have to watch it with him, he really was fragile.

"I will take you through the various stages of our research. It is categorized into a few sections. But, I am afraid we cannot start tonight. You must go and come back tomorrow evening. I must rest. I will prepare it into some kind of order and you can gorge on the gory details then." A half smile lifted his lips and I wanted to argue, but to be honest I knew it was fruitless; we already had more cooperation than we expected so better to play the game. Plus, I was exhausted and the idea of retreating to hide in the secluded haven of Jake's arms was too tempting. The very thought was like a siren's call and my eyes relaxed into a long blink as I imagined his smell.

The three guys stood up and between a few grumbled words and nods had said their goodbyes. Pierre was already at the front door, flanked by Elias and Jake and I stood with Jacques alone in the study.

"How bad is it?" My voice a whisper. I didn't want Jake to hear anything else. I had sensed his tension growing all evening and I knew he was trying to put on a brave face. It was so easy, looking at his perfect exterior to forget the pain he must be feeling and just the notion he was holding it to protect me wrenched my stomach.

Jacques placed a gentle hand on my shoulder and bent down to my ear, his warm voice met the side of my face and his breath hot and tainted with a thousand cups of coffee hung in the air around us. With a voice so quiet I could barely make it out he said words which made me hope I was wrong.

"This is a war of the darkest kind and I don't know that we can win." His hand squeezed mine and he ushered me with a gentle pat to the hallway without a glance or another word. The sentence resonated in my head and the darkness throbbed within me.

PUZZLE

The taxi ride back was silent. A collection of contemplative minds trying to work out their part. I was fixated on trying to sort the details, desperate to make sense of what could be in those dusty piles of books to possibly help me. Something bigger weighed on my mind though; why was he alive and what was that weird feeling I had about Rosalyn's mother? They have proved themselves to be very keen on eradicating threats to their operation; surely he constituted one? Or perhaps they saw how hollow he was and realized that the likelihood of anyone believing him was too small a concern, but it didn't sit right. This wasn't how they did things.

Pierre had left us about four blocks away from Elias' apartment. He had clambered wearily out of the cab with barely a word, just a few knowing glances. Elias was calmer, less fidgety. I had seen him checking in on Ava on the way home and he didn't say anything, she was obviously doing OK.

"Ava has your things; she's already at the apartment." He allowed his head to tilt back onto the headrest and it bobbed gently with the car's movement as he relaxed. His head bounced back up with words on his lips and his gaze was for Jake. "She doesn't know. About any of this, so keep it to yourself." With that he resumed the head back position and Jake turned to me, jaw clenched. I signaled with my eyes just to leave it. After all we were staying in his apartment.

We took the door off the entrance hall where I had seen Elias bundle Ava that night and to my surprise the place just opened out again. Three bedrooms and a huge white wet room.

"You guys take the end on the right." He signaled to the room at the end of the hall, and through its partially open door I could see it was also painted white and I knew at the moment he was consciously putting distance between us. Jealousy? Anger? I didn't know. Elias' personality was proving to be somewhat complex.

We walked by the first two doors; one of which was shut. Elias' room and the middle room was halfway. Before my eyes reached into the space Ava bounded out.

"Hey. You're back. Where'd you goo... oh." Her eyes found Jake who was slightly behind me in the dim hall. "You must be Jake." She arched her neck from her doorway position to greet him before leaning back into the shelter of the room to mouth "Oh my God" at me excitedly. A smile washed over my face and a sense of pride warmed me a little.

"Jake, this is Ava. Elias' little sister." Jake took a step to stand level with me and he extended a hand but didn't speak. Formal, and rude. It was unlike him. I could tell staying in the apartment of a guy he was suspicious of didn't sit well with him and whatever his feelings for Elias, it seemed to stick for his whole gene pool.

"Hi. I've heard so much about you." She spoke with the same light in her voice that she had when she dragged herself into our room at the hostel. The room that was trashed by someone looking for me, to kill me no doubt. The memory caused me to flinch and I instinctively reached for Jake's hand. He smiled back at Ava, still no words and she shrugged it off. I turned back as we walked to the final door and apologized with my eyes. She shrugged it off and blew me a kiss before closing the door. Jake went ahead and walked into the room while my eyes, still fixed on the hall, caught Elias as he moved to enter his room. He sensed my stare and flashed his own up at me, his face pained. Without a sound and with no sign of anything at all he stepped blankly through the frame and was gone.

I closed the door gently to find Jake already in the huge bed. The sight of his bare skin meeting crisp white sheets sent a shockwave of desire through my whole body and he pulled the duvet open and patted the space where I belonged. My bag already lay on the floor and I knew that unpacking was no match for the draw of him, so I peeled away the clothes that had held the smell of Jacques' dusty books and climbed in beside him. He lay on his back and I found my place under his arm, my head resting on his chest. The sound of his heart beating was all I needed to bring me to life again; to remove the weight of the day, all the days where I had learned so much about worlds I never used to know or believe existed. I looked around me, more alien surroundings. White walls, white bedding, and white furniture. It was as if Elias was trying to force the light into the room, create an artificial peace and it was almost blinding, even by glow of a solitary floor lamp on Jake's side of the bed.

I was still trying to wind down when I noticed the lull in his breathing. Slow, deep breaths moved peacefully in his chest like waves on a deserted beach and I clung to him tighter. He was exhausted but even in sleep his grip tightened round me in return and he whispered my name.

Sleep was less than accommodating for me and I lay tormented by feelings of confusion and of growing responsibility. I thought about The Occularis community and beyond them The Collective and realized how many people were watching, waiting for me to do whatever I was meant to. The threat of a guttural cry, a glass-shattering scream, lurked in my gullet and if it weren't for what happened next it may have made it in the room and shattered the white peace.

The bed shook beneath me, or so it felt and the warmth of Jake's skin below my cheek fell away as if he was being pulled from under me. Where my eyes fixed on the wall the paint oozed away from the bricks taking the light with it and it grew dark. The vision consumed my body and I lay paralyzed while my eyes watched it unfold beneath tightly clenched lids.

While I couldn't distinguish why at first I knew it was different. I wasn't seeing as a spectator, I was seeing like I had through Jake's eyes when I watched him find the notes. Then it hit me, I sensed it, I knew those breaths, those sounds. These were Jake's eyes. He was restrained; I could feel the tight, course burns against my wrist and my ankles. The room was so dimly lit it was hard to make sense of it. The walls were stippled with deep black holes and thin brick. My body fought the realization. Skulls and bones. Jake's frame wrenched against his restraints and a hot surge of pain ran through me as they twisted and gnawed at his skin. A voice without a face sparked a memory, a recognition buried deep that I couldn't yet place. He was speaking quietly. I reached as far as my mind would allow, desperate to hear and I caught the last of a hissed sentence: "Just like your mother." What did he mean? Where did I know this voice from? Then it was over. A rigor washed over me and my body convulsed with the stress as I let out a moan. Jake shot up from his sleep, disturbed by my distress, and grabbed my shoulders.

"Scarlett. What is it? A vision?" I couldn't bring myself to say it out loud, as if that would make it more true. Yes it was a vision, one that involved the boy I loved and the very thought that this one would come true, like the others was enough to fold my body into a sob.

"Sorry, just a horrible nightmare." Not technically a lie.

Him, getting hurt? That was my nightmare, no, far worse, my hell. I needed to end this now before such a thing could happen. I waited until I had reassured him I was OK and he fell back into his slumber. If I wasn't terrorized by the thought of anything happening to him I would have stayed and watched him in all his incomprehensible beauty. I pulled one of his T-shirts from my bag and crept as quietly as I could manage from the room. The scream from earlier was back in my throat and more determined than ever as I padded towards the living room, my feet like lead on the wooden floor of the hall.

I had to work through what I had. The darkness. The bones. The words. A computer, I needed to research, be proactive, or I would explode with rage and fear. Luckily Elias had left his laptop on the counter. I pulled it under my arm and sat on the sofa. The unclosed curtains tried to tempt me with the million-dollar view, but even that was of no interest. The colors in my mind had begun to run and the threat of Jake coming to harm had rendered everything gray. Elias would probably approve, on both counts.

My trembling fingers typed simply 'Bones'. To my surprise or maybe horror, the first result stared back at me and I knew it was an answer, my answer. Catacombs of Paris. Click. Caverns, formerly stone mines. Bones of over six million people. A tunnel network below the city's streets. That was where they had taken him. I slid the computer away, rejecting its truths and searching my mind for what to do next.

I had no choice. I need the information now. Jacques.

I managed to re-enter the room, grab my jeans and Jake's hoodie without waking him. I had to be there and back within a couple of hours. He would freak, they all would, if I wasn't there when they woke up.

I made my way out of the apartment building and as the front door clunked to a close I realized I wouldn't be able to get back in without Elias. Crap. I tapped my pocket where I had stashed my phone, reassured that even if he was pissed I would be able to reach him and mildly pleased that I knew he would be more than happy to keep a secret from Jake.

My mind could only remember half an address, much to the annoyance of the taxi driver I flagged down like a mad person and whose English was not as strong as Pierre's or Jacques'. He reeled off a few names and I felt my mind turn over before one clicked and we set off into the Parisian night. Either the cold air had followed me into the car or I was chilled with unease. The latter was more likely. I fed my hands into the pockets of Jake's sweater and pulled the material tight to my body, which sent a gust of Jake scented air upwards to my face.

I paid the driver and watched his lights fade into pinpricks as he drove away before turning on my heels. The gates crunched loudly against the gravel and the noise of the rusting hinges screeched in the air. I winced as I flashed my eyes up to the house. A faint glow appeared in the shutter cracks and I knew he heard me.

I pressed my face to the wood on the door and tried to speak calmly though I wanted to scream at the top of my lungs. He had no choice but to help me. I wasn't leaving until I knew how to save Jake from whatever it was they planned to do with him.

"Jacques, open up. It is urgent." My informality and use of his name in such an aggressive manner was no longer as surprising as it once would have been. I had found a fierce resolve, the kind a mother found when defending her young. I was like a lioness. It hit me, such an obvious thought. I would die for him.

"Jacq…" My voice was cut off as the undoing of the locks began on the other side of the door. Three, four, I got to eight this time before the wood moved in its frame and some small relief found me.

His face was fraught with the remains of fractured sleep and worry. Edward Jacques; this pale, barely there human was my only hope in saving Jake and hundreds, maybe thousands of others. If it wasn't so scary it would have been a little amusing. I pushed the door out of his hand without difficulty and headed, uninvited, into the study. I grabbed the book that was in front of his chair and started flicking through it manically, praying.

"Miss Roth. I told you. Tomorrow." He raised his voice and stormed, in his own, rather slow way into the room after me.

"No. Now." I barked. He sighed as he ripped the book

from my hands and slammed it from standing height onto the desk with a thud. I was startled by the power shift and he had caught my attention.

Inhaling he took a 'seat' alongside me and raised a hand to rub his eyes with his index finger and thumb. He was exhausted, and wanted it to be over. Like me. "You shouldn't come here unannounced. Especially not on your own. Were you followed?" His eyes were incongruously fierce and he snapped his fingers in front of my face to command my attention. I had acted stupidly and selfishly. I could have led them here.

I Scoured my mind in case he had a point. Had I seen anything? No, I was blind with love and rage and horror. I had barely seen anything but the desire to keep Jake safe.

"No. I mean, I don't think so anyway." I was sheepish in the gaze of his more commanding demeanor and my hands tightened in each other inside the sweater sleeves. "I'm sorry. I know I have no right and that there is a lot at stake for everyone, but this couldn't wait."

My throat throbbed with pent up emotion and he wavered as he witnessed the role reversal. I was weak. I needed help. Now it was me who was broken.

"What on earth was so important that you risked your safety to come all the way back here in the dead of night?" He handed me a neatly folded handkerchief from his dressing gown pocket. "It's clean. Go on. I sense we may need it." His thin lips curled into a sympathetic smile and my face replied with a smile of its own, albeit a small and damaged one.

"I had another one. They are going to come for Jake. I have to stop them." I wailed, tears finally coursing down my cheeks. I explained about the bones and the catacombs and he remained silent while I spilled every detail out for him. Without a word he pulled out the book he had referred to earlier; the one Alice left safe for him. Her visions. He flicked through page after page, his index finger running through the script at speed. He stopped and tapped a page before handing it to me. I begged silently for Alice's familiar handwriting to bring me comfort.

I had another. She is in love and he is in danger. More than she knows. I see them in a dark place. She is there, hiding, hoping that she can rescue him and I feel her overwhelming desire to save him. I didn't see the outcome… seeing his fate is not in my vision path. I cannot shake the unease that their love, whilst pure and so very real, might be fated to fail. I cannot see a world where they exist together. The only way she can save him is to offer herself but with that, comes the risk that she will throw off the balance and leave herself vulnerable. She must stay strong, and focused. She must do what is right for us all.

My eyes darted back and forth and I looked up, more confused than ever. "Is she saying that I am not allowed to intervene? That it is better for me to let him fall as a casualty in this war because he might…" I paused, my tone changed, "get in the way?"

Jacques shifted uncomfortably on his pile of books. "I think what Alice meant was there is more than your love at stake here. It is bigger and more complicated. But, I suppose your interpretation is accurate, if not a little crude."

"I will not let him die for me. I need to know what my options are." My eyes pleaded and he shook off a thought that he obviously deemed unfit to share.

"Well. You could go to them. But, that would be suicide without a watertight plan which right now we do not have. You, after all, are the only thing they are really interested in. He would be a pawn in their bid to draw you in is all."

The way in which he so casually discussed the life and death of the boy I loved angered me. He didn't understand, how could he? He had been alone too long to remember how loving someone so much you would die for them was sometimes the only thing that made people feel alive in the first place.

"Well. We need to get one and fast because if getting to me is all they want and that will keep him safe then I might just do it." He sensed the severity of the threat in my voice and my eyes didn't falter.

I didn't allow him time to respond and I think I sensed relief. "I still can't get my head around much of this detail if I am honest." Even I felt like I was accusing him of something unknown. I had risen from the seat and was now pacing; though it lacked the determined pace I would have associated with a pacer, thanks to the haphazard nature of his study and the mounds of paperwork that littered the floor.

"I wouldn't expect you to. There is much to learn and research yet." Very matter of fact.

"No. You misunderstand me." I cleared my throat. "Some of this just doesn't fit. Why are you alive? I don't believe for one moment that they don't know about all this." My hands waved frantically around the room. "And I also don't understand how, after all these years, if someone as clever as you can prove what they have been doing, that no one in the world would take notice and it could still fall on me to be the one to bring them down." I exhaled. "It doesn't make sense."

I was exhausted but still driven with burning curiosity and desire to stop my latest vision from coming to life. Jacques was standing now, leafing through notebooks and papers on the desk. He revealed a small space where you could see the polished wood underneath and it filled my mind with a conjured daydream of how plush and well-to-do he once was. Now reduced to this. I looked around me again. Maybe this was the best I could expect; a half-life, sent mad by the constant threat of being caught.

His eyes widened in acknowledgment of a find and he thrust yet another dusty notebook into my hands. It was small and brown, staple bound and had curled up in submission after years of review. Scrawled in that familiar way on the cover were the words: KNOWN DEFECTORS. So people had tried to out them. People from the inside.

"That..." he pointed firmly against the book, weighing it

down in my hand, "is a comprehensive list of the ones who tried. Mostly those who witnessed first-hand the, shall we say, end of a member of The Collective and decided they couldn't handle it. You will know by now most people are born into it. They inherit this extreme hatred from lines of ancestors, but... the veil has slipped a few times, and history has seen more than a few Standards be initiated." I broke his speech with my confusion.

"Standards?" I repeated.

"Yes. Standards are normal people, with standard lives and no powers to speak of. A few have made it in and almost all have defected once they found out what it really meant to be Venari. I should say tried to defect. They never make it out." Solemnity washed over his face and he slumped in the vacated seat.

"So... what? They just take a break from hunting me and the rest of The Collective for a little while and kill the ones that try to get away?"

"Think about it Miss Roth."

"Scarlett." I corrected.

"Think about it. They already have everything they need to make it all go away so what's a few more in the body count?" He was remarkably calm delivering this grim explanation of their disgusting behavior.

"They have the police, the justice department, and the hospitals. They can pin it on criminals, declare whatever cause of death they want. That is why no one can stop them.

They have everyone they need to eradicate these problems."
His face screamed 'I told you so'.

"That aside, there is a whole special task force for the
defectors." More rifling and another book appeared. This one
was equally worn; the oily imprints of a million half
fingerprints stained its green paper jacket and I couldn't help
but feel a sad pang of guilt for Alice. Here, her fingerprints,
her life's work and I was betraying her with my helplessness.

"Task force?" My God that sounded bad.

"Yes. An elite group of Venari members almost bred for
the purpose. As in the annals of history; treachery always
results in the worst possible punishment. These... beasts, are
power hungry, motivated by inflicting terror and pain and
even more ruthless than their counterparts that issue the
orders."

I couldn't believe it was possible. Worse? How?

"There are many names for them among The Collective,
but Sanguinaries, bloody ones, is the most common." Dark
and disturbing images filled the only space left in my head
that wasn't filled with confusion and/or fear.

"Do you think that is who trashed my room at the hostel?"
I directed it at him without the back story. His face fell.

"Someone came looking?" His eyes wide with fear he
couldn't ignore the urge to glance at the door and he moved
fast clicking, sliding, threading and wedging with a symphony
of metal meeting metal until the large front door was once
again truly Fort Knoxed. If he was scared I knew I was right

to be.

"Yes. Yesterday before we came here. The room was totaled but nothing was taken; just shreds of material and shards of broken furniture and glass all over the floor." The image was burned into my mind. Jake and Elias pacing, whispered words and cautious glances as they scoped out the decimated shell of a room.

"Yet you didn't think that coming here would be a problem?" He was furious. His skin instantly glimmered with sweat and his bony hands twisted into tiny, angular fists. "You and your friends have put us all in great mortal danger. That... visit. Well, that was just the beginning. It is the first sign and they will be back, soon."

This new, frightening version of Jacques shuffled through the debris to a small wooden cabinet that stood at his waist height; its legs concealed by his research. He pulled out an old crystal decanter and a grubby short glass before pouring himself what must have been a triple shot of the brown liquid; brandy possibly. The memory of that meeting with Elias and the warm, alien burn of the alcohol in my throat reached the front of my mind as I watched his trembling hand pour another.

"We need to work fast. There won't be much time." He slammed the glass back into the cupboard and glared back at me. "I will give you as much as I think you can process tonight but you must leave. Now." He frantically began scouring the piles and shelves, his mind clearly knowing exactly which books and papers he wanted. I was baffled as to how he could possibly know what was where.

"And you don't come back tomorrow. I will send for you when I can be sure you won't be followed. There are patterns of behaviors here and we need to avoid getting caught up. That is if we aren't already." Loud, heavy breaths left his mouth as he exerted himself gathering books. He disappeared into the hall and came back with a small rucksack and stuffed three or four books into it along with a handful of loose papers. "Read this. Take it in. These are the ones she wanted you to see most. Hopefully these will help you formulate a plan." A nervous or perhaps disbelieving 'plan' left his throat and I knew then that he thought I was doomed, that we all were. The black space in my stomach expanded like a shadow growing and stretching into every part of me.

"But what about the vision? I haven't asked you about all of it. There were bones and someone said something to Jake about his mother. Why?" He nodded as though he was unsurprised by its content and he patted the bag as he handed it to me.

"It should be in there." His eyes were fixed on the bag as he shoved it against my chest. He was already back to the locks; fiddling and opening, desperate to get me out of his house. He saw me as a curse, a bad omen.

Without another word Jacques practically pushed me out into the night feeling like a half completed jigsaw puzzle. I felt, as ever, like I was drowning in awful, terrifying information that pressed on my chest like a ton of bricks. My lungs fought for position and the air battled to make it in and out enough for me to feel like I was getting any oxygen at all. I needed to get back to the apartment. I walked out onto the road that was deserted and fumbled for my phone in my pocket. I had no more money. Panic hit me. I tentatively brought up Elias' contact and pressed call. I had no choice.

I explained where I had been but not why. He was mad, seething; but he had agreed to save it for when he could tear me down in person. He sent for a taxi and I climbed in, so grateful for the security of the car; separating me from the world outside which was getting smaller and more claustrophobic by the day.

He was waiting at the front door of the building when the car pulled up. He had on some gray sweat pants but no shirt. He stuffed the fare into the cab driver's hand and ordered me inside with an aggressive nod of his head. The hallway felt much longer in silence and with so much anger in the air. I knew he was waiting for the confines of the lift so we didn't wake anyone.

The doors closed with a thud and the swoosh of the upward movement made my churning stomach tighten. I kept my eyes on the floor.

"What the hell Scarlett? Jesus." His fingers dug into my arms and he shook me hard.

"I'm sorry. I had no choice."

"Sure. No choice. What were you thinking? Why can't you

see how much danger you are in?" He dropped his hands. "I can't protect you if you keep ignoring the rules."

"Rules? Elias. I didn't ask you to protect me. I don't want you to." He recoiled at the venom in my voice, not knowing it was taking everything I had not to cry. "I needed to see him so I went. And now at least I have some information to work on. So, it wasn't all bad." I consciously softened my tone and he mirrored me. My eyes studied this strange protector; his skin, the fading bruises on his arms from the encounter he had now yellowing as they healed.

The apartment was silent and I hurried to the sofa to spill out the bag. "Scarlett. You need to sleep." Angry Elias returned. I motioned for him to be quiet; I didn't want Jake in here getting all upset too.

"No. I need to be treated like an adult. One that has a hell of a lot of work to do." He shook his head in silent fury and left me alone. His door closing quietly but shrouded in an invisible – but very real – air of rage.

It was three a.m. and I hadn't been to sleep. I made myself a triple shot coffee and sat cross-legged amidst my fate. The first tome was one of the scrapbooks. A million stories with the same end. I flicked without focus through the book, blowing tormented air through my clenched jaw when I was halted by something. Eyes. Eyes that I knew and loved so very well. Jake's eyes. But they didn't belong to him; they were in a woman's face. A beautiful, dark haired woman and I felt like I knew her. My own eyes dashed through the text under the headline; *TRAGEDY OF DOCTOR'S WIFE FOUND DEAD*. Backwards and forwards. *Mother of one, Juliette leaves behind husband Clayton Mayer, respected Doctor and son Jacob, three.* I was so consumed by the overwhelming heartbreak that I didn't even take in how. Was she? Could he have done that to his wife, Jake's mother? A chilling memory of his cold eyes, devoid of all humanity and warmth, struck me and I realized he could. He did. Clayton Mayer had killed his wife, denied Jake a mother, because she had been like me. I felt sick and cold and desperately wanted to go and hold Jake, cradle him over pain he didn't even know. This had been that feeling, the one from the study when Jacques was talking about Rosalyn's mother; on some level I had known and I was fairly sure they had gone the same way.

I wiped a tear from my eye and put the scrapbook to one side confident that Juliette's murder was the salient point for me to discover. That is what they had meant by Jake being like her I suppose; he would be classed as being as bad for being a sympathizer. He was being punished for sleeping with the enemy and failing to grow into the family business. Why hadn't they recruited Jake? What made him so unsuitable? Apart from his beautiful nature and his ability to love of course.

Book two. Notes on them. Observations, scribblings, ideas Alice had about how to find them. It was like leaping into the cell of a mad person; finding what looked like incoherent rants etched on the walls. Though I knew Alice was sane and the idea this could all be some dark fantasy was just a dream.

It was difficult to focus in such dim light but I didn't want to wake anyone; my head was pounding from stifled tears and squinting. So many words and nothing stood out that I didn't already know or hadn't been told. I was searching specifically for links to my visions, information that could help me steer the course away from Jake.

Secrets, blah. History, blah. Then…

I followed one of the bloody ones to the entrance of the catacombs on Place Denfert-Rochereau and I am certain now that this is the location of the meetings and suspect it may even have been home to the European Council. What better place than a museum of death and decay?

I had an address. That was progress. I scoured my mind to see if I could recall any other details that might let me know how long I had left but I couldn't get beyond the horror of seeing Jake wrestling those restraints, feeling his pain and the sound of that voice that I just couldn't place.

There was a stack of papers I had yet to look at and one other book but even my caffeine and adrenalin combination was faltering against the wall of exhaustion which advanced on me with frightening force. I needed to focus. I needed to sleep, so I tucked everything back into the bag and took it with me to the room where Jake lay sleeping peacefully. Unaware of the horrors that had been and those forecast to come.

His sleeping frame molded instantly around me and I allowed myself just one moment of lust and enjoyment as I relished in the contact of his skin on mine.

Sleep was evasive, my head too full of the search for answers and hope. I took glimpses of Jake to break the growing apprehension about morning coming. Morning meant I needed to find some way to be alone, find time to read the rest of the material and speak to Elias before he outed my midnight escapades to Jake.

Jake's hair fell just that way onto the pillow and I was compelled to touch it gently before I crept out for the second time to the kitchen. I was startled by the presence of a dark shape moving in the dim light. I let out an audible gasp. Elias.

He spun on his heels and a spoon clattered across the hard floor, which was cold under my feet. We both winced, hoping it wouldn't wake the sleeping faction of our odd party and we stood frozen with expectation. Nothing. Coast was clear. We both exhaled with relief and he glared accusatorially at me with a finger to his lips like I was an errant child. I scowled. I resented his patronization; the way he was acting like my father. A wave of guilt cascaded over me as I noted my lack of communication with my parents, with Taylor, Lydia and Brooke. It was swiftly followed by the realization that what really bothered me was how OK with my absence everyone was. I had found the trust and freedom I had been so determined to achieve; and it felt lonely. There was no sense of accomplishment to be had.

"So... You can start by explaining without lying, what the hell you thought you were doing last night." He was still shirtless and that only added to my inability to articulate what it was that I had been doing. He gripped his coffee two-handed and took a sip, his eyes closed as the caffeine made its way to his veins. He sighed.

I stood, momentarily frozen as I tried to organize my thoughts. The inside of my head felt more like Jacques' study; jumbled thoughts and memories jostled for a position and my mouth went into overload as I spilled out the torrent of information; my vision, how Jacques had told me about the bloody ones, the books, his anger, finally the part about Jake's mom being murdered for being like me. That final sentence wracked my body with a cry, a slow and silent one that remained in my chest like a build-up of pressure that caused my ribcage to ache.

Elias looked almost scared, which I hadn't expected. "Whoa. That stuff, I mean, I might think he is a little... well, you know?" I did. "But, his mother. That is really tough. Are you going to tell him?" He swigged another mouthful of coffee with his left hand as he poured one for me with his right. I considered my answer as I accepted the mug. It was slightly chipped and there was a questionable stain on the inside, which made me shuffle it around. My lips found a clean section and I took my own sip, relishing the boost.

"I don't know. Is it my place? Though I feel like if I don't I am betraying him." I studied Elias' face carefully. I had noticed more than one occasion that his eyes often said something very different to his mouth and on this of all subjects I was keen to assess any differences.

He padded out from behind the counter and paused alongside me. He gave me a long, weighted stare, which lasted long enough to ensure I was thoroughly unnerved and he was halfway to the sofa before answering me. "Surely if you have this..." He paused as he searched for the word and I tensed, already knowing that I wasn't going to like what was to follow. He slouched oh so casually onto the sofa where a dip was waiting to cup his form. His body was taut and he hinted at a smirk when he caught my fleeting glance at the way his chest gently rose and then fell. "...This, super connection that you say, then surely you have to. He might sense it. Or you might show it to him somehow. Pierre says that can happen." He was picking a fight, trying to make me bite at his insinuation that Jake and I weren't as close as I made out. He was hoping and he was wrong.

"I know it can happen. I am aware of my powers." He sniggered incredulously and shook his head. I was silenced with anger and some embarrassment. He waited until his drink was back up to his face before he muttered something under his breath.

"What did you just say?" My angry, stronger alter ego had returned and I felt bolstered by her presence. He feigned innocence.

"Nothing. It was nothing." The remnants of his smirk

lingered on his lips.

"You know what Elias? Screw you. You haven't protected me. All you've done is insult me and/or Jake and mock me and really I don't need that in my life." I slammed my drink down onto the counter and turned back to him. "I think we need to end this. This weird thing. Jake and I will find someplace else to stay. Consider yourself released from duty. I am sure there are others girls out there looking for a lame ass knight in shining armor with multiple personalities and misogynistic tendencies." I was out of breath from my rant and rage. I searched his face not sure if I would be met by some smart-ass version of Elias or the humble, apologetic one which tended to follow his more inappropriate self.

"Maybe you're right. You two lovebirds go out there. Into the big bad world and see how you get on." His voice was filled with poison. He was wishing us ill with all his might and I was burning with such disappointment and sadness. I didn't want it to be like this. I moved through the door into the hall where the bedroom doors remained shut. It was cold and I didn't know if it was just me, chilled by my discord with Elias; the strange, dark mystery airport guy that had come so close to being a friend but just never made it.

Suddenly his voice boomed from the room beyond without regard for the sleeping bodies in the rooms alongside me. "You can't save him you know." My spine was electrified with fear. What if he was right? No, I wouldn't let that happen. But my mind backed to my conversation with

Jacques. He had shared that feeling, I had seen it in his eyes. Refusing to show him he had bothered me I continued to the bedroom where, despite Elias' best efforts Jake was still sleeping, he had starred outwards across the whole bed, his left foot dangling listlessly from the side closest to me. I knew I had to tell him, but not now.

"Jake. Jake, wake up. We need to go. We're leaving." I traced the line of his ribcage across his back with my fingers and he shuffled round to let the line find his chest.

"What? Now? Why?" His voice still distorted by sleep he brought his hands to his eyes and rubbed the night away before opening those eyes and burning my soul with a stare that was full of love.

"Let's just say Elias and I have decided his, role, isn't working out and now you're here I don't think we need any extra baggage. So, we need to find somewhere to stay." I was already up and off the bed. Throwing the few things I had out back into the bag. I felt the bag of documents beneath my hands and buried them deeper.

I heard in his voice that his face had hardened and I knew his perfect lips were molded into that angry thin line now. "Scarlett. Has he done something? I swear..." I averted my eyes in a bid to diffuse it but it was the wrong choice and it only aggravated him further. The white room suddenly felt darker and filled with tangible tension.

"Scarlett." He pressed. "Look at me." He had shifted up onto his elbow and his face straightened with ready-to-go male ego. I conceded and met his eyes.

"Jake, no. Nothing like that. I just don't think we need anyone else. Besides, it isn't fair to Ava. She is really sweet and I don't want her getting dragged into this. It's better this way. Trust me." I slid onto the bed next to him fully aware that I knew a kiss would dissuade him from posing any further questions. He allowed his lips to be parted by my tongue and he pulled me towards him, enveloping me in those muscled arms as he tasted me.

"Aaannnnd that's for another time." I laughed as I playfully rolled off the bed, desire still hot and coursing through my veins but needing to keep my head. First things first. Out of here, somewhere to stay and then a way to find out more. It was hours before we could go back to see Jacques and I had to make progress before then.

"What do you do to me?" He smiled as he shifted uncomfortably and pulled the sheet around himself, protecting his modesty as he spun his feet out of the bed.

Within the hour we had packed up and headed out following a slightly heated and definitely testosterone heavy exchange between Jake and Elias. I was certain at one point that Elias was going to punish me for my earlier remarks by revealing my midnight jaunt and all its resulting drama, but to my surprise he barely even looked at me.

Jake needed to pick up his bags from the lockers at the hostel he was supposed to be staying in the night before and we stood for a moment on the street outside which was when he read my mind's silent dream.

"Look. I know there is a lot going on. But, let's have one freaking thing that is ours and normal and exciting. What do you say?" His expectant eyes were alive with something wicked, good wicked and I simply nodded and he grasped my hand. We grabbed a metro and shunted through hordes of people before taking a cab. He had made me cover my ears when he had named the destination and I lost myself in the excitement. Jake's hand burned my skin and teased anticipation and desire to be stored for later as we were driven through the winding roads of Paris.

When the car stopped I looked up from my seat to the impossible grandeur of The Ritz. Jake squeezed my hands and sensed my question. "What are you...?" His finger met my lips and he pressed them together.

"Shhhh." At the same time a doorman opened my cab door and I felt immediately ashamed of my attire. This was not the place for faded jeans and converse. Holy crap, this place was amazing.

Inside, Jake ushered me to a plush seat while he went to reception. I watched him from across the lobby as he spoke to the girl behind the desk. She was immaculate, as you would imagine. Her white blonde hair was swept into a faultless chignon and her necktie fell just so over her sculpted, tanned collarbones. The most noticeable thing was her face. Despite how incongruous Jake looked in his dark denim jeans and creased gray shirt in such opulent surroundings, she was still mesmerized by him and she hadn't even thought to wonder how it was he had come to be here. I was wondering that but no, she was totally immersed in him, you could see it in her eyes. Jake pointed over at me and her face sought me out with a blush; probably as she realized I had caught her checking him out.

Jake sidled back over with the wicked look back on his face. "OK, Mrs. Beck. Your suite awaits." The concierge was already showing us to the elevator and my feet felt like they were gliding in a state of glorious disbelief.

"Mrs. Beck?" I mouthed to him. He stifled a laugh and motioned for me to keep it quiet. All would become clear I suspected.

UNDERGROUND

"Your room Mr. and Mrs. Beck. It is a Junior Deluxe Suite. I am sure you will find it has everything you need, but please do not hesitate to call down to reception should you require anything at all." The door swung open and my mouth followed suit immediately. My God. I stood for so long in wild awe that Jake had already tipped and thanked the bellboy, well man, and only the sound of the door clicking to a close roused me.

"Explain. How... I mean?" I couldn't stop looking at everything. The room spilled out in front of me; a beautiful living room with huge expensive cream sofas arranged around an exquisite turned wood table. Beyond was a bedroom the likes of which I had only ever seen in fairy stories. Huge pillars marked where the living area ended and the bedroom began. The bed would have filled Jake's entire apartment at home and the colors; cream met gold touches everywhere; the bed's headboard, filigree at the tops of the pillars. It was beyond anything I had ever seen and surpassed any hotel I had ever been in for sure.

"Well. I hadn't even had chance to tell you about everything, what with all the drama. I had more money than I thought thanks to..." The pause was to avoid speaking his name. "And I had always planned to do something a little like this, give us, give you, a proper treat and now seemed like a good time. Besides, if nothing else, with an alias and this being the Ritz and all, no one is going to come looking for us here." His smile widened. He had done good and he knew it. Oh the ways I wanted to thank him, this hypnotic, beautiful boy.

"I don't know what to say. How did you even get a room here... surely it gets booked for like, ever?" My eyes were greedily searching the room, trying to see it all, believe it all. So romantic. Even the thought of being a pretend wife was exhilarating.

"I told her we were on honeymoon and that we had reservations elsewhere but that we had been let down and this had always been your first choice etc... blah. She bought the sob story and sorted us out three nights. That was the most they had."

"She bought you, you mean? You must have seen how she was looking at you?" He scooped me into his arms and pulled me flush with him.

"No I didn't because all I could think about was getting

125

you in there." He signaled to where our private living area, scream, met our kingside bedroom. A knowing smile teased my mouth upwards and I let myself fall into him completely. He had me, all of me and I loved it.

It was noon before I knew it and the softness of the hotel robe against my bare, well-kissed skin felt like I was wearing a cloud. Jake was propped up in bed alongside our room service tray strewn with leftovers of amazing fresh fruit, pastries and empty coffee cups. The sensation of him teasing a strawberry against my mouth flooded my body with warmth and I wrapped myself in splendid comfort.

The afterglow dimmed as the need to make some progress and tell Jake the unthinkable returned and I realized I had to find out more. I needed to learn about the bloody ones, the ones who were planning to take Jake and to where. The catacombs. I had to go there but I knew there was no way he would let me out of his sight. Suddenly ditching Elias felt like it might have been a mistake; if nothing else his feelings towards Jake meant it would have been easy to get him on side to help me escape and explore for a while.

I perched on the edge of the bed; its perfect linen now entangled around a perfect Jake. My eyes fixed on where the white sheet met his abdomen and followed his skin up to the line of his jaw. He was beautiful. I leaned over and kissed him, bowing to the compulsion, like I lost all free will looking at him and his hair, the brown lightened by the sun but still perfect, twisted and turned on top of his head where it was longer.

"So... I have been thinking. I know we have all that stuff with Jacques, but we should try to have a day of, you know, touristy stuff. Like you said, no one knows we are here at least for now so we can get out and have a few hours. I have some ideas." I watched for his response. His eyes motioned to the bed and his mouth widened with a smile.

"I have a few ideas too." He patted the bed as he lifted the linen up and gestured for me to get in. I rolled my eyes and threw one of our seemingly hundred pillows at him and he put forward a mock petulant lip.

"OK. Your ideas Mrs. Beck?" We both laughed at the notion, but somewhere deep inside my subconscious unashamedly reminded me how much I wished I was Mrs. Mayer. Idiot.

"Well... and stay with me on this." A twinge of guilt spiked in my stomach because I knew I was leading him there under false pretenses but if he knew that I was putting myself on their radar to save him, we'd never get there.

"I really want to do the whole catacombs thing. You know... forgotten city and all that. There was that film set there with Pink in it." His face contorted from the smile into a kind of scrunched disappointment. He wasn't going to go for it. Crap.

"I remember the film, it sucked." He shifted up to a sitting position. "So, our way of forgetting all the darkness and death is to go underground and spend the day with a million bones?" He shook his head.

"More than six million sweetie." I forced my voice into saccharin sweet mode and he conceded with a look as he got off the bed.

"Hooray. Sounds, well...terrible. But, anything for you." He winked and flashed me a killer smile that stirred me and as he headed for the bathroom I heard his chuckle as he discovered the goofy heart I had drawn on the mirror after my shower.

I pulled on a dress, my first of the trip and went against Jake's preference and pulled my hair up. It was hot and my hair stood out like a campfire at night so the less of it you could see the better. In case anyone was out there waiting.

I felt slightly more appropriately dressed as we sashayed through the lobby hand in hand, my pale blue dress swung just above my knees and I had opted for some cute sandals. Jake moved his hand to the small of my back to help me negotiate the lobby and I watched as woman after woman gorged on the sight of him in his navy shorts that stopped just above the top of his shins. His skin glowed with the residue of the sun from below his impossibly white T-shirt and the girl at the desk, the same one who checked us in, bit her lip nervously when she realized I had caught her checking out my 'husband' for the second time in under twenty-four hours.

The Parisian sun did not disappoint and we were relishing the warmth, the normality of walking down a street hand in hand like a real couple; one whose fate didn't sit in the hands of archaic megalomaniacs.

For the first time I was enjoying the feeling of being a tourist. My self-consciousness had been temporarily subdued by Jake's presence and there was something refreshing about blending in with my map and man in hand. Jake was acting relaxed but I knew he always had one eye on the shadows, checking out suspicious lone strangers and his arm had darted out in front of me on more than one occasion as he shielded me from some perceived threat.

When we reached the address, a queue of short-wearing people shuffled and jostled into position in a line that snaked along a wall. Entrée de Catacombs was marked on the sidewalk in front of large black gates that were filled with darkness and it was hard to marry the image of what was below with the sunny, fast-paced streets above. Cameras clicked wildly as people snapped themselves in poses at the gates below signs in all languages. One of which warned of long queues and the need to book and I knew Jake was thinking we might escape my planned activities and swap them for his. Tempting as that was with the image of him lying in our huge hotel bed, I knew there was more at stake here.

"Ah ah. Don't even say it. If we get in line now I think we might just make this next tour." He rolled his eyes and studied the rest of the info presented for the benefits of the waiting crowds.

"Three hours?" He sighed and pouted. "You have to be

kidding me?" Even I thought three hours sounded too long to be surrounded by the dead but if there was any hope of me working out how to stop the vision; I had to know the territory.

The line moved impossibly slowly and the sun was beating down on us the whole time. We got in just as Jake was beginning to get restless and I brought him back round with a smile and a lingering kiss.

Inside it smelled of damp and dust and the heat radiating from hundreds of bodies trudging down the smallest staircase I had ever had the misfortune of using. One hundred and thirty steps down ensured there was only the yellow glow of artificial light in the rooms at the bottom. We walked through a museum-like exhibition that told stories about the catacombs, their purpose and history. Jake shot me a few looks of boredom or exasperation and he kept loosening his grip on my hand to let some air pass between our clammy skins.

The hum of conversation broke the silence and we carried on through blank walls, no bones just old stone punctuated by the odd street name. There were intersections dotted along our path and though obviously not part of the tour I couldn't extinguish the burning desire to take the less traveled route, I was certain they wouldn't conduct anything in the more public areas; the signs themselves said that half the paths were unused but they wouldn't block them off for fear of trapping people inside. Apparently it was quite common for people to pay local experts and explorers to take them down off the beaten track, in the chasms and depths less traveled by the eight euro tourist tour. Something to remember.

The air felt close and devoid of real oxygen and I couldn't determine if that was my anxiety or fact; the black space in my stomach had been working overtime since we left behind the glorious, comforting sunshine for this graveyard.

The non-descript tunnels were brought to an end by sculptures, carved directly into the stone of grandiose buildings, the impressiveness of which was tainted by the flash of a million bulbs and the angry French guides shouting 'Pas le flash'.

We were halted as the line rubbernecked at one of the catacombs' most famous sites; the warning carved into the Ossuary's stone portal. *Arrête! C'est l'empire de la Mort*, the reassuringly direct, *Stop! This is the Empire of the Dead*. A chill ran the length of me as my last vision flooded back to the fore of my mind. This would not be a tomb for Jake.

"Well. This is cheerful." Jake squeezed my hand playfully and I tried to conceal my face from his by looking deeper into the path ahead. I didn't want him to read the fear in my eyes, not here.

"This is history Jake. It is a little creepy though." I conceded. There was no way of denying it. No one should be surrounded by this much death and decay; it brought an overwhelming sadness through the air, as if the souls of these six million people were trapped here too in this dim, incongruous commercial lighting.

The impact of the bone-lined walls was noticeable on everyone. The din of conversation hushed upon first sight as people worked to get their heads around what they were seeing. The tunnels went on and on with the occasional break for a side room or narrow tunnel. The crowd halted as someone up ahead took a picture and I found myself adjacent to a small room. It was unlit, one of the unused, but I had this weight of fear, this recognition and I knew it was the one from my vision. I had to get in there, to see for sure.

People shoved and jostled us keen to get their next picture of death and read more of the grim inscriptions. I instinctively kissed Jake and nudged him playfully towards the opening. His eyes widened with surprise but I knew with my lips I could pretty much guide him there. The line filled the space we left and it was like we were never there.

I pressed him into the wall, out of sight of the crowd and he smiled through our touching lips. "Well. This tour just got a whole lot better." I winked at him in the dim light afforded by the tour route outside and turned to face the room.

"I just fancied having a little look at what they don't show us." He slumped, dejected against the wall with a thud.

"Oh. There was me thinking it was about to get interesting." I ignored him, lost in my reconnaissance and studied the room. I pulled my phone out of my pocket to use its light. This was the room. I could sense it and the smell in my nostrils matched my memory exactly. I was pained by the image of Jake here, shackled and I was compelled to look for anything that would help. The floor housed a series of drag marks, like a chair had been pulled across it a hundred times. They used this room often. There was nothing else; its bare walls held no further clues and I had run out of time without Jake getting suspicious. I grabbed his hand and pulled him towards the stone arch when there; in the middle of the stone above the doorway was a simple carving made into the stone. V. It could have been coincidence, but something deep within me, an untapped, primal intuition stronger than any I had ever had stirred and told me I knew, it was them. What was this place? A kind of rent-an-office for cults? Jake followed, still disappointed in my failure to deliver on the passion front and I playfully smacked his behind to lighten him up. He turned and smiled and I was back on track though weighed down by the knowledge I would have to come here again, alone.

We trekked through the rest of the tour, me totally preoccupied with the 'V' and Jake dragging his feet like a sulky toddler. By the time we reached the ascent to the street several others on the tour joined us in a collective sigh of relief. The feeling of the light as it hit our skin, the warmth of it coupled with the revitalizing lungfuls of real air was amazing. We scrunched our eyes as they adjusted to the light and took in the surroundings. It was the weirdest thing; a side street with no signage or reference to the horrors below, we were just outside and back to reality.

The afternoon was spent in blissful normality. Jake and I

had found ourselves a patch of grass and eaten a picnic of cheeses and beautiful French bread under a blistering sun which I watched move beyond the outline of his hair from where I lay on his legs. We were breathing Paris and it was certainly the city of love where we found ourselves. I happen to know I would have been appalled by our public displays of affection if I were one of the many passers-by subjected to our outpouring of lust. We were simply appreciating each other, for hours, sometimes with hands and a simple touch and sometimes with kisses, which were like a silent translation of love and fear and all the things we couldn't dare say or even think about.

I knew we had to get back and ready to go for round two with Jacques and see what the rest of the deal was. I hadn't yet figured out how I would get round the fact I already had so much stuff from him and the memory of my reckless midnight adventure plagued me with yet more guilt.

Jake's head was tilted up towards the afternoon sun and through the sepia lenses of my sunglasses he looked like a modern day Grecian god, bronzed and sculpted just for me. My eyes ran down his throat to his Adam's apple and I was filled with an insatiable need to kiss him there, all over his neck where his pulse gently throbbed and made me feel like I was the hungriest I had ever been. A symptom of my mind's wanderings, I stroked his thigh, which was firm and taut beneath his shorts and he was roused from a sunny dream, his reactions slow and sleepy.

"We have to go baby. I need to get showered and changed before we go back to see Jacques this evening." That house. I didn't want to go back, especially with Jake. I needed someone with whom I could talk freely about the vision and sound out my options. There was only one person and he wasn't an option right now and then it struck me that Elias and Pierre may still turn up; after all they were involved now. If I were them I would probably not be able to pretend I wasn't interested and go back to reality to wait for some ancient war to reach the streets. Jake nodded in agreement and shifted from below me to rise into a stretch. His arms hoisted me into him and we stood; that sweet smell of warm skin and grass combined was intoxicating.

"Let's go back to our suite Mrs. Beck," Jake said in a ridiculous accent that brought me out in a fit of laughter and we swung into each other as we headed back.

Our room was beautifully tidy and the made bed screamed at me to throw Jake on it and cling on to today's bubble for a little longer, but I knew it was time to face whatever the hell was coming and my lack of a real plan was starting to be a concern to say the least. We left the tranquility of the hotel for another muggy cab ride and something just felt different, like we were riding into the eye of the storm. There had been a tectonic shift in our mood too; though unspoken, we were both mourning the end of our time as 'tourist couple' and our re-assimilation into 'couple with the weight of the world on our shoulders'. I released the window, which brought a sobering blast of cool air as the driver wound through the city to the house.

The huge gates were open and my growing sense of unease reached a crescendo as I shot a look at Jake, who, only having been the one time, knew this meant something was off. This man, the one with twenty locks, would not leave such an invitation when there was so much unrest and so much at stake. Our hands were wound tight and Jake took the lead as we walked cautiously up the path. The door was intact and closed so that was a better sign. Jake knocked firmly and we waited, but Jacques didn't come and there was no sign of that familiar metallic clash as the locks mobilized into action. Silence, more than the last times I had been here. A shared sense of concern hung between us in the air and Jake stood in front of me in defense of whatever he perceived the threat to be. His worry only fed my own and I recognized the quickening of my pulse as the sound of it in my ears drowned out Jake's voice.

"Jacques. If you're in there you have thirty seconds before I kick this door down." I watched his lips, the lips that had kissed me so many times and it was strange to see them working in more serious circumstances. Even in fear I took a moment of longing. The time we had spent together in the last few days had been so wonderful in spite of everything and his protectiveness over me and mine over him had resonated between us. We would do anything for each other. My mind flashed to the dark room with the 'V' and I conceded again to the sacrifice I was so prepared to make if it came to it.

Jake, unappeased by the continued silence, took a step back and launched a powerful foot charged with frustration and fear at the door. The wood buckled and my eyes winced as shards fled the scene like sparks from an explosion and the door swung open into the lit hallway. The noise of the door's chains and locks swinging in the aftershock was the only sound to be heard. The déjà vu of watching Jake tread silently by the shattered wood at the hostel was at the front of my mind as I followed him, my hands tightly wound round his arm.

The hall was clear and there were no signs of foul play. The grandfather clock chimed the hour and we both flinched at the drone of its bells, feeling like we were in some lame horror film. This was the part where the tension music started to build and the teenagers met their end at the hands of a chainsaw wielding madman. But no one came and we didn't move, still recovering from the clock's interruption. Jake peered off to the right as he took another tentative step forward and habit, if you could call it that, forced me toward the study. From my position in the hall the room looked its usual, messy state but the second step stopped my heart and a guttural, primal scream rose in my throat and invaded the air. I felt Jake spin behind me as I dropped to my knees.

The mess was beyond the recognized chaos, the piles of papers were scattered and ripped like the curtains and glass in my hostel room. The air felt cold as my eyes processed what they saw.

Jacques' body lay in an impossible, twisted and contorted heap on the floor; his left arm was bent back and round, broken in at least two places and his legs were splayed, with deep red blood staining and pooling, still new, from below his chinos. A slow slick of blood was still advancing on the floor from an unseen wound on his head and his eyes were wide open, completely stricken with terror and bloodied from multiple cuts and slashes on his face. I felt Jake walk by me but I couldn't register anything but this body, the man I had seen hours before, now hollow and broken on the floor. His words about this being a war resounded in my head, which was pounding. I hadn't noticed I was sobbing and rocking on my knees, papers below me. Words on my fate, the tasks ahead destroyed by blades and blood, were strewn everywhere.

Jake pressed his fingers to Jacques' neck and without looking at me simply shook his head solemnly. Dead. He was dead and I couldn't pretend this wasn't another message. "This is all my fault." My hands shrouded my eyes as tears streamed down my face. Jake's hands met mine and he dragged them away fiercely.

"No. You hear me Scarlett. This is not your fault." His hands groped desperately at my face, forcing me to meet his gaze and they ruined me. I felt like I was disappearing, fading in the abyss of emotions I had been so sure I could keep in. I pulled myself up to my feet.

"They have let him live this whole time, even when they took Alice. The second I show up he is dead." I walked in apparent slow motion to where Jacques' body lay limp on the floor.

"This is all my fault." Jake was silent as I crouched next to the body. I was rocked by a shiver and my hand found my mouth as it stifled another moan at the horror. It was worse up close and the metallic tang of blood hung in the dusty air. His mouth was open in a frozen scream. No one should die this way. I went to turn my head when a flash from the open scream caught my eye and the shock made me recoil across the floor.

"Jake. There's something in his mouth." He appeared beside me and ushered me, hand under my armpits, further from the body. I waited, suspended in confusion as he leant over the body, his trembling fingers hanging over the parted lips. He glanced at me with a look that suggested he couldn't believe we were here doing this and I found myself asking the same question. His fingers moved swiftly and he produced a tiny black and silver square that glinted again under the study lights. My mouth opened to ask but we were both startled by a sound; there was someone in the hall. Jake motioned for me not to move and stay silent; his fingers still clutching the mystery object. He crawled, avoiding the pool of blood to reach me and his body shielded me as we held our breath. If it was the police we'd be arrested. If it was them, we'd both be killed. I wanted to run, for us to both make for the open door and run so fast we would be away from this, but my muscles and nerves were rigid, weighted with pure and overwhelming fear to the point I couldn't be sure my heart wouldn't just give out.

Footsteps approached and the owner was treading carefully, hoping not to be heard. Jake was holding me back and I was shaking behind his touch as we waited. The shadow moved into the room before the body and all I could think of was how I had failed him, the beautiful boy in front of me who had lost a father – admittedly not my fault – flown across the world and been thrust into living hell for me and I hadn't been able to stop it. Maybe this was how they got him in the vision; I led him right into their hands.

A hooded figure, all in black, stepped with silent purpose into the room and Jake rose to his feet in front of me. My view was obscured by my desire to hide; I didn't even look up ashamed of my role in this disaster.

"You." Jake spat the word.

"You," the hidden voice responded. I stood from my fetal crouch and saw their eyes locked. The mystery man was Elias. His hands pulled down the hood and his eyes found me. They were hollow and angry, still shrouded with thoughts and emotions I couldn't decipher. He was like a foreign language, mysterious and frustrating; I didn't know what was with him and I didn't know why he was here.

My hands were on Jake's back and his muscles were fraught with tension; he didn't trust Elias and as I studied those dark eyes for the hundredth time I wasn't sure I did anymore. Elias looked beyond me and his eyes widened the way mine had when I first found this scene, in the place where we had all stood and idly chatted about this situation like we naively thought we could control it and now it felt like I'd never have control over my life again.

"Holy Christ. What the hell?" His face was angular and his stare held a weight of judgment. He thought we had something to do with this. "Is he dead?" His eyes were confusing; dark and conflicted.

Jake mocked his adversary with a round of forced, slow applause and Elias scowled. "Yes and I don't like your tone."

"Well I don't like walking in here to see this guy looking like road kill and you two just hanging around." I knew I had to interject; it was only going to get uglier. If that was even possible.

"Elias." It was a command for him to give me eye contact. "Calm down. We got here about twenty minutes ago. Jake and I found him like this. We were just processing it, trying to work it all out when you scared the crap out of us, creeping around in the dark."

He sniggered and broke the look. "What are you doing here anyway?" The tension was almost unbearable and we were all doing a terrible job of concealing it.

"I was here with you remember? He told us to come back. And based on the crap he intimated was likely to go down I thought I had every right to find out what was next." He took a step closer and squared up to Jake. I pushed my way between them and shoved him back, forcing him to clench his teeth, and the sound of scrunched paper broke the silence.

"OK. I get it. Enough. Put the attitude away. We need to get out of here before the police show up. We can't trust them, or anyone else and we don't want to be implicated." I turned between them and they were still frozen.

"So... your great plan is to just go... leave with no information and leave this guy, whose death is basically on you, alone in his own blood. Classy." He was already turned, poised to go but Jake had other plans. He shoved me towards the desk and grabbed Elias' shoulder. Elias turned, already smirking; he wanted this, the fight, and he made sure I saw it in his eyes. Why was he so calm?

"Come on Jake. You want to go? We can go." His mouth spread wide into a smile but I could see the fear. Always so confusing with him. "If I were you..."

"You'd what? Please, enlighten me with your wisdom." Jake was seconds from losing it and I touched his hand with mine but he shrugged me away. It cut me like a knife and I stepped away.

"Well... I am pretty sure I'd be more worried about the fact my girlfriend was being hunted down. I'd probably have put some effort into finding out what I was up against and I definitely..." Emphasis was on the definitely. I was so angry at him it was almost enough to make me forget where we were, what we were standing next to. "...Would have steered her the hell away from this hell hole. And you can hate me as much as you want. But you know what, Jake? You are watching her play into their hands and you are failing her." I knew there was nothing worse he could say to Jake than that. Jake shook out his hands and balled them into tight fists. He swung at Elias, who laughed as he ducked and Jake ploughed his fist into the doorway, which stood resolutely against him, and he grasped his hand with the other, blood oozed down between his knuckles. Elias shook his head and tutted sarcastically. Jake turned to him but Elias was kneeling beside Jacques.

"What are you doing? We need to leave!" He didn't answer. He was studying the body, moving his eyes across him from his bloodied hair to his strewn limbs. He was looking for something. Jake and I acknowledged the shared thought in silence and I watched him pat his jeans pocket checking the mystery square was still there and he shook his head under Elias' radar; he wanted to make me understand, Elias wasn't to know.

Elias came to his feet, an unrecognizable expression on his face. The staunch determination on his face had faltered and his eyes were wider, the white standing out against his skin, which looked almost gray. When he thought we had averted our gaze he casually brushed open the cold fingers on Jacques' hand, looking. He walked out, overtaking us, his sweater pulled over his hands.

"Have you touched anything?" We were both thinking,

calculating. "I said, have you touched anything?" The absence of whatever he wanted to know or find was obviously an issue and his tone was aggressive. Jake looked at him directly, his own hands wrapped in his jacket to avoid spilling any of his blood. "The door. But no prints." Elias nodded and ducked out through the frame into the night. Jake gently tugged my wrist and paused. I needed to take more information. I pulled my shirt over my hands and scooped up some untouched books from the far corner of the desk. My arms heavy with exhaustion and pages I glanced back to the body, it seemed somehow older now. The red of the blood was browning but the smell of it stained me and my clothes so much I had to give myself a look over to check there was none on me. We stepped out into the night leaving the door gaping open. Elias had paused on the path, waiting for us. The light had gone and the air had lost its summery warmth. Paris twinkled beyond, oblivious to what was happening in its suburbs and I rebuilt the human wall between Jake and Elias as I bought time. Under the glow of the streetlight Elias looked even paler, almost ill, while Jake had reddened, eager for another shot at his nemesis.

"So. What is our story?" I sounded like a bad actress on a crime drama but it seemed important to me that we at least made some kind of plan. Elias stared at me with such disdain I had to look away. "Well... it seems to me that we need to agree on our story," I muttered.

"Jesus Scarlett. Get a clue. We don't need one because we

know who did it. If the police wanted to come then they would, they own them. When will you get it?" Jake's chest inflated with fury. Elias had a finger poised; pointing at me and it was pink with something. I wanted to be wrong, but it looked like blood. When had he touched him? I remembered the attempt he had made to open the dead hand and it settled the hideous train of thought I was running away with, but there were still too many questions about his being there, his behavior that didn't add up.

"Back away Elias. I mean it. I won't miss a second time." Jake pushed me along the sidewalk and back off in my direction. "We're going our way. I suggest you go yours and we didn't see you here and likewise. OK?" He turned his back and pulled me with him.

"Fine." Elias set off on foot in the other direction. "I pity you." He whispered it, but I heard it. Jake couldn't have because he would never have let it slide the mood he was in. Jake took the books from me and passed me his phone. "Call us a cab in a few minutes when we are further away. Why'd you take these?" He looked so deep into my eyes that I almost said it all, the vision, the last visit, but if anything what I had seen tonight only made it more important for me to make a move. I shrugged. I wanted to say why; desperation.

BALANCE OF POWER

The plush surroundings of our hotel room were so far removed from the horrors we had just seen it was hard to associate the two. I felt jet lagged, like there must have been a time difference or parallel universe in motion. Jake spilled the books from his arms onto the cream sofa and they left dusty gray lines as they tumbled across the perfectly plumped cushions. My mind recalled the blood and the cream turned red in the light of my memory. I shook it off and sat on the edge of the bed. We were sharing thoughts, no powers, just knowing each other and thinking the same. Something was wrong with the way tonight had been, apart from the obvious discovery of a body – that was really wrong – but there was more and we weren't saying it because even the idea felt so preposterous.

I was lost in my myriad of thoughts and hallucinations about the pool of creeping blood when Jake tossed something onto the bed. "Scarlett. Check that out." He pointed to the object he had just discarded, the square. "It's a memory card. For a camera or phone or something." I took up the tiny shape in my hands. On inspection it was a rectangle not a square and it seemed so obvious now that this was what it was. Did I want to see what was on this? I was obviously meant to. For reasons I wasn't sure of I knew that Jacques left it for me. He knew I was coming and he needed to be sure I knew more. It had been clear from our brief meetings that his time with Alice meant he knew me well, the same way she seemed to and within the confines of my tortured mind I suddenly felt very isolated; the ones who knew me, my role, my fate. They were all dead.

He placed a hand tenderly on mine as he all but fell into the spot next to me. He pushed his lips into my neck and I leaned into him. "Thank you," I whispered, my voice stolen by grief and anxiety.

"What for?" He genuinely had no idea what I thought I should be thankful for and that was half the reason; he really felt like this was normal, well not normal, but just what he needed to do and I loved him but resented myself for making this our reality when it was only ever destined to be mine.

"C'mon Jake. You can't honestly be OK with this." I waved the tiny card in the air. "You could have anyone, without all this crap. We cannot go on pretending like this is fine and whatever happens to me we just expect you to go with it. It could be, well, worse, you could get hurt and I'd never be able to forgive myself." My hands possessed with love ran down his face, tracing the stubble on the line of his jaw, which was clenched. His hands found mine and grabbed them. His eyes burned and they widened like he was hypnotizing me; it was working.

"Scarlett. How many times are you planning to have this conversation with me?" His eyes became glassy, as if he were fighting back tears. "I don't know how to prove to you that I am staying, fighting, whatever you need." His lips moved on mine and I traced his teeth with my tongue; I was powerless. I needed him in every conceivable way. A pleasured groan left his mouth and flowed directly into mine where it echoed. He pulled away.

"Please. Look at me. I will say it again and I will keep saying it, every minute or every day if I have to. This isn't some misplaced guilt or sense of responsibility. I love you." His hands held mine tight. "I can barely breathe if I think of those freaks getting their hands on you. I won't let them. I promise I will protect you. I mean it. At all costs." The last part hung between us. At all costs. Even the thought of what he was saying made me sick to my stomach. I traced the edges of the card with my fingers and placed a kiss on his lips that lingered long enough to say so much of what I wanted to but couldn't.

"OK," I exhaled. "We need to get this somewhere we can look at it." Jake reclined and grabbed the room phone with an outstretched hand.

"Yeah, hi. Can you tell me where the nearest photo shop is please?" There was a pause while the person, probably Jake's new pal downstairs, found out and he fumbled across the bedside table for the Ritz paper and pen. "Thank you. I mean, Merci." He replaced the handset and tore off the note.

"It's like two blocks. We can go first thing. No arguments. You need sleep." I nodded as I stood up off the bed and pulled the chain across the door. It was a futile move but I needed to do anything I could to bring my pulse down and survive the night. I padded into the shower and turned it on, leaving the door open so I could feel closer to Jake. I saw him recline on to the bed before the steam enveloped the room, concealing him from view and hiding my tears. Time was running out.

When morning came I woke with my arms entwined with Jake's but felt like I had barely been to sleep. I kept seeing Jacques lying on the floor and three or four times in the night I had the strangest feeling, like my head was filled with static and white noise. I felt like a human radio, but someone else was trying to tune me in to something. I had thought at first it was the start of a vision but no images followed, just fuzzy shades of gray and a distant hum and I knew it must mean something – everything was a clue at the moment but I was damned if I could figure it out.

We ordered coffee to the room, neither of us able to handle food and consumed it in silence. Jake had perfected his 'it will all be OK' look and I had perfected the one which made him think I believed it was possible. Jake grabbed the card that had been clenched in his fist all night and we headed out. The morning was predictably beautiful and the people who weren't recovering from the sight of a mutilated acquaintance, simply, went about their day in the warm morning light. It was true that the sun helped; it made everything softer and brought more hope but with every step I knew we were walking over that place, those rooms and it cancelled out the daylight's power and brought to the fore how easy they found it to disappear and get away with murder.

We found the shop. It was tiny and the walls were lined floor to ceiling with cameras, old and new. However it looked like the kind of place that might shun the digital. A bell sat on the counter next to a handwritten note in French. "Errm. Hi." Jake called out to get the attention of whoever was lurking behind the retro beaded curtain. A spoon clinked in a cup and a small dark-haired man, maybe in his late fifties, shuffled out through the rattling strings of beads carrying a steaming cup of coffee and ignored us entirely until he had taken residence on a small wooden stool which put him barely above counter height. It was weird. Jake slid the tiny card onto the glass and waited for eye contact.

"American?" The man eyed us both suspiciously.

"Yeah. French?" Jake replied, teasing. The man's face softened and he nodded in appreciation of the humor. He picked up the card between two stubby, hardened fingers and pulled the glasses down from his head onto the tip of his nose. He shook his head and slid it back over.

"I think errr. Dis is, how you say? Video. Large memory, usually video." His accent was strong. "Best way is put into laptop for quality. Or you can buy this." He swiveled round and pulled a box from the more modern row of cameras. He opened the cardboard, pulled out a petite, expensive looking video camera in front of us like a game show host. He opened the side out to reveal a screen the size of the camera and tapped his index finger on the edge of the glass.

"Good size."

Jake reached for his wallet and pulled out a stack of notes. "How much?" He was already thumbing through the notes.

The man turned the box over and peered through his glasses. "Three fifty." I tensed and shook my head at Jake, too much. But he had already handed over the money and the man smiled as he re-packaged the camera and put it into a nondescript paper bag with twine handles. Jake took the bag and nodded before he turned to the door. I smiled at the man, already back to drinking his coffee, and we stepped out once again onto the streets. We headed back to the hotel eager to discover the mystery without the risk of prying eyes; we walked at speed and without speaking.

Once inside, we sat facing each other, cross-legged on the bed, which had already been made, and re-opened the box. The camera, which Jake knew instinctively how to operate, wasn't charged; he fumbled around and connected it to the power, it sprang to life with a beep and the screen lit up. Jake pressed the side, gently allowing the memory cardholder to spring open. He pressed in the card and spun the camera round so we could both see whatever was coming.

The screen stayed blank for what felt like an eternity and the room was completely silent apart from our labored breathing. It burst to life with some flashing images in a bright room. The study. Jacques' voice was cursing in the background in French and it was an innocent, beautiful moment to think of him doing such a normal thing. I remembered my dad doing the same every year at Christmas; fighting with the camera, the new toys that needed batteries to make a cacophony of terrible sounds and a faint smile stayed with me until the change in light brought me back. The screen went black and the sound of rustling, like a phone accidentally calling from a pocket burst out from the speaker. Jake's eyes narrowed as he tried to work out the images. Focus improved. It was very dim light and the view was obscured by a wall; it looked like stone and was taking up at least half the screen. Wherever he was, he was hiding from what was beyond.

From the fuzzy distance in the picture two voices and two figures to match. One tall, thin, the other slightly smaller, both all in black. More rustling and a glimpse of Jacques' hand as he tried to up the speaker's ability to capture the conversation. He was shaking. The volume increased and it was clear voices were raised. They were speaking French, arguing with words being spat through tense jaws. The tall one was pointing at the smaller one, his bony finger pressing aggressively into the other's chest. The smaller one was nodding and he looked like he was wiping tears from his eyes; he kept dragging his sweater over his face but his tone held his anger.

The mumbling turned into shouting but we couldn't understand, it was too fluent and too fast. Our ears sprang into action when suddenly the conversation turned to English. "What do I have to do? Just tell me and let's end this." The smaller one suddenly found his authority and both of us stiffened. We knew that voice, those clothes and once he spoke in English there was no room for doubt. Elias. Jake sprang from the bed, pacing. "I will kill that son of a..." He was incandescent with rage.

"Jake. Sit. We need to see this." He retreated and sat alongside me. His knuckles white from balling his hands into tight fists. The taller one was rustling. He handed Elias some sort of bag. He unrolled it to reveal what looked like a giant syringe. "Bring her here. Do not hurt her. We want her alive and co-operative. If she is not the deal is off and you lose." That voice again, the one from my vision and sometime before that I still couldn't place. Lose? How could Elias be with them? Despite my instincts, I had tried to see the best in him. The weird, tortured boy, who seemed at one point like he might even like me, was in fact the enemy. It didn't make sense. I paused the video, desperate to collect my thoughts. The house, the weird search of the body, the blood. Could he? I was cold with fear and I looked to Jake who wasn't faring any better than me. His beautiful cheeks were devoid of color, of life. He looked hollow and different; his teeth clenched and grated in his jaw.

I hit the button to play the rest. Elias nodded and took the bag, concealing it in the pocket of his hooded sweater. The same one he wore when we all went to Jacques just two days before. This was recent.

The conversation lulled and the tall one, still too shrouded in shadow, moved back beyond the reach of the camera. Jacques panned the camera up as he stepped back, fearful of being caught. The stone wall became an archway, the archway I had walked through with Jake. It was that room again. I glanced at the date in the corner of the screen. This video was taken two days before I arrived in Paris.

"He knew." My hands shook uncontrollably and Jake, still wound so tight, held me. "From the beginning, he knew I was coming and everything he said. He was going to lead me to them. Oh God. I've been so... so stupid." It didn't make sense, surely they just wanted to kill him too, he too was part of The Collective. He had his own powers. Unless that was the deal, his life spared for the delivery of mine into their hands? "What now?" I whispered, having never felt so helpless.

"You mean other than me going over there right now and kicking his ass?" Jake paced until he met the desk. There his fist hit the wall and it buckled, dented below his hand. He called out in pain as the previous injury reacted to the force. I stood to go to him but the radio like interference in my head crackled and hissed in my ears making me dizzy. I stumbled back, my legs hit the bed and I collapsed onto it; my hands cupped over my ears.

"Scarlett? What is it? A vision?" I could hear him but it sounded like he was talking to me through a kids' tin can telephone. His voice was muffled, distant and competing with the sounds in my head. The distorted crackling clarified momentarily and hissed into what sounded like whispered words but nothing I could decipher clear enough. The noise was accompanied by a fierce shooting pain that rippled through my brain and my eyes closed tight in a bid to shut out the ache. Then suddenly as soon as it had appeared it shut down, like the radio was unplugged and the pain disappeared with it.

"Scarlett. You're scaring the hell out of me." He was knelt next to me with his hands either side of my legs. I was working on how to compose myself. It was the strangest feeling; like my head had been taken over for a moment but I had returned to the room with no message, no image, just the lingering feeling that I should be able to recognize the sensation, that it meant something.

"I. I don't know. No. I guess not. I couldn't see anything anyway." I shook the sensation away from my head and his eyes were burning into me, observing, checking for withheld information. "I'm fine. I promise." He withdrew his hands and joined me on the bed.

"So now what? The tape. Elias." I needed so badly to go, take the drama away from him to keep him safe. Every muscle in his body was rigid with fury, it radiated from him with such presence it felt like a force field. I attempted to break down the wall with a touch but he flinched and a stab of rejection shot through my chest.

"Don't." His tone shocked me and I felt myself shift back defensively.

"Don't what?" Panic had risen up my throat and made it into my voice, which was now a hollow whimper.

"Don't try to distract me." He glared at me; his usually beautiful gray eyes were narrowed and sad. "Why are you trying to protect him?" The air between us was green with his jealousy and while I would normally take some small joy in his proving how much he cared; this was different. It felt like things were changing and I didn't like it.

"I haven't even said anything Jake. I would never side with him." I moved towards him. "But you have to trust me. You have to let me handle some of this myself. It is the only way. I will not let you endanger yourself for me." I watched the tension flex in his perfect jaw as his teeth clenched at my words.

"What does that mean? What don't I know?" Now he was suspicious and I was realizing how stupid it was of me to think I could keep anything from him. The more he knew the worse it would be.

"Jake. Look at me." He conceded to my command and his eyes fixed on mine. "I love you. There is nothing I wouldn't do for you." I kissed him briefly, urging him to feel the truth in my words. "But, I need you to trust me. Do you trust me?" I shook him by the shoulders and he wrestled free.

"Of course I trust you but I get the feeling you're about to ask me something I can't agree to." There was just a pregnant pause. The air filled with tension and our overarching need to protect each other.

I smiled a half smile. "I need to go somewhere. To help end this. But I have to go alone. This has nothing to do with Elias, though I am as mad as you are at his, I don't know, call it whatever... stupidity."

"Betrayal," Jake spat and he was right. That is exactly what it was but of all my concerns Elias was the least. I knew he was weak when it came to it. I had seen his childish behavior first hand and I knew I could outsmart him. Right now I just had to make sure he didn't get the chance to hand me over because for this to work, for me to avoid ending up dead, I needed to hold all the cards.

"I know you want to protect me. But I can do this. It has to be me Jake." He was still silent and I thought he was accepting it; my secretive plan. But I felt what was coming before he said it and it was like a tsunami building. He stood up from the bed calmly and paced to the wall where his clenched fist had burrowed into it just moments before. He struck it again, causing the weakened plaster to buckle further.

"Jake. Stop." I buried my head in my hands. It was frustration, pain, anger, complete terror all rolled together.

"Please."

"I can't Scarlett. I can't let you walk into this alone. I..." His trembling voice softened and he broke off, choked by the words we both knew were coming. "I can't let you go, knowing you might not come back." He collapsed into a heap on the floor, his back resting on the desk and his head in his hands. A tortured scream of frustration escaped from him but it wasn't his mouth, it was a primal, instinctive sound that came from somewhere much deeper. The room, once blissful and a symbol of something so pure and exciting felt darker. It had been tainted by the very thought of them; the band of monsters that lurked outside its beautiful walls in wait for me.

He didn't move. I slid into the space next to him and wound my arms around his hunched frame. He wiped pained, angry tears from his eyes before they could fall and I kissed both of his cheeks in turn.

"I need just a few hours tonight. Once I know for sure where I can find them I can really set things in motion. We can set things in motion. Together." I held him so tightly. "Together," I reiterated and he kissed my lips until I was alight with desire for him. We were entangled and I knew he was kissing me with fear. This was his prayer that I would come back. Mine too.

I waited until it was getting dark. Jake hadn't spoken for over two hours. He had accepted but not consented to my decision to trace them tonight. But I knew I would have to move fast as he would be moments behind me. He would never have allowed the conversation to end that way if he had truly thought I would be alone. He kept switching between pacing and re-watching the video; despite my pleas for him to stop. Elias' voice slithered out of the speaker and it made my flesh crawl. I hadn't even been able to entertain how it was possible for him to be on their side yet but I would be dealing with him at some point.

When I had built up enough resolve to leave without crumbling in the wake of the obvious heartbreak I was causing Jake I slipped out without a word; only a silent kiss, during the length of which I know we were both fighting back tears. I had released him from a vice grip when his hand grabbed mine; he planted a parting kiss on my knuckles and it sent a shot of white-hot adrenalin through me. I was doing this for him; that made it easy and impossible to fail.

Jake's admirer was on the desk and I knew there was every chance he had somehow managed to get her to watch out for where I was headed. I left the hotel and took a left. I peered round to find her distracted on the phone and made my move to the other side of the door. I was starting to feel like I really knew my way around but I wished that it were in different circumstances. Tonight was our last night at the hotel and it dawned on me we had made no provisions for what we would do next but that was a small, normal problem compared to the rest.

The air was warm and maybe because of the burning threat to my mortality I felt like I was feeling the dimming sun's rays for the first time and my eyes closed in muted appreciation. My hands were locked by my sides in the pockets of my jeans and I couldn't help but think how crappy a wardrobe choice I had made; what a thing to wear if this were my end. Surely I should be bowing out in some gothic masterpiece; a sacrificial gown of epic proportions, all taffeta and black lace, but if I went today I would be found in grubby cut offs and pumps. Classy.

I had become so suddenly accustomed to the Parisian sounds, the way the smell of petrol and diesel fumes hung on the dense summer air and I recognized a love for it, despite never having been able to enjoy it sans drama. I made a silent promise to myself to not let this be the last time, not this way. I wanted to come here again with Jake, maybe we would get engaged up the Eiffel Tower with the city sparkling below like diamonds and he would sweep me into his arms and we would somehow have shaken off all previous memories of the place and be lost in the possibilities held by the future we were yet to share. My teeth were clenched with determined hope.

My fuzzy daydream was abruptly snuffed out by the radio interference in my head again. Waves of crackling white noise and sounds from eons away traded places in the space between my ears. It was like holding a giant seashell to my ears; a deafening tidal wave of hissing sounds and crashing waves. Don't. The noise was speaking to me. It said don't. Don't what? Then as soon as it had arrived it faded into oblivion and the sounds of cars and conversation took its place.

No one batted an eyelid watching me walk alone through the streets and I wondered if any of them would even remember seeing me. I always wondered that. When kids turned up on milk cartons; there must always be someone who had seen them, sometimes there must be tens or hundreds of people so how can no one remember anything at all? How was it possible for people to simply disappear? All those taken at the hands of The Venari were slightly easier to understand but it still brought its own questions. Why in hundreds of years had no one been brave enough, committed enough to make sure people found out and stopped them? Unless they really did own everyone of power, but the thought was too sobering, too terrifying. I had to believe there was hope.

I was almost there. I could see the entrance to the tour. A young girl, probably my age, was pulling in the sign boards that hung outside with the times on. She stacked them inside the large doors and started fumbling around on a huge set of keys, which rattled like money in a purse. I had to distract her and get inside. I hung back out of view while I came up with something passable. I started to run, I picked up my pace and headed towards her commanding tears to form, which came easily after I pictured the gray of Jake's eyes glassing over with fear, the sound of Elias' betrayal on the tape and the fact that I was once again hurtling towards the unknown but this time I was thousands of miles from home. "Forgive me." I hadn't meant to say it out loud but the words had built their own momentum and my need to leave something in the air, a prayer for my parents, for Jake if I didn't get out, had grown so great it was an involuntary action.

I felt the clamminess of the skin on her arms as we collided and my body met hers. My weight threw her like a doll to the floor and I found myself almost on top of her, my heaving chest pinning her down. Her eyes wide with shock bore into mine.

"I'm so sorry. You have to help me. There's a man. That way." I pointed to the street I had been lurking in moments before with a trembling hand. "He was chasing me." I drew on the rest of my emotions to bring more tears and they were more than happy to oblige.

"Mademoiselle. Are you OK? I see no one now." Think faster I chided myself. I forced the rest of the fake tears over the brink and onto my face. I fixed my eyes on hers and winging it I pleaded, "Please. I will be fine. I just need to get back to my hotel. Can you call me a cab? I don't want to walk alone while he is out there." She stroked my arm affectionately as she scanned the street again for the fabricated assailant.

"You like for me to call the police?" God no. That would ruin everything and probably wind up with me restrained on a gurney again. I shook my head adamantly and she smiled politely before she stepped into the small ticket booth that stood next to the door. It was barely a meter square. Its walls were plastered with ticket information, postcards and leaflets. She turned her back to me as she made the call. I took my chance and moved as quickly and quietly as I could through the wooden doors and down the stairs. The acrid smell of dirt and sulfur filled my nose and every nerve ending in my body tingled with the rush of adrenalin. There was something different, it felt different, darker somehow and I fought the realization that I knew why. They were already here.

I ensured each step was silent and the only noise I heard was the call of the attendant on the street above as she frantically searched for the fake damsel. Her cries faded out and I could only assume she had written me off as a nut job and locked up as the light seemed even dimmer down in the passageway than it had the last time.

There were no sounds yet, no hushed voices or screams of innocents, just an odd, eerie calm that wreaked of them, their secrets. I felt the dust in the air as it traveled on my breath and into my lungs; it only added to my suffocation and claustrophobia.

I walked cautiously and it didn't go unnoticed that the lights were all on. Surely no one had sanctioned the use of this 'attraction' for such purposes. Though I knew now that I shouldn't be surprised by anything at all.

My subconscious slowed my pace as I re-approached the room I suspected was theirs and took in how completely isolated I felt in comparison to the last time when Jake was here too and a million other people hurried around me, cameras in hands.

Something made me stop just ahead of the door and I couldn't put my finger on it but my instincts were sharper now than they once were, or I was just more suspicious of everything. I knew someone was close and I was battling fear with determination to fight back. My hands quivered and my legs threatened to give way but I kept a fixed eye on my surroundings, scanning left and right to look out. Still no sound, but the sensation that I was being watched had intensified and every hair on the back of my neck stood to attention like a row of tiny pinpricks. My breath was held prisoner in my chest while my brain tried to figure out a plan of action but it was released involuntarily and suddenly by a hand, firm and rough wound tight around my mouth from behind. My legs buckled at the shock and I struggled, my feet shuffling fruitlessly in the dirt. Another arm gripped my waist and elevated me so the only sound was my clothes rubbing against that of my very real attacker. I was being dragged back the way I had come and even though nothing had changed around me and the wall lights still glowed against the stone, it felt like I was now in pitch darkness. The hand round my mouth was warm and left a salty taste of sweat on my trapped lips. I tried to make a sound but my vocal chords were paralyzed by the pressure of the alien arm round my neck and the weakest of protests escaped to be met with such startling proximity. A pair of lips brushed my ears. "If you want to ever get out of this place alive you need to. Be. Quiet." The air from his lips brushed over my skin and my fear dissipated and quickly morphed into anger so hot, so powerful it burned me from within like I was being branded with rage. Him.

Bolstered by a sudden burst of strength and adrenalin I wrestled free and felt my feet find the floor below. I spun round, still encircled by his arms and saw him. His black hair hung limply over his right eye and he looked weary but incredibly angry. Elias looked like a broken man. Angry but irrevocably broken.

He spoke but his voice was barely a whisper, a blur of hushed vitriol in a confusing turn that saw him enraged with me. "This way. Shut. Up." Interesting that he felt he had the right to be mad. I stepped towards him and planted repeated thumps against his chest. Relentless hollow thuds echoed from where my clenched fists met his ribcage. Again he dragged me backwards, fingers boring into my forearm, hundreds of yards away from the place I was supposed to be going to and we were in some other room, one I hadn't even spotted at the base of the stairs. It was some kind of store cupboard; mops and brushes and catacombs memorabilia stacked against the walls, all swathed in thick, black dust.

He unceremoniously dumped me down on a discarded chair, which wobbled below me on the stone floor, before sliding the door to a close with the delicacy you would afford to a sleeping child. Once we were enclosed he strode toward me, palpable anger filled the space between us until he was knelt in front of me with his hands pinning my shoulder to the chair's wooden back. The wooden spindles forced their way into my ribcage and I shifted uncomfortably, still furious with him but frightened by the intensity in his eyes.

He moved his face to within an inch of mine and his breath smelled sour in my nose; all old cigarettes and warm alcohol. Same as ever. He was so close I felt panicky, like there was no fresh air, his breath had taken it all and my lungs strained to breathe.

"You. Stupid. Stupid. Girl." He spat the words and his saliva landed on my face in a fine, unwelcome mist. My head was enraged but my gut was wrenched and warped with fear. The darkness reared up like a rogue stallion and overpowered me completely.

"Didn't you hear me? Haven't you been listening? Jesus. To think. What were you?" He stood and leaned side to side on each leg, his hands were entangled in his hair, pulling, twisting and his face contorted in some indistinguishable emotion. Through clenched jaws he repeated, "What were you thinking?" His eyes were now fixed on me, expectant.

Then in his moment of silence I found my strength.

How dare he? "Don't. You. Dare." The need to be quiet didn't conceal my formidable disgust and anger. "I found the card you spineless coward. That poor man. And for what? So you could play teacher's pet with..." I motioned to the hall beyond and his eyes followed my accusatory finger. "With those monsters. And now what? You planning to hand me in as part of your little deal?" I pushed my face as close to his as he had been to mine only moments before. "You. Make. Me. Sick." My hands copying his early behavior, I grasped his shoulders in my hands, which swept forward, soldiers of my will, and before I even realized what I was doing I had yanked my knee into his groin and he was buckled in pain, folded between my hands. His teeth bit down on his lower lip as he struggled to contain a yelp of pain. He crumpled onto the floor and rocked like a child. I could have run but I wanted to hear his explanation. His reasons for selling me out, for pretending that whole time that he was on my side when he really planned to sacrifice me.

"At least you've found your fight. You're going to need it." His words were hushed but that smug smile was back, I could hear it in his voice and I was tempted to go for a second blow. He stifled a snigger but his head remained bowed and I couldn't see his eyes. I was still silenced by indignation and indecision. I wasn't sure whether or not to beat it from him or wait for the unedited version. The feelings I was having were so alien to me. I had never been violent in my life. I despised it. But the thought of Jake getting hurt because of this weakness made me sick to my stomach and sick in the head apparently. I literally wanted to punch him over and again.

My horror film fight sequence was cut short when he decided to offer his side.

"You're wrong." His voice a whisper, I could hear the sadness had returned. "I didn't do what you think I did and I am not what you think I am." An indignant snort left my nose.

"Scarlett. I didn't kill Jacques and I don't want to hand you over." His head fell again and his shoulders convulsed. He was crying. "I have to." My breath stopped again and I spun on my feet to meet his gaze as he stepped up from where he fell.

"The whole thing. They have been blackmailing me. They said they were going to kill Ava if I didn't co-operate. They wanted bait, someone who would get you close enough that they could get to you." Sobs rippled through him and his back heaved with the emotion. Tears pooled in my eyes. Could it be true? Every tortured look. Every bizarre moment. Because he too was trying to protect someone he loved.

"How though? The tape. That was before I even came to Paris." I stared at him; just a mass of black hair resting on hands bound into balled fists.

"Everyone knew you were coming. It wasn't hard for them to pick out some of The Collective. I was just unlucky. Wrong place, wrong time. They sent Sanguinaries. A kind of henchman type..."

I interjected. "I know who they are."

"Well. They sent them to find me, to my house; they knew I knew the city well and we are a similar age. I guess I just fit." He wiped away tears onto his sleeve and I was overwhelmed with sadness for him and for me. I had been so wrong.

"I have been trying to tell you. I have been listening.

Hoping to keep you safe. Haven't you heard me listening?" The white noise.

"That radio noise was you?" He nodded solemnly.

"When you told me about the vision, the one with Jake, I knew it was too late. That I couldn't stop you. I have seen how you look at him. So I tried from further away. But then tonight I heard you and realized what you were going to try and do." I leaned against a stack of old leaflets in boxes and he rested alongside me.

"I had to. It would have been him here tonight if it wasn't me. I cannot. Will not. Let anything happened to him." He sighed.

"You really are love's young dream aren't you?" His eyes rolled. He was never going to let it go.

"Elias. Stop. Don't use that tone." We had been here before and we were never going to agree. "Ava? Is she safe?" Lovely, sweet Ava. She didn't deserve to be embroiled in this nightmare. Elias was brushing great cobwebs loaded with dust from his sweater, black of course. He nodded.

"For now." He approached me and extended his arms. At that moment it seemed the most natural thing in the world to do, to hold him and let him hold me. We embraced and his anguish was seeping from his pores. His arms were so tight round my back.

"Sorry. Scarlett. I am so, so sorry." His arms contracted around me.

"Shhh. I know. It isn't your fault..." I paused, unsure if my next question would tip the new found equilibrium. "I need to know. What happened with Jacques? Why were you there?" His arms fell from my back and he lifted his head from where it had been on my shoulders.

"Wow. Still thinking the worst of me hey?" He created a distance between us and collapsed onto the chair I was sat on when he dragged me into the room. "The whole thing was a warning... they knew you would see it and I guess they felt I hadn't moved fast enough. By ensuring you saw him and the card they knew you would start to make your own way. It was a matter of time." Eyes, heavy and pained stared at me.

"And I played right into their hands. But why did they let him go if they knew he was filming you?" I sighed. I had thought I was one step ahead but turns out I was wrong. The pain of feeling so helpless, like I had the last time, washed right over me and I looked to him, silently pleading for answers.

"Scarlett. They know everything. The only reason he lived as long as he did was because they knew eventually you would trace Alice here and want to know more. That is the problem. They know you better than you know yourself."

"What happens now? I don't want to just lie down and die." Elias didn't want to look at me, he knew more, if that was possible, but whatever it was he didn't want to share it.

I glanced at my watch. I had been gone three hours. Jake would be here soon if I didn't do something and I could only hope at this point I had done enough in coming that the vision wouldn't come to fruition. I had kept Jake away and that was surely something? I looked back to Elias. We needed a plan. Now.

THE FALL

Elias' knuckles glowed white with pressure as his hands gripped his knees. "Scarlett. Didn't you read the rest of the stuff you took?" He stood again and tried to pace but the space was too small. Nose to nose with a battered metal shelving unit he gripped a side with each hand as though to steady himself.

"They don't want to kill you."

"But then... why?"

"They want to use you." Finally he lifted his head. "Come on. You are a smart girl. Think about it." He kicked the dusty ground and sent a plume of gritty fog swirling into the air, causing us both to cough involuntarily.

"I don't follow."

"You are so much more use to them alive. The whole Venari organization..." He made them sound like the mob. "It's about power. These are relics, megalomaniacs of historic proportions. They have grown up thinking what you have is a disease. Until this generation. Now it is changing."

"Changing how?" I couldn't hide the confusion on my face. The amount of information people expected me to be able to take in while under immense stress was growing but my capability to do it was not.

"These guys see what you have as an opportunity. For people seeking power foremost but also money, fame, political prowess and control; what you have is a key."

"A key. Elias, enough of the riddles. Spell it out." He huffed childishly and sulked towards me heavy footed. Hands back on my shoulders, eyes back on mine.

"I thought I was. You are a pawn in a massive game, Scarlett. If you'd read all the stuff you would know this." His hands squeezed me in what I imagined was pity. "What they want is to harness your powers, unlock your potential. If they did that they could have whatever they wanted." His eyes didn't move but behind them I could see he didn't want to be the one telling me all this.

"Unlock what potential? They know what I can do and how limited it is. What use are random visions and very occasionally being able to see through someone's eyes? Even then it seems only to be Jake and that happened one time." This to and fro was exhausting and I didn't feel any wiser for it. His exasperation was noted and he shook me in frustration.

"You are the one Scarlett. Your visions? Just the tip of the iceberg. You are the one, the leader. You can do anything any member of The Collective can do and then some." Elias widened his eyes in a 'get it now' kind of way and I was terrified, mostly because I think I did.

"How? I never have..."

"I don't know. I know you can be trained to unlock them and if you'd had more time you would have been able to figure that out for yourself." He offered a consolatory smile but my mind was ablaze. Was it better or worse that they wanted me alive? The idea of a lifetime with them, like some kind of experiment, was completely intolerable, it made my skin crawl but my desperation to avoid that end yielded no suggestion as to how.

"What can I... we do now... I have to think. We don't have long before Jake follows me down here all guns blazing." I didn't even give him time to respond. The words were coursing through my synapses like tiny flashes of light. "It has to be tonight. Whatever it is. Tonight." My reaffirming of the word did nothing to illuminate his expression. For the first time I saw the weight of his burden in its entirety. It glowed like a dark blue aura, a fuzzy outline of desperation and sadness clinging to his being; an unwelcome passenger of my creation. "Do you have any idea how it is that I am supposed to end this when everyone is in with them? Is there anything about it anywhere?!" I didn't know why there would be. I mean, they have successfully evaded exposure for centuries so I was sure it wouldn't be as simple as a few damning photographs and some missing persons reports.

"I have never heard anything about what it was you had to do. I'm sor..." His voice trailed off. We both froze. There were heavy footsteps coming down the stone steps where – just above – the streets of Paris were alive with twilight and sparkling lights. The contrast was ridiculous, incomprehensible. Muffled voices; three, maybe four men and the rattle of metal chains sang out from the distorted sounds. My lips parted of their own accord, poised to scream but Elias forced them closed with a firm hand and pulled my body against his.

"Shhhh. Not. A. Sound." He shuffled me slowly, ushering me to a small space behind the door. We maneuvered into a narrow hollow and I found myself cowering into his chest, praying. Our breath was held, an awkward ache between us and our struggling chests heaved silently.

Elias dropped a foot back to steady himself against the weight of me and a box filled with pamphlets fell in slow motion toward the floor. The contents exploded to life, escaping into the air where they danced in front of us like colored snow. The sound was echoing, the cardboard tumbling to the ground, the whoosh of the paper and the yelp of fear that escaped my mouth when I realized an irreversible course of events were now in motion.

It can't have been more than three seconds from the box hitting the ground to the ear-splitting crash of the door being forced open into the room. Our position meant we were initially hidden from their view, which only served to overdose me on adrenalin. My veins were white hot with an odd kind of furious terror and I felt as though I was watching my body from above. The door moved and a face I had committed to imprisoned memories stepped forward with a look of shock etched across his face. Sutcliffe. His eyes widened and narrowed as they adjusted to the dim light before his face exploded with a euphoric, haunting smile. His head fell back and he laughed maniacally into the air; the sound reverberating within the room's four tiny walls. Even from that noise I knew it was his voice I had been hearing, in the vision, on the tape. He had been here the whole time.

"Well Mr. Mack. Seems you kept your end of the bargain after all." Elias stepped forward and I thought he was rebuilding the human defense he and Jake had created so gallantly the first time we went to see Jacques, or the day the hostel was broken in to, but he took another step and stood almost nose to nose with Dr. Sutcliffe. Was this him abandoning me again or was he working to some plan he had devised on the spur of the moment? I really hoped it was the latter. My heart raced at a speed that made me worry it may explode in my chest.

Sutcliffe's face had aged. He was covered with white, wiry bristles, which started on his cheeks and only tapered off when they reached his long, thin neck. Conversely, his attire was smart, an expensive navy three piece suit with an old fashioned pocket watch chain contrasting the fabric on his waistcoat and pointed, black shoes that were impossibly shiny and totally unsuitable for our subterranean location.

He peered round Elias' frame, which was still facing away from me and grinned a sickly smile.

"How wonderful to see you again Miss Roth. Delighted we can be reacquainted."

"Well?" Elias had found his voice at last and I waited a tangle of anticipation, fear and confusion for what was coming next.

"Am I free to go?" I couldn't see his face but a change in angle meant I could see the tendons in his jaw clenching and releasing while he waited for a response. My heart dropped like a lead weight. He intended to get away from here with no concern for me, despite his crocodile tears just moments before. I couldn't even bring myself to say anything. What was the point?

"I see no reason why not. I had worried you may have lost your way Mr. Mack. But, here she is." Sutcliffe's eyes were wide with excitement.

"And my sister?" Elias squared up to Sutcliffe, prompting the muscle either side to move forward. Elias took the message and stepped down.

"We have no need for further concern. You may go and she will not be troubled." Sutcliffe waved him away as if he were a Monarch and Elias a servant. "Bailey. Orson." Those were the names belonging to the Sanguinaries. Huge, mountains of men, both easily over six and a half feet tall and almost as wide. They wore floor length black coats and stood still like stone, gatekeepers either side of their master.

"Ensure Mr. Mack understands the need for total discretion before you release him." He turned his face back to Elias. The one on the left cracked his knuckles loudly and the other smirked as he arched his neck until a large popping sound echoed in the air.

"Mack? Don't make me find you again. I have been most accommodating. It would be such a shame for you to sour this little, arrangement, now by doing anything stupid." With that Bailey and Orson moved in unison and took an arm each, lifting Elias off the ground. He didn't struggle. He was leaving me here, with them. I wanted to scream, to cry, to run but I felt like I had the last time I was in his proximity; frozen.

The muscle moved Elias out the door and he made a fleeting, furtive glance at me. Was it his apology? I didn't know but I would kill him myself if I ever got the chance.

Sutcliffe took a step closer and gripped my arm. The memory of his hand on me in that sickly asylum room flooded my mind and I could smell the acrid scent of chemicals as though it was yesterday.

"Walk with me Miss Roth." It wasn't a suggestion. He led me back out into the hall and down beyond the room with the 'V'. He glanced at me as we passed it as though he was silently acknowledging my awareness of its purpose. My silence was my protest.

"No. That room is for little interrogations. Scare mongering. No. For you we have an altogether more...

sophisticated facility. I think you'll be impressed." I felt like he genuinely believed I might be privy to feeling flattered by their obsession with me. We walked through the tourist exhibitions and I longed, ached for Jake. I cursed myself instantly; this was what I had come here for, to learn. I needed to get to grips with whatever it was they wanted and figure something out. After my revealing conversation with Elias I was relieved to cross 'avoid death' off my list even though I still had the seemingly insurmountable issue of escaping them on my mind.

"Of course had we received a visit from your little, love interest, we may have treated him to a stay in there. But you, no not you. You are practically royalty." The sound of our footsteps was drowned out by the addition of two heavy sets close behind. Bailey and Orson were back from disposing of Elias. I could feel their craving for a tussle; they thrived on conflict so I assumed my currently stunned co-operation would displease them and a crescent of a smile formed on my lips at the thought.

We broke away from the path I recognized and took a turning down a dark slope cordoned off with a chain. Sutcliffe tore it from its hook and left it swinging from the other wall. His hand was still forcibly gripping my forearm and the constant pressure had made my hand tingle and throb. The artificial lighting stopped within ten feet, signifying an altogether too horrific realization; we were going where we definitely wouldn't be disturbed.

Sutcliffe pulled a tiny but immensely bright flashlight from his inside pocket and flitted it left to right to light our way. Bailey and Orson had stepped up their pace to match ours and I could have sworn I felt their breath on my neck.

We took a sudden left down a path I hadn't even noticed and I grew more painfully aware of how much deeper we were going which meant I was losing track of how to get out. The air further down was damper and the putrid scent of the death housed in the rooms all around us was lingering, haunting the maze like a horde of ghosts.

Sutcliffe stopped at a large wooden door that ran flush with the stone wall. It was thick, old timber with heavy metal adornments and a huge door knob. He placed his hand over the handle and it split in two, one half separating from the other as the top slid to the right. Beneath what had appeared to be a normal handle was a small gray pad, not unlike what Elias had at his apartment. They had been making modifications. I guessed this is what he was referring to when he used the word sophisticated. The door came to life with a loud thunk. It moved back a few inches before sliding to the left and revealing a bright white laboratory style room. The luminescence of the clinical strip lights burned my eyes and I squinted to adjust. He dragged me forward and the room expanded before me into huge space that glowed white. To my left there was a bank of steel work benches with complex looking machinery and microscopes. Straight ahead there was a large dentist style chair with restraints on the arms and legs;

a huge brace hung above it which looked like some kind of futuristic helmet and a hospital gurney, just like the one I had experienced the last time I lay in wait, at the back of the room with unused IV machines lined up alongside. On the right hand side there was a bank of monitors mounted on the wall above a control panel of blinking lights and switches so vast it looked like it could have been lifted right out of air traffic control. The wall of blank screens stretched ten deep and three high. There was nothing to suggest at all where we were stood, not a single bone or trace of stone. I had been in hospitals less equipped than this. If the circumstances were different I might have been impressed at what they had been able to achieve in these underground tombs, but the reality jolted me back into the moment and the darkness I had been fighting since I first learned about any of this twisted; we both knew that this room was set to bring about some form of conclusion.

My eyes were greedily trying to take it all in, desperately searching for clues of a way out, what exactly they would do with me in this room. The door had long since closed behind us and a glance confirmed my worst fears; there wasn't just a code to get in. There was one to get out.

I turned my head, my body still frozen within Sutcliffe's grasp, and saw Bailey and Orson flanking the door like gargoyles. They were exactly like Jacques had said. They looked angry and hateful, everything about them screamed violence, from their shorn heads marbled with pearlescent scars to their dead eyes. They looked black, empty, like there was no soul behind them at all and it was abundantly clear why Jacques had called it a war. The Venari had an army fit for purpose and right at that moment, I had nothing in my arsenal at all.

Sutcliffe released his grip and with a smile bending his lips invited me to explore with an over eager gesture. He was beaming, delighted in the elements of his game playing out. "So? Miss Roth. What do you think of our little, shall we say, learning hub?" He looked to me expectantly, like he really hoped I may just strap myself in the chair and say "Sure. Mess with me all you want."

Then I realized. It became abundantly clear; this was the way it was supposed to be. I needed to let them learn what I could do, so I could find out too. If I had the potential Elias thought then the situation wouldn't be quite so desperate. I just had to be patient and find a way to keep Jake safe until I could get out of here. It was the only way I would be strong enough to bring them down; when they had unlocked my supposed potential for me. The realization made me suddenly more confident and for the first time I felt like I had a part to play; that I could change something.

I felt the pinch of Sutcliffe's hand return to my arm and he directed me to the chair. "Please. Sit." I found myself complying without question. "Well Miss Roth. I have to say, I am surprised by your willingness to participate in our little experiment... and having you just arrive, well that was a bonus. I had expected, well a much more complex process." He looked into my eyes and I could almost hear his mind whirring. He was desperate to get inside my head and work it all out, but most of all he wanted to know what was making me so calm, so collected. His lasting memory of me would have been one of discord, chaos, fanatic and futile fighting. But here I was, sitting perfectly still as his papery skin brushed my own as he tightened the restraints. They weren't like the leather ones from the hospital. These were heavy, inch thick cuffs that reached from the base of my thumb to beyond the ball of my wrist. The stainless steel was new and reflective. I watched as Sutcliffe's face was distorted by the metallic surface into a ghoulish, elongated incarnation and it seemed like I may be seeing the real him. A man whose soul was lost a long time ago.

"Well. I figure you are going to kill me so you may as well do it. It's not like I could get out of here is it?" I flashed a glance at Bailey and Orson who were still on guard. Hands poised by their sides. I could only guess what manner of archaic, torturous weaponry they were concealing beneath their floor length trench coats. Sutcliffe seemed delighted by my misdirection and I took my own pride in harboring the knowledge I knew what they wanted and that it would end up being the one thing I needed most to fulfill my role in this power struggle.

"Oh... now, now. Who said anything about killing?" He smiled broadly as he connected the restraints round my ankles. "You misunderstand my dear. This is a means to a wonderful end. We will make a partnership the likes of which you have never seen. The likes of which no one has ever seen." He was alluding to what I knew already but it sounded so poisonous, dangerous when it left his lips. He couldn't be allowed to succeed. If I were as powerful as they thought then I would be a weapon of mass destruction in his hands and with this man on a power trip it would be catastrophic.

I didn't respond. It was more important now that he thought I was slightly resistant, unyielding to his demands or he would start to get suspicious. I turned my head to face the wall of screens and felt the air alongside me shift as he got to his feet. Bailey and Orson stiffened slightly at his movement and he joined them at the door.

"We will be back later, with company Miss Roth. Please make this easier on all of us, especially you, by staying put." His eyes checked the four points of restraints on my limbs and he nodded to himself. He turned on his feet and I heard the bleep of the door before it slid open. He stepped into the darkness beyond, Bailey and Orson fell into line and followed him out like he was a king in some medieval procession.

There wasn't even a cursory glance. Just me, strapped down in a sterile room. I wrestled against the restraints for a moment before relinquishing to a sigh. Co-operation – or the fabrication of it – was uncomfortable and terrifyingly silent. I closed my eyes, desperately trying to see Jake and see through his eyes like I had before. My mind was too full; a montage of pixilated news clippings, broadcasts, weary, weeping faces. That was the reality if I failed. The Venari would spread chaos, loss, torture; perhaps in modern ways, with the graces of technology, but history would repeat itself and this would lead to the witch trials on a grandiose scale. Concentrate. I willed myself but the images faded and in their place a scratchy, black and white snowstorm of static erupted behind my eyes. Elias was trying to contact me.

"Breathe Scarlett. Focus." I felt surprisingly little concern for talking to myself. Focused on opening my mind with what little experience I had I filled up with aching lungfuls of the room's clinical air. "Try."

It started as the faintest whisper, like words carried miles on a breeze. But it grew and with it the sound created shapes in the static; swirling shadows as the syllables merged as if they were literally spelling it out. One more deep breath was all it took. The moment my lungs reached capacity a stillness washed over my brain and with it the sounds rang clear. It was like he was in the room.

"Scarlett. That's it. Well done. Now, stay focused. Stay with me. You have to listen. We will get you back. I am so sorry I had to leave you. It was the only way." We. *He must be with Jake*. "Yes. He is right here." *Holy crap. You can hear me too?* I surprised myself as these were thoughts not words. It was a confusing, exciting feeling to engage a new power and I held no resentment to this gift. I felt in control; something I never felt.

"I told you. When you really think, really concentrate you can do much more than this." I couldn't believe it. I was having this silent conversation deep within my headspace and my redundant mouth was gaping with awe. "I'll let you talk to Jake in a minute but right now I need you to listen very carefully. There are probably cameras in the room. Look around. Can you see any?" I was terrified to open my eyes in case it was like pulling out the plug, but miraculously Elias' voice stayed with me. My eyes darted to each corner of the room but I couldn't see any equipment that looked like a camera.

"Keep looking." He was panicking more than me which was odd considering it was me tied to a table in a lab of experimentation. I looked up and directly above me was a glossy black sphere suspended from the ceiling. A tiny red light flashed every few seconds. *I found one.* My mouth was still veiled in silence as my mind took over.

"OK. Don't look at it anymore. It won't take them long to figure out what you are doing if you keep checking it out. Just be natural and try to look at least a little anxious."

I thought you could just hear me? It sounds a lot like you can see me right now. Can you? I was still hesitant about whether or not he had told me everything. I had learnt a lot about Elias in a short time but so much of it had been thrown into question.

"No. But you will find out for yourself that it isn't just sound. When you practice it kind of becomes a whole series of sensations. You can sense, feel more. I can hear more in your voice than just what you think or say. Like, how much you are desperate to talk to lover boy for example." I closed my eyes and the static kind of fell away as Jake's image came to my mind. All of a sudden I could feel him, his hands on my face; a phantom touch but almost as delicious as the ones that make the blood run hot in my veins.

Jake? The end of this bizarre telephone connection was dead and I wasn't prepared for it to be over yet. I needed the company. I needed him.

"Baby?" His voice acted like a soothing compress to my head, which ached with the concentration. My heart raced in the best possible way and my hands pulled in vain against their restraints, searching for my eyes as I desperately willed my memory into glorious three-dimensional Technicolor.

Jake? Can you hear me? Elias how is this…?

"I can hear you baby. Are you hurt? What have they done to you?" His voice was breaking and fraught with despair and far above anything I felt. It was the darkest hell to think of him in pain. My chest ached for him and I wanted to fix it for him.

Jake. Jake, listen. Hear my voice. Well, mind. This is so weird. I am fine. You have to listen to me. You can't come here. They want me alive Jake and I need to be here so I can find out what it is that I can do.

"Elias told me about them wanting to draw out some of your other powers. So, you think you can do even more than this hearing thing?" It would have been so easy to lose it; be undone by the sound of him and the thought of not being able to get close. I forced my mind to focus. I wanted Elias to be right. I wanted to be able to really feel him here or it might be too much for me to see through knowing his feet could be walking just meters above me while I festered in this room.

I sensed Elias listening. I guessed as the conduit he must hear both sides. Lucky for me Jake only heard what I put out there and chose to say to him. It was a complex but intriguing system.

I don't know baby. I hope so. It is impossible for me to imagine that I can do enough, have enough power to make them want me this much. But, if it is true, then it must be the only way I can be strong enough to fight. I have to learn as much as possible. Trust that I can do this. You believing I can is one of the few things I can rely on to see me through. There it was again; deathly silence.

"I know you can do it Scarlett. But, that isn't the point. You shouldn't be there alone like this. It is all wrong." He planned to intervene in some fashion, it was obvious. My sharp-tongued retort, a warning, was cut short by the sound of muted steps in the hall beyond the fortress door.

They're here. Elias? Keep Jake safe; away from here at all costs do you hear me? The movement beyond the door broke our connection before I got the chance to hear the reply but, if nothing else I had learned with the right amount of concentration I could speak into people's minds. It didn't really matter what came next. I had my focus now and there was nothing else that mattered.

The door moved with what felt like a strange familiarity and Bailey and Orson marched in, their eyes scanned the room's perimeter for threats and I couldn't help but smirk; these grown men cautiously edging by me. No doubt they were intimidating but the perfect beads of sweat that negotiated their pitted faces suggested that on some strange level they were wary of me and whatever this hidden potential meant. I had a good hand now and it was imperative I played it well.

AN EDUCATION

Sutcliffe waded in from the corridor and the door closed behind him. He paced without speaking to the space behind my chair and I was engulfed with vulnerability without him in my line of sight.

My heart reached my mouth as the chair beneath me dipped backwards at speed, leaving me horizontal and back in a powerless position I remembered all too well. His eyes burned into mine the exact same way; only the surgical mask was missing. I flinched at the memory and thought of all at stake, all that I had to learn. When my eyes opened he had stepped away towards the wall of monitors. He hit a large white switch embedded in the wall and a short bleep brought them to life; a montage of flickering screens as the power surged through them. They turned from black to bright white to dark blue, but then just hummed with an electric glow.

"I think it is time we started to make some progress Miss Roth. Don't you?" Before I could answer he swung the chair round so my face was below his hunched frame. "These." He gestured to the wall of dimly illuminated glass eyes fixed on me. "These will tell us how that marvelous brain of yours works." A smirk spread across his face and he swept a bony finger across my forehead; tantalized by the potential beneath.

"With a little help from some clever little electrodes, a few concoctions of my own design, we will be able to track your responses to a whole array of stimuli and hopefully, we can work out just what it is that you are so capable of." He turned away from me and walked to the other side of the room. He pulled open a large, deep steel drawer. I could no longer see what he was doing, but I could hear the tearing of cellophane, packaging opening and the hideous slap of latex gloves around his wrists.

When he turned around his gloved hands were holding a neatly coiled hoop of delicate colored wires, each leading to a small square patch; the kind you saw stuck on sick people in hospitals. The only time I had ever seen them not on the TV was when my grandmother died. She had been hooked up to what felt like a million machines that beeped in haunting unison. The small, pale squares pinpointed her pulse across her body before there was just a haunting, indescribable silence as they could no longer find it. A rogue tear burst from my eye and rolled down my cheek. It was met with a finger and a cackle.

"Now, now. There isn't any need to cry. There is no reason we shouldn't all get what we want from this little arrangement Miss Roth." He rubbed my stolen tear between his index finger and thumb, his face awash with something undeterminable but chillingly sinister. "For you I suppose it would be the safety of that pointless Mayer boy. Yes?" His eyes were on me and I turned my face away. My expression of horror at the thought of him laying a single finger on Jake's beautiful face was too clear to hide. Where he was concerned I was an open book and therefore, weak.

"Don't tell me what I want. You know nothing about me. At all." I spat the words and felt my fists simultaneously clench so hard I felt the razor sharp bite of my fingernails as they broke the soft skin on my palm. "I don't need to bargain with you. He has nothing to do with this. I am here. This is about me."

"True. We do have you rather where we want you." He moved toward me and slid a hand inside my T-shirt. I flinched at the touch of his latex clad skin on mine; in places only meant for Jake. Bile rose in my throat as he placed a tacky square over the exact spot where my heart was furiously beating. "Ahhh. I see you too are sharing our anticipation at what may be to come?" Another disgusting smirk rose from his thin lips and he pressed another pad firmly on my temple. I shifted my face and he grinned at the futility. For a megalomaniac, a lonely girl, far from home and tied to a chair, with the potential to unlock world domination, was about as exciting as it got and he wasn't concealing his delight.

Five more pads later and I looked like some kind of alien

clone from a sci-fi movie while he started pressing buttons on the mysterious control panel until the monitors sprang to life. Their bluish glow hit the fluorescents and turned the air in front of my eyes a putrid green. The monitors made incessant beeps as they recorded my heartbeat. I didn't know what the hell the others were doing. They were just a blur of neon lines and numbers. A needle etched jagged patterns on a piece of paper that spooled at a million miles an hour; the paper reeling off crazily onto the floor.

"What is all this stuff? What – exactly – are you looking for?" My tone had been even more laced with hate than I had intended. My insolence would no doubt leave me in even more trouble.

He ran a finger along my jaw before pinning my head back into the headrest with such force I felt my neck twinge under the pressure. I shifted uncomfortably but held his gaze.

"We are going to test your worth Scarlett." My name sounded empty and unfamiliar said from his lips and my mind clung to his choice of words. My worth? "You see, as I am sure you are starting to figure out, we think you can do an awful lot more than just see a few accidents and follow clues. We think, based on earlier volumes of research in this field, that you may well be able to do all sorts of tricks." His face was close to mine and his sour breath turned my stomach. "So." He snapped back to an upright position and I jolted at the quick shift. "Let us not waste anymore precious time on this inane conversation." He maneuvered the whole chair to face the screens and moved behind me to the surgical cabinets. I heard more packaging opening and his shadow cast over me plunged me into a temporary twilight before I saw the glint of the syringe in his hand. I involuntarily shook my head; desperate to dislodge the memory of Clayton Mayer desecrating my sacred space, my room and his eyes as he plunged the needle into my arm.

"Now. I don't need to be like you to know what you are thinking now Scarlett. This isn't like the last time. We need you compliant. This is just to take the edge off. Make you more… open to the experience. Once you let this little guard of yours down we should be able to unearth all sorts of weird and wonderful things." He patted the skin on my arm and a deep bluish vein rose to the surface, betraying me with its willingness.

Before I had time to think I felt the burn of the point entering the tender skin in the fold of my arm. A cold rush of liquid soared through my veins below the skin and dissipated before I could trace it beyond the confines of my arm. I lay in wait for the drowsiness, untrusting of his earlier promise. It didn't come. I just felt soft, like I was melting into the chair and some of the weight was being lifted from me. Even my stomach, which had been dominated by the dark the entire time I had been in the room, was somehow easing. This would have made me uncomfortable or anxious on a normal day but whatever it was had made me a much more relaxed captive.

"OK. Let's get started." Sutcliffe pulled on a white coat from a hook on the wall I hadn't even noticed before and buttoned it at an incomprehensibly slow pace. My eyes were riveted. It was like I couldn't look away. I was just absorbing all the minutiae around me without even intending to.

"Bailey. Orson. Secure that door. The exhibition security will be patrolling soon and we don't want any uninvited guests now do we?" Bailey turned and pressed some more buttons on the control panel and a gunmetal gray screen appeared from the top of the doorframe and closed over the entire doorway.

"Secure Sir. Soundproof." He went back to his on guard position and stood motionless. It was like they were both bound to him. These huge men, who could snap Sutcliffe in an instant, were so, obedient. Like trained Rottweilers.

"Good." Sutcliffe bent down to tap something on a computer keyboard, which made up part of the flight deck style panel below the monitors. The central four screens turned blue and an image appeared across them. Each of the four screens a part of the picture. My eyes focused on the image and I swear I actually felt my pupils dilate. Jake? In my haze I felt only a huge surge of love and tingling desire in all of my nerves. The rest of the screens remained resolutely scientific; and neon spikes of activity danced to life.

"Interesting. I thought it best to start with an easy one, but this is even more than I hoped for. You really do have a thing for him. Look at this heart rate boys." He looked jovially towards his pets but they remained stony faced, eyes forward. "He could prove to be very useful." I didn't speak but the needles on the monitors went crazy as my brain processed the insinuation and even in my drug-induced state of calm the message broke through and I fought the urge to shout out. It took three huge breaths before the needles returned to normal. Sutcliffe kept making notes but I couldn't see from the angle of the chair what they said. The text on the screen was too small and the only way I knew so adamantly that that was what he was doing was the sound of his too-long fingernails on the keyboard. I had a fundamental distrust of men whose fingernails featured anymore than a millimeter of white. His, I had noticed during the button saga, were yellowed and overgrown. It was just another thing about him that made me sick to my stomach, almost literally on a few occasions.

"Very good. What about if I show you… this." His nails tapped briefly on the keys and the image of Jake's face was replaced. A dark room shifting, shapes and muted colors. It was a video camera. I made out a bed and was hit with a sense of familiarity. I knew the pattern on the comforter. My clear mind put the pieces together cautiously; I was fighting the realization. Hot with panic I thought I had lost, my forehead started to sweat and a fury spread through me like fire.

"Mom? Is she there? Who is that in my house? I swear to God, if you…" Sutcliffe kept his eyes fixed on the wall of screens as he pressed a button, which erased the neon lights and bleeping and spread the grainy image full, cinema size.

They had someone in my house. In my mom's bedroom. His fingers tapped impatiently on his lips and I feared he was waiting for what he thought was the best bit. The camera panned across the bed and I could make out the shape of Mom's sleeping frame below the blanket. The lens met her peaceful, unsuspecting face and stopped, watching. It felt terrifying, voyeuristic and whatever they were hoping for was irrelevant. The paused image taken by some intruder in my home set off a chemical reaction in my brain and all I could think of was the words 'I have to get out'. They repeated over and over again. The only monitoring equipment left were the needles scratching at the paper and it went into overdrive with each silent repetition.

The final time I said it my head was light with exertion and my limbs were quivering with anger or adrenalin. Suddenly there was unbearable heat around my limbs. The pressure where the restraints were holding me down was replaced with a growing heat. Searing, skin-peeling heat which was so real the smell of parched flesh started to mix with the chemical air.

I let out a scream as the mounting pain became too much to bear. The site of the burning flesh turned into bright white flashes of light and a thunderous rattle as the metal restraints burst from my limbs like they had been axed. Shards of metal and sparks flitted into the air and fell to the floor like the embers of a vast explosion. In my periphery I saw the statues flinch at the flying sparks.

I didn't move for a moment. The burning was less now but in its place there was a deep throbbing agony and I glanced to my wrists where angry burns the exact shape of the shackles had been. My skin was marbled with crimson and maroon sores where blood and tissue were torn by the heat. My vision blurred for a moment as the scale of the pain sent my body hurtling into a state of shock.

Next thing I knew, Sutcliffe was alongside me. His face lit up with the most joyous expression I have ever seen. His hands worked around the wounds, expertly attending to them in an almost tender manner. It was unnerving but all weirdness was dwarfed by the excruciating pain that continued to surge across my ankles and wrists. I was fading in and out of consciousness as I struggled to cope with the agony but the glint of another needle in the light was the first step to me regaining my composure. Morphine.

It wasn't instant, but the pain started to wane, just enough that I could cope with holding open my eyes. Maybe half an hour passed, I couldn't really tell, but while I was writhing, Sutcliffe had finished seeing to me and was maniacally making notes on the computer. I had never heard anyone type so fast.

The chair had been shunted back to an almost sitting position so I used my elbows on the arms of the chair to raise myself up. I was woozy and unstable; standing wasn't an option. I just shifted on the spot until I was sat almost normally. I looked to the floor and saw the remnants of one of the restraints. The metal was charred and contorted beyond recognition and tiny, diamond splinters lay on the ground like dew. Had I really done that?

The pain was hard to process and I dipped my head to inhale a breath for restorative purposes. Sutcliffe spun around at the sound of my discomfort and another wide grin spread over his face. He was ecstatic.

"Aren't you a little firecracker? Pardon the pun." He used his feet to wheel his own chair over to me and sat directly in front of me; giving me enough room to keep my legs outstretched in front of myself.

"My mother. Where is she?"

"She is perfectly safe Scarlett. And she will be for as long as you co-operate. Our little home movie was simply a test. A seemingly brilliant way to test what we hoped you may be capable of." He glanced at his watch. "We may have to wait until tomorrow to proceed. I am not sure we can work with you in this state. I will dose you up and we can continue tomorrow."

"What. What was that? How did I?" I didn't finish what I was saying as the very idea seemed absurd. Could I possibly have willed that inch thick steel off my body? It was insane. But the strewn remains on the floor suggested it had in fact been the case.

"You responded to emotional stimulus in a way we could only have dreamed. This is the beginning Scarlett. I think you may be even better than we first thought. We will harness this, help you control it and when you can use this, and any other gifts we may find you have in a measured, on demand fashion, we will proceed to the next step." He moved to his feet.

"Next step?" He just looked at me and tapped the side of his nose with that horrible, bony finger.

"I am going to have Bailey and Orson sort you out some food and we will make up your bed. You will of course be sleeping here. We can't afford to let you out of our sight. They will be on watch throughout the night should you need anything." With that he paced to the soundproof screen, peeling off his lab coat and gloves, which he thrust into the waiting hands of Bailey as he went and waited silently to leave. The screen buzzed to life and disappeared into the recess above the door and the entrance to the corridor beyond groaned to life. Then he was gone.

Bailey and Orson leant closer to one another and muttered inaudibly before Orson went out of the open door. Bailey closed it behind him and walked by me to the back of the room. He pressed a square panel that was flush with the wall and stepped back as the wall shifted and tilted before falling flat into a double bed with stark white sheets tightly tucked into it. He said nothing, simply nodded at the bed and me before pacing back to me and scooping me into his arms. He laid me on the bed, his face slightly softer like he might speak, but the light behind his eyes dimmed again and he hardened, returning to the door and staring beyond my gaze.

I managed to lie myself down flat. It was the most comfortable position in a selection consisting of varying degrees of agony. I closed my eyes and sensed the room lights dim. I had no idea what time it was but could be certain that I wasn't going to bother asking my minder, even after his courteous carrying and room darkening acts.

Sleep tried to compete with my myriad of thoughts as I attempted to make sense of what had happened in this weird hospital facility come prison cell. My brain won. I hadn't been to the bathroom in hours and I didn't even know where the hell I would be going if I asked so I pushed the thought and growing need into the back of my mind and honed in on the buzz of the burns that made itself known even through the morphine. I thought about Jake and longed for him. I had managed to derail the course of events that I had seen where he had been here instead of me and for that I was thankful; but it didn't ease the guilt I harbored. I still hadn't told him about his mom and I knew it was going to weigh on me until I did.

The mechanical swoosh of the door opening disturbed me and my pulse quickened. Orson stomped back into the room clutching a crumpled paper bag in each hand. He thrust one into Bailey's chest forcing his eyes to spring open and a surprised groan to escape his throat. Orson's hulking frame was larger than Bailey's and he lacked that potential for softness I had seen in Bailey. He dropped the other bag on the bed next to me and immediately turned away without a single chink of warmth in his steely façade.

I shoved huge chunks of the warm pastry in my mouth. Ham and cheese and butter tasted like they had never tasted before. I barely chewed, desperate to fill my aching, growling stomach and ease the griping cramps I had been enduring for hours. I washed it down with the bottled water he brought me and slumped back onto my pillow. I allowed my eyes to close and the room and my food high sent my head into a sleepy spin. The bed felt like it was bobbing around on an ocean and my ears popped and crackled.

The faintest whisper found my ears and I cocked a lazy eye open to find my minders both still standing at their posts either side of the entrance, their eyes closed. Bailey obviously had spidery-sense; his eyes flicked open and glared at me at the very moment I clocked his on-duty nap. I snapped my eyes shut and returned to my head. I thought about how much I had achieved today and it gave me the boost I needed to focus through the pain and really listen. The world fell eerily silent at first and the faint hum of the equipment dissipated into nothing. I couldn't even hear my own breath or heartbeat. It was like someone had hit the mute button. Focus. The crackle started somewhere in the distance. It grew closer with every breath I took and soon I felt like I could almost reach out and grab the sound. It wasn't as strong as earlier, but I had found the connection. I managed to reach into the nothing and find Elias.

Elias. Can you hear me? There was a pause; nothing.

Elias? Please be there. Please.

Then from the darkness I heard him. "Scarlett. What happened? Why are you in so much pain?" His voice trembled with concern.

Elias. Something happened. Sutcliffe, he started doing these tests. He showed me a picture of Jake and then some creepy footage of one of them in my mom's house and I just got so angry. I have never felt such rage. Then I kind of willed the shackles from my wrists. If it hadn't been so gut-wrenchingly painful I would have been impressed. I just blew them to pieces, with my mind. Sadly my wrists and ankles were caught in the molten crossfire. Hence the pain.

"Wait. You can control physical objects with your mind? That is going to come in handy Scarlett." That's what Sutcliffe had thought too. I was growing tired of being seen as this rare commodity. I longed for a complete lack of attention, for the ordinary and mundane. What I wouldn't give to be sat being bored senseless by my teachers on subjects in which I had little to no interest; or to be sat back in the school lunch room complaining about undercooked fries and rubber omelets.

It would seem so. But it isn't enough. I need to know what else there is. This stuff isn't it all. It can't be. But I don't know how long I can cope with being down here. I need...

"He is fine. He's sleeping. It has taken me three hours to convince him that I would wake him if anything happened. He was all for storming the place and trying to whisk you off fairytale style. He is one stubborn mother..."

Elias. Enough. It is hard for him. He feels responsible. Go easy on him and keep him away like I asked. When I am ready I will tell you, but I can't leave yet. It isn't time.

"I get it. But I think it is best if we start to mount some kind of counter assault." Boys.

Elias, this isn't a game of Risk. They will kill you. In fact, you got off too lightly before. I didn't really believe they were going to let you go.

"I am not talking about me and lover boy storming the place. I am talking about harnessing the power, all of it." I let my brain work through his words one by one. I was starting to get it.

The Collective. What are you going to do? Light a freaking beacon?

"You mock but it ain't so far off. There are meeting places and messengers. A kind of ancient contact circle that has evolved and with the wonders of modern technology I reckon I could bring together a couple of hundred within the hour."

Then what?

"Then we work it out. Together. Some of these guys can do things I have never seen in person. Useful things; mind control, hypnosis type stuff. If we have it all at our fingertips we might just be able to pull something out the bag."

Is pulling something out of the bag supposed to fill me with warmth and confidence? Because it doesn't. We need something better than should. Don't you think if it were as easy as getting a load of freaks together it would have happened before now?

"No. Don't you get it? What's different is you. Whatever it is they are hanging on to you for. Whatever this other stuff is. That is why this time it is different. We have you."

I'm getting pretty sick of everyone thinking they have me. I was a person before I became the poster child for The Collective and the most wanted on the Venari hit list.

"Jesus Scarlett. Calm down. Get some sleep. Do what you need to tomorrow and by then we will have worked something out. And yes, before you ask me, again, I will keep him away. Heaven forbid…" I cut off the connection. I didn't even know until that moment that I would be able to but I wouldn't be able to keep my words in my head if we had carried on and since my earlier experiences the idea of getting mad didn't seem so clever.

I released myself from the space in my head and gave into the nagging pull of sleep.

The night was dreamless and short. I had been beyond exhausted and somehow managed to sleep in spite of the burns. I wasn't so lucky once I was awake though. The meds had long since worn off and as soon as the weary dreamlike seconds passed as my eyes opened the pain hit me like a wall as my body remembered the trauma.

"Holy crap. Mm." I bit down on my lip hard to hold in the expletives. The fierce, sharp pains had been replaced by the dull tightness of the warped skin and I felt like I might throw up. Bailey and Orson sprang to life and one of them – though through screwed up eyes and clenched teeth I didn't catch which one – administered another Morphine shot into my arm through a cannula I didn't remember being there. They must have been topping me up all night.

I waited until the relaxing wave of relief passed through me and shifted myself up. Now I really had to go to the bathroom.

"I. Need to go to the bathroom. Kind of urgently." I blushed uncontrollably; they on the other hand barely blinked but managed to communicate silently and Orson drew the short straw; I was secretly hoping this was yet more evidence of Bailey's struggle to keep up the act but I couldn't take any risks yet.

Orson helped me to my feet with as little contact as he could manage. We made it to the door and he leant me against the wall facing away from him so he could unlock the door in secret.

The passageways were cold and the smell of chemicals had faded in place of dust. The emergency lighting was visible in the corridor ahead; we were almost back in the public side of the tunnels. The urge to scream was almost unbearable. I fought with everything I could muster to stay calm. Orson was steering me, bearing most of my weight on one arm. We turned into another unused room; he ushered me forwards and produced a miniature flare which he placed on the floor. The stone walls were illuminated with bright pink light and lit up a makeshift toilet in the corner. He made sure I got there then turned and patrolled the doorway. All I could think of was how hugely undignified this was and how crazily uncomfortable. It looked like a crate with a toilet seat on top. A bucket of water next to it which could only be the high-tech flush system; it was a million miles from the lengths they had gone to in the creation of the one-room medical research facility down the hall.

I tried to take into account the route – how far we were from where there would soon be throngs of people – and it weighed on my mind, the absurd significance of their operation. How this kind of thing had been happening time and again for years, right under everyone's noses. Right now there were people above me, planning their days in Paris. Being in love, fighting, eating delicious food and without a single clue that I was down here, desperately trying to find a way to stop this hideous cycle. The worst was the guilt that came with knowing I wasn't doing this for the world; I was doing it for a chance to have something real with Jake. I wanted to look at him in a few years and feel safe; like I had done everything in my power to heal the pain his father's death caused, protect him from the Venari and make it possible for us to live. Like I had promised months ago on the bridge in my mother's back yard.

By the time we got back to the test room, Sutcliffe had arrived for another session. He looked positively beside himself with joy to see me.

"Ahh. Miss Roth. I trust the pain relief is still sufficient?" I nodded as I limped toward the bed; Orson had long since abandoned his post as my crutch and was back to being the gargoyle impressionist alongside the doorframe.

"No. No my dear. Back to the chair please. We have a lot to get through today and our guests arrive tomorrow. There isn't much time." He was hurriedly flicking through a worn leather notebook. I had seen one like it before; in Jacques' study. Alice's notes.

His index finger scanned the page and his eyes chased its path down the paper.

"Guests?" My eyes were boring holes into his temple and he didn't even look up.

"Yes, Miss Roth. We are expecting the full Council and we have to have found out as much as possible by then. They will be expecting a comprehensive list of your particular skills. The bidding won't start until we know exactly what we can offer. So, sit." Council. Bidding. This did not sound good and it meant I had even less time to gather my own info and get out of here, somehow. The wounds on my limbs pulsed as my anxiety started to peak.

"What Council and who is bidding?" His eyes finally met my own and his expression was one of extreme frustration. A deep slow breath left his lips as if he were swallowing pure rage.

"Look." The word erupted from his throat, a vicious growl. "I do not have time for anymore of this polite drivel.

You know as much as you need to. What we need to focus on now is getting through the rest of these tests. Last night's little incident threw us off course and cost us precious time." He grabbed my arm at the elbow and pulled me into the chair. The sudden twist in my legs broke the fragile membrane on my burns and I let out a yelp. He didn't acknowledge. The pleasantries were definitely over.

I kept my mouth shut and waited to see what was coming. Rather than restrain me he lifted the back of the chair into an upright position and motioned at his henchmen who promptly unlocked the door. A small dark-haired girl similar in age to me with pale skin in an all-black ensemble scurried in like some kind of timid prey. She didn't make eye contact with anyone. She was pushing a bed tray on wheels which she pushed until it was resting over my knees. Without a word or a glance, she hurried back out of the door and it closed behind her. Who was she? Why would anyone work for them? She was obviously terrified so it was possible she was another of The Collective being blackmailed or even held prisoner. I hoped for her sake she wasn't, but it was the most appropriate explanation.

The tray was shrouded in a starched white sheet, which smelt like fresh laundry. The smell brought an overwhelming surge of homesickness over me as I thought about the simplicity and pleasure of climbing into bed and new sheets. The image in front of me tainted that somehow and I resented them so much at that moment I couldn't help myself. I spat at the tray and promptly turned my head away in defiance. No sooner had my head faced the wall of screens to my left than those bony fingers pinched the skin on my face. He didn't say a word; he just firmly forced my head back to the forward position and kept my chin within his grasp.

"I am going to remove this sheet in a moment and I want you to look at the items on it. That is all. Just look until I tell you otherwise. I hope we are clear. If I have reason to believe you are not to be trusted or will not co-operate; I shall engage orders to ensure your mother doesn't sleep quite so soundly this evening." Vomit rose in my throat and a spasm of panic gripped my stomach. Mom.

He slowly pulled the sheet away revealing a bizarre bric-a-brac collection of items that were so obtuse together I couldn't even begin to think where he was going with this one.

A key. The kind to your average house, nothing special or ancient, just a gold key. A hardback book; a copy of *Macbeth* in green binding. A mirror; the kind you found on vintage dressing tables, the ones that had intricate crystal backs or melamine images of birds and flowers. My grandmother had one just like it.

Sutcliffe was watching me like a hawk and for reasons unknown he clocked the tray and flashed his eyes back to me; something in that moment made him decide to move the tray further away. It was now almost further than my toes.

As my eyes found the final object my heartbeat accelerated

and I felt my fingers curl into a tight fist. My bracelet. I knew it was mine but I was compelled to check my wrist. The bandage was blocking my view of the skin but I knew; I could feel its absence now. When had they? I knew for sure it was mine. The same beautiful charms Jake had picked out. The ones I had kissed when my heart was breaking for him at the start of my trip. I held my breath for a moment and my head was dizzy with anger. That was mine. It was my piece of Jake and it belonged with me. Sutcliffe didn't move. I wanted to bolt forward but his eyes were studying me and he didn't give me a chance. A flick of his head brought Bailey and Orson to my side where they exerted their full power on my shoulders. I was bound to the chair again but there was shuffling and the mechanical clink of the door. If felt like there were others here too.

The eerie silence in the room and the pressure against my frame only spurred on my anger. It was bad enough they were keeping me here but taking my personal things was a step too far. A strange atmosphere descended and I felt like my mind was separated from my body. The pain was gone and all I felt was the accumulation of all the resentment and disgust I had ever felt for them, for Sutcliffe. Alice. Jacques. Threatening my mom. My fingers flexed from their tightly wound ball and they began to tingle and burn. The room began to swirl in a mist of glowing white light, which formed together in whorls that channeled through the air and into the tips of my fingers.

The three men stood by my head didn't flinch or speak so I

could only assume they weren't seeing this. I didn't think even they could remain stony faced in the light of something this bizarre. The weirdest thing was how completely at ease I felt. Something deep in my mind was reassuring me, urging me to give in.

The mist fed into each of my fingertips and set them alight with a glorious, other-worldly glow. My mind cleared of everything without me even trying and all I could see, think or feel was that the bracelet was mine and I wanted it, immediately.

A distant rumble moved closer and the chair was vibrating like there were seismic shifts directly below me. My pupils burned at the sight of the bracelet and with a rumble it moved into the air with a delicate grace and hovered above the tray. Then as quick as it had all happened it appeared in my left hand and the light, the rumbling sounds and the peace in my head disappeared.

A slow, loud applause started behind me and Sutcliffe sauntered into view. "Well. You really are as good as they say you are." Bailey and Orson followed some invisible command and left the room without a secondary glance. I stroked the symbols between my fingers before stuffing it into my jeans pocket.

"You knew I could do that?" I was thinking so many thoughts I could barely concentrate on waiting for his answer. I could hear people in my head, I could break and move objects with my mind. This was insane; suddenly the odd premonition didn't seem quite so extraordinary.

"No. I didn't know for sure but I had hoped that was one of your gifts. You can move objects, manipulate or in your case obliterate them and now that we know your stimulus is anger we can adapt that to be a more simple process. It will take time, of course, but we will get there. You'll be a little more raw tomorrow than I had wanted, but we can show them the basics. The potential will be clear for all to see." He pulled a leather strap across my waist and went back to his books. He scrawled quickly on its pages and before throwing it down onto the counter.

"Let's continue. Shall we?" I was concentrating on the latest additions to my repertoire and the tiniest hint of light that lingered in the tips of my fingers. God knows what else I could do; but I was making real progress. Less than a day and I had uncovered a whole lot more than I had ever thought possible and the books I read as a kid, the ones filled with magic and bad guys and heroes? They didn't sound so far-fetched anymore.

My train of thought was broken as Sutcliffe brought the screens to life and spun me round to face them.

"Look at them. I want you to focus. Show me…" He rubbed his chin playfully. "Show me what you think of when you see Jake." I smirked. He was a lunatic.

"You expect me to what? Project my thoughts?" I couldn't help but explode with laughter. Some of it was nerves but most of it was the notion that he felt he owned me. I had already proved I was more powerful than him but his arrogance knew no bounds. I might have no idea how to wield them yet, but I was drawing some confidence from the fact I knew if I really had to I could take control. "You're crazy."

"So… even after all you have seen. All you have done, you are still a skeptic. How odd."

"I don't understand why this is only happening now." My partially mock concern and questioning was two-fold. These were questions I wanted, no, needed the answers to but in asking them I was maintaining the façade that I was as clueless as he hoped. It was a balancing act but I was pleased with my performance so far. He was not only handing me the gifts I didn't know I had but he was handing over all the information I needed to piece the puzzles together.

"We have spent years trying to find out what makes all of you sideshow freaks tick. It seems there are no hard and fast rules for what makes you react but you, as we thought, are the only one we have seen in decades with quite so many talents. I am willing to bet there are a lot more where they came from." He gestured back toward the screen. "It is all a case of finding what works to evoke the right reactions. And it seems you Miss Roth are a sucker for emotions; bonds between people. It would be pathetic if it weren't so… useful." He nudged my head with a finger to face the screens again. "Now. Think. Hard. Picture him." As he spoke he brought out some more of the sticky medical pads with colorful wires. As he rigged me up to the machines a familiar crescendo of beeps and whirrs sprang into action. "Are you trying?" His voice had lost the smug expectation and was filled with frustration.

I wasn't trying. In fact, I was trying not to think of Jake. Bringing him into this room under these circumstances, even just in my head, felt like I was dragging him through hell. He was too pure and too wonderful to be embroiled in this and I was frightened of what might happen if my love for him transformed into something physical.

The screens paused, a blur of gray that occasionally flickered with a pulse of electricity. Sutcliffe was staring at me intently. Waiting. Challenging. I was looking at my wrists, focusing on the dull throbbing pain and trying to do anything but let the image of his perfect face into my mind. In trying so hard not to I was blindsided by my memory of the last time I was trapped in a room and he burst in. The memory of the fight, my paralyzed body was too much and a supernova of memories and images of him flooded my head without permission. It was the first time I had ever had a thought of him and felt that it was unwelcome, but this was the wrong way, the wrong time.

My head ached under the weight of the war I was waging on my thoughts. Sutcliffe shifted in his seat in my periphery without speaking and I looked up at the screens, conscious that if anything was going to happen I had already opened the floodgates.

A silence befell the room, aside from the bleep of the machines, and we both stared at the wall in front of us. The gray mass twitched with white flashes of light and I began to feel dizzy. A familiar nausea washed over me and my skin turned clammy as my mind span. This was bad. Rather than project anything of Jake at his request I was in the throes of falling into a new vision and he was going to have a front row seat.

I screwed my eyes so tight my head pounded as I desperately tried to hold it off, force it back into the depths of my mind. I knew in the pit of my stomach that it was impossible. I had never been able to stave one off since the beginning and God knows I had tried. As the room span I watched through pained eyes as the vision spilled out of my mind, through the fine, neon wires and started to unfold on screen.

A dimly lit amphitheater or lecture hall filled to capacity with hordes of smartly dressed men. Their conversation was loud but there were too many voices to determine a single line of coherent speech. The conversation stopped dead as another man took to the stage beneath a glaring spotlight. I couldn't make out his face in my head or on the screen but the silence that befell that room meant he was of some significance. I had surrendered to the vision and even conceded to trying to focus to satiate my curiosity in spite of its public nature, but to no avail. There were a few more flickers but the image had already paused, stilted mid flow and faded to a spot like there had been a power outage. My mind was empty now and I was left feeling hollow and spent like a visiting host had just left my already weary body.

A tear rolled off my cheek. Now the confidence that came with my discoveries was paling in light of the vulnerability of the last few minutes. He had been in my head. There was no space safe and as much as I wanted to believe it, I wasn't strong enough to retain control of this situation.

A KIND OF FREEDOM

With my eyes closed in silent grief for my sanity and most likely my safety; I felt him before I heard him. His face brushed the skin of my ear and I shuddered. The frequency of his proximity to me was increasing and the extremity of my reaction correlated. My skin crawled.

"How beautiful to see what you can see." His voice was feigned and sickly sweet. "I didn't expect to get that far today. Much more interesting than gushing images of your pathetic beau. And so good of you to show me the turnout of our guests too. They will be pleased." It made sense now. The crowd. They were the bidders. They were the ones coming for me. It was apparent that whatever I was going to do to get out of this place it had be soon.

"I think you deserve a short break. I don't want you giving out on me. I will send Bailey in with some refreshments and we can continue when I get back. I must tend to a few matters ahead of our guests' arrival." He placed a hand on my wrist and pressed down. The touch spread the pain of my burns the width of my arm and I cried out in pain. "Let's not spoil anything by forgetting what is at stake here." As he released my hand he met my eyes with a firm gaze; silently and unnecessarily confirming what he meant. He slithered toward the door and spun on his heels just before he activated the lock. "I really am delighted with your progress." I was appalled that he felt his so-called praise would be of interest to me, let alone please me.

He slipped out of the door and I heard the muffled sounds of hushed voices just before it closed. Bailey and Orson hadn't been far it seemed so it wouldn't be long before they were back and I was on total lockdown.

I closed my eyes and tried as hard as I could to clear my mind. My senses felt weak. Every vision I had took a little from me, but these new forms of madness; they really stung me. My subconscious was worried for us and my current apathy for making a move and I was served a fleeting memory of the forthcoming guests as a reminder of what the alternative was if I stayed. It spurred me on enough to make contact with Elias. I prayed he had the plan.

I cleared my mind as best I could and waited; drawing on the silence of the room to move the process along. Come on. Come on. The sound of energy clicking through the air, around my head and somehow finding its way into his was all I could hear. Whooshes and whirrs of sounds in my inner ear before a scratchy blank was filled with his voice.

"Scarlett. You there? My God. I heard some crazy stuff. Are you OK? What the hell? We have been worried sick." Trying to process his questions in turn was too much for me so I tackled the bits that I could remember and forced out the salient information from my end of the situation.

I'm here. Look we don't have much time. I am alone but not for long. I have found out all sorts of crazy crap that I can do and I think there is more; I mean... I just feel it. But, there is some kind of huge Council meeting come auction tomorrow. I had a vision and Sutcliffe mentioned something about it. They are planning to sell me off to the highest bidder.

"Whoa. Whoa. What?" He wasn't so hot with the quick fire information either, though he had no excuse.

I think they are still Venari; but that is just a guess. Regardless, you were right about the harvesting my powers thing, but they are going to showcase me and sell me on as a, as a weapon or something and the way he keeps grinning and looking at me; the price on my head is freaking huge. I have to get out, tonight. Tell me there's a plan.

"Well. Not exactly. We have managed to get some maps of the routes through the tunnels and even if I knew exactly where you were, which I don't, I think we would have trouble outrunning them. They know these places. Their forefathers are the ones that built them. Trade secrets passed down through generations."

My stomach lurched at the realization it had to be me. That meant finding some way to get through Bailey and Orson and find my way to the tourist section and out. Without being followed.

Great. OK, thanks for that. Where are you guys now? I need to know if I get out of here that you'll at least be waiting to offer some kind of back up.

"We are at my place but I am not entirely sure we aren't being watched. A black SUV has been camped out front all night." All I could think of then was Jake and how Elias' priorities had to shift to make sure, if nothing else, that he got out OK.

Find a way out. I need at least an hour from now. Is he...

"Here. Speak to him yourself, figuratively. Hell, you know what I mean." As Elias had explained my senses suddenly opened and I felt Elias reach out for Jake's hand. I couldn't see it, but I knew it was happening. As soon as their skin touched his face filled my head and I could smell his scent in my nostrils. I couldn't hold back the tears, but I reined them into silent sobs that hurt my chest with restrained emotion.

Jake? Listen to me. No heroics OK? I am going to be fine. I am getting out of here but you two need to be ready and you need to source somewhere safe for us to go because they will not stop until they find me. We need to buy some time to work this thing out. And we have to find a way to get my mom out of the house for a couple of days. There was no sound on the end of the line at all but I could feel the ache in his chest and sense the weight of the lump in his throat as it threatened to consume him. Tears streamed down my face.

"I hear you baby." That word from him was too much now. "I swear to God I won't let anything happen to you. We will find a way to put an end to this I promise. I will sort your mom, don't worry. Just be careful." I still didn't know how all this worked but if anything I had learned how miraculously powerful my mind was these days. I didn't have any anger to draw on though, only unbridled longing, but the pain felt almost the same. Perhaps, just perhaps. I focused as hard as I could and thought solely about placing my lips on his. Softly tracing the line of his jaw with my mouth and planting a series of kisses so loaded with love and desire onto him in the hope it would carry him through. He smiled in my mind's eye and on some level I knew he felt it too.

I have to go. There's someone coming. I cut the connection short and closed my eyes to shake off the remaining tears just as Bailey strode in with more food and a soda. He avoided eye contact and a plan I hadn't even thought out was set in motion as he placed them down on the tray table.

BEYOND REACH

"Bailey? I can call you that right?" He nodded, eyes still fixed on some imaginary distraction across the room. "I have to use the bathroom again." His eyes rolled and he clenched his fists. I hadn't really looked at his hands before but the potential for an imminent fight made it seem logical to know what I was letting myself in for.

He had huge, worker's hands. I could see the tips of callouses on the edge of his palms and his fingers were stocky and bore the remnants of dirt and grime; no doubt from the other Venari business he was assigned to do. He wore a wedding band, which really threw me. How could anyone keep me locked in here as a day job before casually going home to play family man? Though that was the trick wasn't it? Everything looked so normal; the secret was hidden in plain sight.

The door unlocked and I limped through. The feeling of

the dusty, stone floor beneath the skin on my feet felt somehow encouraging and I inhaled a gasping breath of air that lacked the close, chemical tang of the room behind me. Feeling something real, solid and breathing new air reminded me that there was a street not far above me and soon I could be on it. Most importantly I could be on it and in Jake's arms.

I hadn't yet seen Orson. He wasn't in the room, he wasn't outside. Not being able to account for his whereabouts made my flimsy plan all together more terrifying. I squinted to try to make out more shapes in the dim light but I couldn't see anyone. I could however, hear the distant mumble of excited chatter. Tourists. I could definitely follow their noise back to the tour route; if I could get away. Possibly the biggest 'if' in history.

I walked even slower than my injuries demanded. Twice Bailey stopped ahead of me and turned around looking furious. I grimaced in response and he turned back to face the dark.

The makeshift bathroom smelled awful as if somehow the warmth of the sun had penetrated the soil and stone to warm it up just enough to make me want to puke. My mouth was filling with saliva as I swallowed the urge to wretch. I pulled a hand up to my face and Bailey stood at the doorway, un-phased. I really did wonder if he and Orson were human.

By this point my heart had begun to race as I realized my window for making something significant happen was open for the briefest of moments. I shifted myself into the dark haze of the room; this time lit by a small hand torch Bailey had kindly thrown in across the floor from the doorway.

"Can you move out of the door just a little? I really could use a little privacy in here." Bailey didn't respond other than to produce an awkward throaty cough come chest clearing sound before shuffling a couple of feet to the left; covering the exit towards the tour of course. Always on duty.

I sat on the makeshift toilet and panicked in a way that was incomparable to anything I had ever known. Never had anyone felt so utterly terrified, confused and weighed down by responsibility but not been able to make even the slightest sound. I trapped my convulsing hands beneath my legs. Think. Think. All I needed was extreme emotion and a thought about the end result. Admittedly it was a sketchy and flawed plan but all I had at that moment was the belief that my mind could respond when I asked it to with something out of this world. I needed that now.

I didn't have long. I could hear Bailey's shuffling feet. Any minute he would be in here checking up on me, irrespective of the situation he would always check. The panic flooded my system and the sick feeling came back. It rose in my throat sending simultaneous hot and cold chills through me that left my skin glistening by the torchlight. I turned and put my head towards the bowl just in time to vomit my fear out into the stench-ridden hole below. I wiped a sleeve across my mouth and spat the taste from my mouth. I hadn't thought this through. I didn't even know what I wanted to happen, other than that I wanted to be out of this place. I needed some kind of miracle and possibly the kind of power it would take to teleport somewhere else but this wasn't the time for wishing, I needed to evoke action, realistic action.

Shuffling in the hall beyond disturbed me from my anxiety attack and I clambered to my feet and stumbled towards the door. I held my breath as the sounds of labored breathing and a struggle echoed into the room. I shifted the torchlight to the corridor and there was a sudden thump as Bailey's head appeared on the ground. I stepped back, my hand clasped to my mouth in shock and terror. If someone could do that to him then I was in big trouble.

I stepped towards the doorway and swung myself against the wall to give myself the best chance to make a swing at whomever it was that was lurking in the shadow beyond. I could still hear the throngs of people in the distance and lost myself in the escapist dream of being one of them. Camera flashes and souvenir maps would be a welcome alternative to this.

Footsteps in the hall brought the sound of the assailant's path to the doorway. I braced myself with the torch and hoped it would be enough for my one shot before I ran.

The crackle of a flare startled me and illuminated the room before they even stepped in. A long, thin, warped shape of a shadow entered the room and stretched out in a ghoulish snake across the stone floor, twisting around the stones and broken slabs.

I raised my hands above my head and my wrists began to instantly throb as my heightened pulse worked overtime. Breath still held I braced myself for impact. One foot, then the other. They entered the room and I went to swing but my movement spurred a reaction in them I hadn't anticipated.

A piercing scream filled the space between us and I found myself echoing it with my own. We both stopped and our eyes locked onto one another. It wasn't some other-worldly gangster or another of Sutcliffe's cronies. It was the small, dark-haired girl who had brought the tray in during the experiments.

She thrust a firm but delicate hand over my mouth. "Shhh. Don't have much time." She grabbed my hand and led me through the door before I even had a moment to speak. We both stepped over Bailey in such a callous manner but I had no time to question. Instead I was left with a cocktail of fresh panic and confusing relief; was he dead? Did I want him to be? My brain could not keep up. My feet were moving as fast as my pounding heart and the blur of stone walls was making me dizzy as I hurried, following the lead of another mysterious stranger.

"Is he?" I looked at the back of her head as she dragged me upwards. She didn't turn to answer me but her voice, still a whisper, carried on the air behind her.

"No. That is why we hurry. The other one will be back any moment. We have to get out of their route down here." She was speaking hurriedly and her accent made my ears strain to understand the words. I didn't even ask how she managed it. This tiny young woman, no more than five feet tall had floored Bailey – the man mountain – and broken me free. I was beyond grateful because I had known in that room that it was too soon; I didn't know how to harness what I needed yet, not in every situation. She had saved my life and I didn't even know her name. Or what she wanted. An unwelcome afterthought courtesy of my paranoid subconscious. I pushed the growing urge to be suspicious out of my mind; after all, it was run with her or take my chances. If she turned out to be another undesirable, or worse, one of them, the odds were more in my favor with her slender frame than his gargantuan one.

We twisted and turned; my feet resisting the prod and scratch of the rough floor. She had such a firm grip on my hand, but she loosened every few yards as she turned back to me. It felt like she was checking it was really happening to her too.

She was whispering hurried, breathy words in another language but I didn't need a translator to know they were prayers. I joined her silently. The sounds of the tour were closer than ever and we were venturing back into the strip-lit tunnels that glowed. She dragged me off to the right into a tiny room and flicked the light on as she slammed the door behind us.

We were in a janitor's closet. The smell of bleach and wood polish clung to the air but it was so much better than the test room or the smell of anxious vomit in the hideous make-shift bathroom. She pushed me gently into a questionable looking padded chair and slumped against the door; sliding down it until she reached the floor and her head fell into her hands.

"Who are you?" I rubbed the bandages gently wanting to ease the pain but it only highlighted the need for me to see a real doctor and as I couldn't trust them I pushed the thought and the agony out of my mind for another time.

My heroine looked up at me and only then in the light did I notice that she was wearing a tour T-shirt. She worked here.

"I am Celeste. You are Scarlett, oui?" She produced a small bottle of water from a linen bag slung over her shoulder. My mouth ached with thirst and she instinctively threw me the drink. I swallowed huge, greedy mouthfuls of the chilled liquid and relished the sensation of it cooling my throat before hitting my stomach in an icy tidal wave of satisfaction. I nodded through my breathless gulps.

"How did you? What did you do to him, to Bailey? And who are you as in what do you know? Why are you helping me?" Even in these circumstances I had to remain a little cautious. She smiled; probably the same way I had the first time Lydia questioned me incessantly.

"First. He is fine. I, how you say, acquired something to help him sleep a little while. He is fine in say three hours tops. His friend will find him before then anyway. What was your next question?" She reached back into her backpack and pulled out a power bar, which she tore in half. It didn't go unnoticed or unappreciated that she threw the slightly bigger half to me.

"Who are you and what do you know?" I greedily stuffed the bar into my mouth the moment I had let the question out. She had a slightly bemused or perhaps disgusted look on her face as she watched me chew.

"I am Celeste. I work here," She pointed to the badge on her polo shirt to authenticate the information. "I struck a deal with these guys about a year ago for that room. They paid me good money to let them in, get them keys and not ask questions and it seemed OK." She glanced at me for approval or for acceptance, I wasn't sure.

"OK?" I didn't conceal my failure to understand how she could even think about being involved.

"I know. My judgment may not have been correct. I see them bringing all sorts of strange equipment, medical supplies and then they ask me to bring in those objects the other day and they paid me such good money I couldn't say no. They have, the, err, the…" She screwed her eyes as she shook her head in frustration. Language was yet another barrier we could little afford in a tense situation and I was trying not to press her for the words but the wait was torture.

"Slower…think." It had been so supportive in my head but outside it sounded nothing short of patronizing.

She took a long, slow breath. "They have the people who own it. This place." She gestured to the ceiling and the hall with weary, outstretched arms. "They have them all too. Money. No one cares what they are doing, they only want the money. But, once I saw you I realized I couldn't play along anymore. So, we are here." A sound in the hall beyond jolted us both and we hushed as we retreated instinctively into the same corner. The sound passed by and we unfurled as the tension left us. We didn't have long.

"There must be more. They wouldn't just trust anyone to keep their secrets?" I demanded her gaze with my eyes and she conceded to the pressure; she looked down to her feet.

"It was simple at first. They wanted simple things. As everything began to change they started threatening me about keeping quiet, about how much time they needed, how much access. Then one day I went home and they were there; the two, how you say…errr henchman. They…" Her voice broke and she fought back tears. Her head fell into her hands for a brief moment as she shook away the threat of the emotion on her composure. "They killed my dog, torn up all the pictures of family and said if they had any cause to doubt my, my…errr. Reliability. They would be forced to… act in a certain way. So I let them have what they wanted. I am so sorry. I know it was wrong, but I couldn't get out of it. I was too scared." Tears welled again in her dark brown eyes and she hurried them away with her sleeve.

"What changed? The risks are still there… why save me now?" I couldn't control the part of me that didn't trust anyone but Jake these days and even though I could see she was offended I didn't feel like backing down. I needed to know the deal.

"You. I saw you and realized that whatever they were doing to you was against your will and if they could do that to you then the promises and bargains I made with them were most likely hollow. They would be as quick to kill me as soon as they had no use for me. So I came for you." She looked up at me all doe eyed but I could see it, the truth, and she was genuinely laying it all on the line for me; a total stranger that was almost undoubtedly dragging her headlong into the single most terrifying experience of her life. All I could feel was guilt and sorrow for her. Whatever she thought she had experienced so far was the tip of the iceberg.

"Well. Thank you and I am really sorry about your dog and all of this. I didn't want for any more people to be dragged into this nightmare." I reached out and placed a hand on hers. "Really. Thanks." She smiled at me again and looked at her watch. Another sound from the corridors beyond invaded the tiny, suddenly claustrophobic space.

"We have to move. A tour will be passing through in about five minutes. We can mix ourselves up in them and follow them out to the street. Then I am afraid I have no further plans." She was massaging her temples with her index fingers. Her hands were adorned with about twelve rings each, the silver intricately placed the length of most of her elegant fingers glistened in the light. Her nails were painted black and they were chipped and picked at. She and Elias would probably get on well; dark and damaged was his thing.

"Oh my God. That would be amazing. I don't know how to thank you." I stood up and glanced at myself in the solitary mirror tile hung on the wall. I barely recognized the person standing there. The dark circles under my eyes reached almost as far as the middle of my nose and my red hair was lank and greasy with sweat and dust; curling into sticky rat-tails at the end. "What about you though? They will not let you just escape. There will be someone coming to look for you?" Her eyes filled with sadness and in that moment I identified with the look on her face; she was terrified and lonely.

"I know. I knew that before I even left this morning. I brought a bag; I will find my way." She stood too and yanked the bag back over her head; with another glance at her watch she mobilized and the sad, lonely look was gone; now she was calculating the best route.

"I will help you sort something. It is the very least I can do. When we get out of here you'll come with us and we can work it all out. I won't let you run scared from them, especially not on your own." I turned away from the mirror and offered her a reassuring glance. She was tightening the laces on her pumps and she looked over at my bare, raw feet, battered by all of the running. She reached up to the third shelf of the unit to her right, which was so tall she could barely hold her balance, and pulled down some god awful plastic cleaning clog style shoes. "Here; these look about right." She hurled them to the floor at my feet. They were at least a size too small but in light of the situation; small shoes wasn't such an awful price to pay to get out and I couldn't exactly wander through the Parisian streets like I looked; without shoes I would have been confused for a hobo for sure. "Who are they?" She stared at me hoping she was wrong about them; hoping it wasn't as bad as she had imagined and I felt the weight of the truth bear down on my stomach.

"Let's get away from them first. Then you can know as much as you want." She nodded and pulled the door ajar. She took a glance left and right before signaling for me to join her; with the door open the rhythmic thump of footsteps could be heard and it sent my pulse racing. Orson would probably be here soon and he would find Bailey discarded in the corridor. Then all hell would break loose. I shook the thought away. Focus on Jake. He is waiting.

We picked up a strong pace and hurried through the passageways. We twisted and turned left and right and I hadn't realized how far down I must have been it seemed like years since I had come down here with Sutcliffe and my memory was clouded with all that had occurred since.

There were sounds of a struggle or hurry from the darkness we had emerged out of moments before, deep down in the tunnels. We looked at each other, eyes wide with fear and it went unspoken but we knew it was them. We had just seconds and instinctively matched pace. Faster and faster through the maze.

Suddenly the volume stepped up and voices were clear.

The air was cooler, still rank and filled with dust and age but better than where we had come from. Celeste held out a cautionary arm, holding me back from my desire to run to the tour and cry with joy to see such normality. She was right though, we had to wait. Pick our moment. I couldn't help but check behind us and while the sounds I had heard were no longer nearing I knew better than to think they would just have given up or gone back. It was more likely to mean something worse was happening and I had never wanted to leave a place more.

The tour guide passed the end of the passage. "This way please." He was wearing the exact same T-shirt as Celeste, but she had pulled a red hooded sweater over hers to make herself less conspicuous.

I watched her intently, waiting for the order. "Now." She grabbed my hand firmly and yanked us into the throngs of people. Snippets of conversation about the mundane flooded my head and it was completely wonderful to hear people discuss the inane – celebrity gossip, shopping trips for later in the day, the quality of coffee. I felt my breathing quicken but it was exhilaration not fear. It was the thought of the moment I would see Jake just minutes away.

She weaved through the crowd, shoving gently to help us progress. The tourists were stopping to take photos and read the inscriptions but we powered through, rushing to the exit signs. Neither of us looked behind, we didn't dare. We pushed and pushed until we reached the bottom of the ascent and then we instinctively ran. Up and up. Me, no longer even aware of the pain in my limbs, the bloodied mess of my feet and her, just running from a mistake she struggled to accept she had made. We were both in denial.

When I saw the light of the open door that exited onto the street I started to cry. Sobs of overwhelming relief rose in my chest and exploded from my throat in loud cries. Endless tears started to stream down my face as the sunlight hit it and its warmth permeated my skin.

I grabbed the exit doorframe with both my hands and heaved myself from the heat below. My eyes were frantically scanning the street for him but I couldn't see him. I turned to check Celeste was behind me and I watched her step out into the street to stand with me. She pulled the hood down from her head and hooked out her shoulder-length dark hair. She stood by my side in a show of some unspoken allegiance.

I spun round at the sensation of his approach. I knew he was there because a kind of serenity I only associated with him was passing over me. He ran round the corner toward me and Elias followed closely after, but with a little less urgency.

I was rooted to the spot as my eyes devoured the reality of him. He slowed to a walk and matching smiles spread across our faces. I wiped a tear away with the back of my sleeve and self-consciously ran my fingers through my hair. He reached for my wrist and pulled me into him as he kissed me hungrily on the mouth. His lips parted mine and he searched my mouth for the missing moments; he demonstrated in the most perfect way possible how he'd missed me and it was all I could do not to disappear into him. I buried my face in his neck and inhaled him completely. I had never wanted him more and even locked in this embrace he was too far away. I couldn't do that again – willingly part myself from him – it was too much. I examined him. His beautiful eyes were deeper set than normal and were encircled by gray; he hadn't been sleeping properly. He had the bed hair that I loved so much and his tight T-shirt and chino shorts showed me enough of him to ignite my lust for him in spite of our company. I swallowed those impulses along with a sigh and ran my hand longingly down his chest.

He held me at arms-length and inspected me all over. "Did they hurt you?" His fingers were interlocked with mine and he caught sight of the bandages on my wrists. "What's this? Are you OK?" He pulled me back and kissed my hair.

"I am fine Jake, really. But we can talk about all of this later. We don't have much time." I span round to Celeste who was averting her gaze from the shameless public display of affection and pulled her closer. "Jake, this is Celeste. Celeste, my boyfriend Jake." She offered an awkward smile.

Jake extended his hand. "Hi. Pleasure. Err... How did you two?" He looked at me for an explanation.

"Again. We can talk about it all later but she comes with us. Elias?" I looked beyond Jake's shoulders and Elias was his usual self; leant casually on a wall he was lighting up a cigarette. The sound of his name raised an eyebrow before he sauntered over. He smiled at me and patted me on the back, which I had to assume was his affectionate way of saying he was glad I hadn't been massacred or something else terrible. He shook his wrist out of his sleeve and glanced at his watch.

"We need to move, now. I have lined us up somewhere to go." He headed back down the street and we followed without question. Jake held my hand so tightly and Celeste followed just slightly behind. I slowed until she was level with us; conscious that she was feeling alone.

Elias kept looking back to do a mental roll call and we kept pace. "Where are we going?" I shouted toward him and he glared at me. "OK. No questions, I get it. Nice to see you too," I muttered under my breath and he echoed the sounds but it wasn't English. His mind was closed to me too, he was angry and guarding his thoughts.

We weaved through the streets and I received more than a few inquisitive glances for my interesting footwear and the bandages on my wrists which told an all-together different and obvious incorrect story to the unknowing.

I was taking long, drawn out breaths of city air. While notably smoggier than home it was welcome and far removed from that clinical hole I had been residing in. Full lungs and the constant reassurance of Jake's lips on my hands were enough to keep the worst of the dark anxiousness at bay. We reached the end of a long street, dappled with coffee shops and well-dressed Europeans sipping lattes in their work clothes. We looked about as much out of place as was possible for four twenty-something's with nervous, darting eyes, scurrying down a street in broad daylight while scouring the faces of strangers for signs of danger.

Elias came to an abrupt stop and we fell into line alongside him. None of us were speaking; we were just waiting and exchanging curious glances. Celeste was nervously playing with the sleeve of her sweater and biting her lower lip. I placed my hand on hers. "It is going to be OK." Her lip started to tremble and I knew I didn't need to say anything else. She was in that delicate place where one more word said or spoken would just tip her over the edge. I had been there on more than one occasion and if it weren't for Jake grasping me so tightly I would have been there too.

"There. Come on." Elias pointed to a blacked out van parked across the road. Its gunmetal gray paint twinkled in the sunlight as we ducked between the waiting traffic to reach it.

Elias yanked the door on the side of the van open and inside there were two rows of seats empty except for one at the back where Pierre was sat playing with his phone.

"Guys you made it. Scarlett, are you OK?" I nodded but was too distracted with the final periphery check. So far so good. I felt Jake raise me into the van and he herded Celeste in before he climbed in himself. Elias had jumped into the front; apparently he was our getaway driver. I scanned the streets beyond in what felt like slow motion as Jake sat alongside me, his arm outstretched to pull the van door shut. My heart stopped as a glimpse of a hulking, dark figure turned the corner we had passed round a moment earlier, his frame faced me head on from a few hundred yards and two lines of traffic away. Not enough distance. Orson? I couldn't focus, the tears I had been holding back were precariously wavering on my eyelids and my breathing was so hurried I felt like I might pass out. But, before I could confirm the sighting the door was moving and the light outside closed to a strip then with a click it was gone.

As the door slammed we were cocooned and invisible to the world outside thanks to its dark glass and we breathed a collective sigh of relief, but the possibility of their proximity was enough for me to reserve any excitement. There was no time for procrastination. Elias stepped on the gas and we blended into the hustle of the Parisian traffic.

Pierre finally broke off from his phone and nodded in acknowledgment at Jake before smiling at me. His smile fell when he clocked Celeste; he obviously wasn't comfortable with the addition and he didn't hide it. I stepped in to placate him and offer the explanation I knew Jake and Elias were both eager to hear too. She retreated to her sweater so keen to get through the tale of her bribery and misplaced trust in the Venari, who it was clear by this point, even to an outsider, had negatively impacted all of our lives.

Pierre softened at the explanation and he and Jake both made a conscious effort to include her after that which it was clear she appreciated.

"So. Let's focus a little. Where the hell are we going to

go?" I looked to Pierre, then to Jake and their faces didn't fill me with confidence.

"Well." Elias piped up from the front seat as he looked back at us in the rear view mirror. "I have called in some favors from The Collective. We are staying at an old safe house way outside of the city. As long as we get out of the main routes quickly enough we will be fine. I'll stick to the quiet roads and we will disappear. They won't find us where we are going."

I wanted to feel reassured by that but my first thought was that they'd find me anywhere. I knew the lengths they were willing to go to and my recent revelations had only made Sutcliffe's thirst for power and money that bit stronger. He wasn't going to just let me go especially as my absence would no doubt put him in a less than desirable situation with the 'bidders'. I looked at Jake and he nodded as he squeezed my hands.

"Then what? We get to the middle of nowhere and then what? They will be coming. The embarrassment that my disappearance will cause them will not sit well. They won't stop." Elias rolled his eyes thinking I couldn't see. "Yeah. That's right. I am overreacting. Me, the one who has just spent the last couple of days watching them plot what they might want to do with me."

"Jeez Scarlett. Calm down would you. I know we need more but right now what we need most is space and the ability to sleep safe so we can think clearly. You didn't give me much time to sort anything out." His eyes were on the road again but I could see the side of his jaw flexing with anger.

"Elias is right baby." Rightly or wrongly I felt a little twinge of anger, like Jake was betraying me by standing up for him. I knew I was being childish and selfish but I was scared and I also knew they couldn't possibly realize the lengths the Venari were likely to go to this time. "We need space first then we can work it all out." Everyone else seemed able to cling on to some shred of optimism, but my time in that room had given me the kind of perspective on their intentions that even I had been naïve about.

I had been so preoccupied I had completely neglected to ask about Mom. "Jake. My mom?" My eyes were wide and he wrapped an arm around my shoulders.

"I took care of it. I booked her a room in a hotel and spa. Three nights. Called and said it was our treat to thank her for all her help, you know, with Dad." That didn't sound like the kind of thing Mom would drop work for. In fact, there were very few things Mom would drop work for.

"How did you get her to go along with that? What about work?"

"I called her boss… explained it was a special occasion and how stressed she had been since all the stuff with you. He was really great. Practically pushed her out the door. I also took the liberty of booking it under another name, not that she knew that, and they'll make sure she will be busy for the full seventy-two hours. So we have time to work out that too." He kissed me gently. "Don't worry about her. I will sort anything we need to keep her safe. Let's focus on you, OK?"

I nodded but I couldn't help but feel sick. How many people would I end up dragging into this? As abhorrent as it was I couldn't help thinking maybe I should have stayed and let the bidders make their play for me and come up with something later. The only small hope I could cling to was that everything else but me was small fry to them; they had no real interest in torturing the normal people and they would know by now she knew nothing. They only wanted me and at this point, the fact that every single resource they had was likely to be on finding me, was a positive thing. It meant everyone else at home was safe.

"Are you freaking serious?" Elias snapped. He was listening, uninvited.

"Get out of my head!" He glowered at me then turned to Jake and tattled on me.

"She thinks she would have been better off staying there. Keeping us all out of it." Pierre, Jake and Celeste looked up at me in unison. Jake looked broken at the mere suggestion.

"Is that what you really think? That we would all be better off? That I would be better off? You're insane Scarlett and so…" he groaned in frustration, "so selfish." I was wounded by the sharpness of his tongue. It wasn't like him to speak to me that way. "I don't want to hear you talk like that. Ever." He moved his face close to mine and Pierre and Celeste pretended to busy themselves to lessen the air of awkwardness of this private moment playing out in front of them.

"You and I. When will you realize that is what matters to me? Why isn't it enough for you?" I allowed my forehead to meet his and my breath mixed with his in the space between my lips. I wanted to kiss him so passionately and so fiercely to show him he had it wrong; that actually that was what I meant. It was all that mattered to me but it mattered most that his life; his chance to survive was more important than mine. I knew that now; that I would lie down and hand myself in if I thought for one second that my actions would spare him.

"Jake. You are enough. You are more than I could ever have hoped for." My breath was a longing whisper. "I didn't ever mean or think for a second you weren't worth me fighting for. You are all I am fighting for. I just can't carry this weight. The burden of your life. Their lives." I looked at our co-passengers and sank my head into my hands. "I want all of this to stop hurting people. I just want it to stop."

"Scarlett. Don't you see? We are here because we care. Me because I love you and the idea of anything happening to you tears me apart. I haven't functioned for the past couple of days. I can't without you, not again." He kissed my cheek and I slid my hand along his thigh. I missed his skin. "You wouldn't be achieving anything surrendering yourself. They wouldn't spare me or Elias for the sake of having you so you wouldn't be helping anyone, you'd be the one hurting them. Me, your mom, Lydia, Taylor. We all need you and what we are doing now is the only way we are going to be able to find any possibility of keeping you safe."

"He is right." Pierre was glued to his phone screen but had obviously heard every word of the conversation. "In fact, from now on... we ban all of this. This, you being the martyr, and just focus on sorting this crap out. I have faith in you and us to come up with something, how would you say? Epic?" He smirked at me and winked. Jake was smiling too. The four of us burst into spontaneous laughter either through nerves or exhaustion but even Celeste, who had been silent for the entire ride so far, managed a smile. We may be a group of misfits but she would be just fine and I hadn't forgotten the possibility I spotted for a little matchmaking with our dark-haired mystery man of a driver.

SAFE

Elias had driven us out of the city in exchange for a blissful slice of the French countryside. It was glorious and somehow rejuvenating to see the world whoosh by in a watercolor blur. It reminded me of some of the work I had seen in the Louvre and it struck me how very long ago that felt now but I took it in all the same. I had learned to grasp any hint of reality as it struck; it was impossible to tell how long it would last. The landscape gathered into focus as the van slowed. We were there.

A long, gated stony drive paved our way to a house with red tiled roof with outbuildings and what looked like stables. The sun was low in the sky and a beautiful orange light bathed the house and the endless forests beyond.

"Where are we?" Celeste shocked the group with her first words since Paris.

"The nearest town is Rambouillet. We will be fine here for

a few days." Elias lifted a huge bag from the trunk as we all stood in awe of the surroundings.

"It's beautiful." Celeste stood a few feet away; arms outstretched and her face tilted up to the warmth of the sun.

"Whose is this place?" I was fixated on the house. It was a double fronted stone house with window boxes and a roof of burnt orange tiles that glowed in the sunlight. Its dark green front door was preceded by a wicker mat. Jake swept up behind me and his hands tied together around my waist. It was almost perfect.

"It belongs to a couple I know. They are both members of The Collective so they were very sympathetic to our plight. We can have it as long as we need but I think we need to keep it to three days tops and then either have a plan or simply move on." Pierre fumbled in his pockets and pulled out a key with a Russian doll key chain. He threw it up in the air and caught it as we all fell in line and walked to the house.

"Whose is the van? It's awesome." I rolled my eyes at Jake. Guys didn't change even in the most extreme circumstances. Elias raised a hand and turned round to face us.

"That, I am proud to say, is mine." We all rolled our eyes in unison and purposefully deflated his ego by failing to ask any further questions.

Inside, the house was equally as beautiful. It was the idyll of a family home. Wooden floors bathed in soft rugs with a huge wooden dining table in front of a dresser with the mixed match china like the one in Boston. A living room big enough for ten of us drew me in with not one but three sofas and a huge armchair with high back and footstool in front of an exposed brick fire. It was amazing.

Pierre strode off ahead and made the stairs. "I call the best bedroom." He started to run and Elias marched up two at a time and shoved him out of the way with a cackle. They both landed on the top step at the same time after a few playful shoves.

"I suppose it doesn't really matter. The lovebirds get the best room right?" Elias looked down at me and Jake stood at the bottom of the stairs appreciating the house from the hall's advantageous position.

"A great and valid point." I laughed and ran up the stairs, leaving Pierre and Elias behind me, and scoped the landing. I turned right and back on myself and with luck found what had to be the master bedroom. A huge double bed with a cream metal frame dominated the room. The linen was just cream with pale blue cushions, one for each pillow, and there was a giant bay window with a beautiful seat lined with matching blue material. Clean towels lay in perfect piles on the end of the bed, which were intended, I assumed for use with the mind-blowing en-suite.

I padded round the wooden floor, relieved to feel such warmth beneath my feet as my hand ran along the side of the cast iron, roll-top bath. It had center taps and with that my mind was lost in a fantasy of soaking up his shape, his skin in a bubble bath. Nothing had ever seemed like a better idea.

"Jake. Get in here." He stepped in behind me and our brains synchronized immediately. "Later?" He smiled as he enveloped me.

"Definitely." His lips found mine and the passion from our reunion spilled out into a greedy, lustful kiss. He moved against me, until he had backed me out of the room and lined me up with the bed. "Hmmm. You... just..." He never finished the sentence.

Elias walked in hand over his eyes. "Save it for lights out kids. We need to eat and think. See you downstairs in ten." Camp leader Elias was weird but a little more fun than tortured city boy Elias.

I went to leave, to break away and go downstairs, but a nagging sensation washed over, followed immediately by a sadness so vast it took the breath out of my lungs. My chest ached; the way it did when I woke up from dreams I wasn't ready to leave behind. The newspapers, the information about his mother. I couldn't keep that secret, it was just too much. I needed to tell him at that moment before I broke and even though I felt sick, I knew I wouldn't be able to relax until I had put it out there. I battled with myself. Was it selfish to tell him? Would he be better off not knowing? Probably. But the fact was I knew I would want to know and I had to trust that he would understand. He was in the bathroom now and I could hear the faucet running.

I sat on the edge of the bed nervously fiddling with my

hair. "Jake?" He was still in the bathroom and wandered out rather distractingly wearing only his jeans. Water was dripping from his face. He pulled the towel from around his neck and caught the beads of water hanging from his nose and chin. "What is it? A vision?" He sat down next to me with such care, like I was a china doll. I shook my head. No, not a vision, actually it felt worse than that.

"I have to tell you something. Something I should have told you the moment I found out. It wasn't my secret to keep and I am so, so sorry." His hands cupped mine and he kissed them so gently.

"Shhh. I think I know what you are going to say." He raised a hand and moved my hair away from my eyes. My head was dipped; it was breaking my heart.

"I don't think..." I hoped he did know in one way. I wasn't sure I could face uttering the words out loud.

"My mom?" He raised an eyebrow and forced me to look at him.

"How?"

"Elias showed me the clippings. It's OK baby. It wasn't your job to have to tell me that. You have been through so much. Please don't worry." He leaned forward and kissed the tears away from my cheeks, my head in his hands. How could he be so strong?

"But..."

"Nothing. I think on some level I knew. After everything with my dad; then thinking about our house. How it completely lacked any sign of her. When I saw them everything kind of fell into place. I have spent my life grieving for her and I don't think that will ever change. There will always be a void left by her absence but in one way it has helped me come to terms with what I did; my dad, you know?" He pulled my face to force my averted eyes onto his. "I feel like I can let go of them both now. In the right way." He half-smiled in an attempt to lift my mood.

"I'm just so sad for you. I love you." I moved my head to his and kissed his lips slowly. His courage and proximity made me feel weightless. I wanted more of him but there was always a time and a place and there were three other people waiting on us. I stood up, smoothed down my clothes and wiped the tears from my face.

"I'll see you downstairs." He looked at me, nodded and proceeded to ruffle the towel through his hair.

"I'll be there in five minutes. And Scarlett..." I couldn't avoid staring at his skin. He was absurdly beautiful all the time. I had never seen him look more perfect. "Let it go, please... for me." I nodded and headed across the landing to check on Celeste. I found Pierre's room first and then the one with all the black clothes strewn on the bed; which was obviously where Elias was staying. I peered round the doorframe of the last bedroom and found her curled up asleep on the bed. Her bare feet poked out of the quilted comforter. This room was more like a kid's room with its single pine bed sandwiched between two painted bedside cabinets. There were shelves in there which drew my attention, full of beautiful books with illustrated spines, accompanied by a variety of carved animals. I crept out and pulled the door to a close; she needed to rest.

Downstairs an amazing smell of garlic and basil was filling the air. Pierre was in the kitchen clattering pans and cutlery amidst the sizzling of something hitting hot oil. I realized I was beyond hungry and I wandered in to see what I could pick at. It all felt so normal. I pulled up a stool at the breakfast bar as Jake arrived and sat alongside me like we were students on a summer trip.

Elias joined us and lifted himself onto the counter. "So? Where's new girl?" He looked at me and I mimed sleeping owing to the fact my mouth was stuffed with chips. "OK. Well, I guess she can just play catch up later. We have a few days then we need to move. We need to work out a way to get this public or just show them having you will be more hassle than it's worth." Jake let out a dismissive pffft sound through his teeth. "What? You don't agree lover boy?" Seemed the love-in wasn't permanent; there was still some good old-fashioned rivalry there after all.

"Well. If you want my opinion both of those options are lame. Who the hell would we go to? If they are talking about selling her off to the highest bidder… who do you think they will be genius? They will be the politicians, the rich, the ones who have a chance at calling the shots and making guys like us, disappear. That's the clever part. They know we have nowhere to go."

Elias flicked his head to clear the hair from his eyes and shook it in disagreement. "You're wrong. There is a way. We just haven't thought of it yet."

Jake couldn't drop it; it had become a male pride-off and neither would back down. I let my eyes plead with Pierre silently for a break and he graciously obliged.

"Guys. Guys. You are both kind of right. We do need a way to get this out. Let's face it, the hundreds of years of secrets thing isn't working for us anymore, but, Jake has a point. It isn't going to be as simple as picking out a friendly neighborhood cop and telling him everything. We can't be too trusting." Elias and Jake nodded in silence and I guessed that was my cue to enter the debate.

"I am with Pierre. You guys weren't there and I am sorry to sound a little self-centered here but this is a bit more to do with me than you. I am the one they are planning to sell off. You didn't see what I did in that room. I showed them how valuable I could be and they won't rest until they have cashed in on that somehow. Now, my vision was brief, but I would hazard a guess that the guys in the room, the ones who came to buy me…" I shuddered at those words, but how else could I say it? That was the reality. "…They were wealthy. That room stank of money and power. I think we are talking world leaders, billionaires. Power-hungry men who will put down whatever it takes to get a pet like me that can change the course of their future and ultimately everyone else's." Pierre snapped his eyes back to mine.

"What the hell can you do that makes you so desirable?" I felt Jake's smirk, coupled with the urge to make some loaded comment and Pierre noticed it too. "No. No. Not like that. I mean, The Collective has existed for years. A huge pool of people with all sorts of powers, so for all of this, for the stories and premonitions about you and them to be true, it has to be spectacular." I shrugged my shoulders. It didn't make all that much sense to me either.

"Well. So far we have the visions. I can move objects with my mind, or blow them up it would seem. I can hear people's thoughts and I can project my thoughts and mental images." Their expressions told me they didn't know whether to be impressed or a little scared. "But…Sutcliffe was adamant that in proving that I could do those things that meant there was more. Problem is… Well, first in a long line of problems, is that I have no idea how to summon them without extreme emotion. I don't know yet how to handle them or use them so it isn't even like I can tap into all this supposed talent. It is useless."

"Pierre knows people who can help with that. Don't you?" Elias hopped down and grabbed a handful of chips"Well I certainly know people who have trained themselves to get the best out of their powers. It's like anything; you can better your skills." He stirred the sauce and flicked the stove off. "Dinner is served." He started serving and Jake and Elias descended on the counter top like wolves.

"Err. Guys. If that's true we need them out here, like now." Jake was present but the other two were lost to their stomachs. "Guys!" They jumped and stared at me apologetically. I had their attention now.

"Pierre. Make the call tomorrow. Get them here." He nodded and I motioned their permission to eat. It was like feeding time at the zoo and the fantasy of this being a holiday of friends seemed plausible without the conversation hanging over us. It wasn't a great plan, but it was a plan and it was the best we'd had for a while.

I couldn't have articulated before how incredible an evening of laughter, great food and board games would seem after everything. We all lost ourselves and it was amazing to feel normal even if only for a bit. The darkness was never far away and I fought it off a few times but the main point I suppose was that I won and having Jake next to me made it so much easier. Every stroke of his hand teased in the anticipation for that bath,that bed; having his skin on mine and his lips to myself. My stomach fluttered with the need for him and I gave him the look that let him know it was time to escape.

I patted some concealer onto the pallid skin below my eyes. I scooped my hair up and rubbed moisturizer into the back of my neck; my eyes closed as I let the knots in my back unfurl. Jake strode into the bathroom, my eyes flicked up at his reflection as his hand slid round my waist. He flipped me round in one fluid movement and pressed me against the sink.

He had taken off his T-shirt and his shorts were unbuttoned so it was borderline impossible not to look at the trail of hair that moved down from his navel to the exposed elastic of his boxers. He pressed his mouth against mine and gently parted my lips with his tongue. He moved expertly and I was lost. My hands were in his and he led me out of the room toward the bed. I fell into it and into him and my mind was the complete opposite to how it had been the past few days. I saw only his face; felt nothing but his skin against my hands, his scent filled my nostrils and I was completely intoxicated by him. In my mind they had it wrong; they needed him. That was the one sure-fire way to make me do whatever they wanted and I prayed silently that they never got the chance.

I kissed him hungrily and let my hands rediscover the curves of his back, the length of his hair and the roughness of his chin against my palms. If The Venari didn't exist, this would be utopia, a sensory overload of everything Jake and the sensation of us giving in to each other. The pull between us felt divine and I believed, without doubt, that I was meant to be here, with him and even fighting the fight, if that gave me him.

He had undone me completely and my body and soul had surrendered to him. "Jake." My words were breathless whispers between our faces as they touched. "I'm so scared." His arms tightened around my waist.

"Don't be. I will never let anything happen to you. Ever." I knew he meant it. With that his mouth returned to mine and his hands slid up my arched back and through my hair. That was the moment I gave in. The night was ours then and nothing else mattered.

I had been in the most spectacularly deep and peaceful sleep until about three a.m. The irony of finding myself the only one in the house awake at the Witching Hour was not lost on me. I uncurled myself from Jake's sleeping grasp and headed for the kitchen.

The house felt calm and safe, even in the dead of night and I enjoyed the feeling of freedom, however fleeting it might be as I grabbed a glass of water and sat down at the long dining table. I sat at the head of the table and placed the glass in the center of my line of sight.

I stared at it and willed it to move. Come on. Now. It didn't. It mocked me with its precision motionlessness and I rubbed my eyes and tried again. My gaze was locked onto the glass and I thought of nothing but making it tip over. I envisaged over and over again the liquid marking the route of a rivulet across the polished oak and meeting the edge before cascading onto the floor. I could see that so clearly but nothing was happening. A twinge of frustration caused me to clench my fists. I wanted to learn to do these things at will, without danger or anger. I had to be in control. I had to win.

I cleared my mind and went back to the glass. I was focusing so hard that I had pains behind my eyes but I didn't break my attention. A building sense of determination was spurring me on and although I was clueless, I felt like if I waited something would surely happen.

After about two minutes of staring at nothing but the stillness of the water level and how it looked like it turned up ever so slightly at the edges where it met the glass; a ripple moved across it as though someone had shaken the table. I checked below me and my bare feet were crossed at the ankles below my chair. My eyes bore back down on the glass and it happened again, so I stilled myself and then the glass started to tremble. Sweet gratification rushed over me. They were just tiny movements in the base, but enough that I could see for sure it was no longer sitting flat. My satisfaction seemed only to increase the effectiveness of my attempts and the ripples grew stronger, as did the movements. Now a slow rumble could be heard as if a tiny drum were being beaten by my fingertips against the dead wood.

I didn't break away. I couldn't. The ripples stopped and the rumbling faded to nothing. Then with some kind of ethereal grace the glass fell onto its side; submitting to my will and the water traced the path I had envisioned for it just moments before. I didn't flinch, or make any attempt to slow the gush of the advancing liquid. I watched it play out and the glass that had fallen unnaturally still acknowledged my thoughts as it rolled in an arc until it too fell off the table and hit the soft rug below with a hollow thud.

I had done it. I had made it move. I held my breath, conscious that I didn't want to wake anyone up especially not in the pitch black. Everyone was a little too on edge to accept things going bump in the night right now. I exhaled after a pause to check there were no imminent footsteps, but the house was silent with the exception of my pounding heart and the almost audible rush of blood through my veins.

I snapped out of my trance and mopped up the water before placing the glass on the counter. I felt like I had to harness the strength while I felt it. It was so real. I was caught up in a rare moment of feeling powerful and there was a white-hot ball of energy in my stomach where I usually felt only fear; so I took the chance to use it and went through to the living room.

I sat cross-legged on the floor and closed my eyes for a moment trying to figure out what I wanted to try next. I didn't know what things would be the most useful in the fight, nor did I know what unlocked powers may be dormant; I wasn't sure if I posed a risk to myself in practicing this unorthodox way, but owing to the lack of textbooks on my particular predicament, I continued.

High on the power trip I thought I might just flex those particular muscles again. My eyes found the books piled high on shelves behind the TV and I focused on the spines, despite it being far too dark to see what they were. The concentration was the same, but the pains had gone; it was easier already and I couldn't help but smile to myself. The path of the energy from my vision fell naturally into place and it took just seconds for the book I was watching to vibrate free from its row and fall out of line onto the shelf. Small victories.

Moving objects I had managed but the challenge associated with the power of projection spurred on the excited flurry of activity in my stomach. My fingers wrapped impatiently on my knees. Clear your mind, I demanded my brain to keep still as I flicked the TV on and typed in an absurd number so the screen filled with busy white and gray flecks of static. With the volume down the room was silent but illuminated.

I stared at the TV for a moment but it made me feel nauseous, so instead I closed my eyes and thought about what I would want to see there. Jake. Always Jake. I allowed my Technicolor memory to kick in and the evening's reunion passion was the first and only memory that came to mind. I immersed myself in my mind's re-telling of events and to my surprise, it pointed out things even I hadn't remembered in the throes of it all. There had been a moment his lips drew a line of wanting across my collarbone and I had shuddered at the delicious softness of it. I had kissed each of his fingers in turn; appreciating all the times they had wound through my own to comfort or protect me. It was strangely blissful to recall the intimate details this way, though it felt somehow voyeuristic, despite the memories being all mine to re-live.

I sensed a change in the light and without wanting to lose whatever may be happening on the other side I focused just on his face. Every detail in perfect, sharp focus and the glow from the other side changed again and the white luminescence was gone and the glow was warmer now. I slowly let the light in; concentrating the whole time on his very being and I could see him. The image was no comparison to the glory of it in the flesh; but his face stared back at me in muted colors, it was there. I had projected him somehow to the screen. The mystery of it all remained but I had learned to take control and make things happen. This was good news.

The sound of wood flexing behind me broke the intensity of my concentration and the image flickered and faded back to the chaos of monochrome static. I turned to see Elias in the doorway; his eyes heavy with sleep were squinting at the bright light from the TV.

"Sorry. Did I wake you?" I flicked the TV off to spare his eyes and pulled myself up onto the sofa. He came and sat alongside me, his dark hair ruffled from what I guessed was a restless sleep.

"No. I wasn't really sleeping. But I heard a noise and then with the light I just thought I had better come down and check. Seems there is always some drama when you are around. Better to be safe." The corners of his mouth curled up.

"Ha ha. Very funny. I was just..."

"Practicing?"

"Yeah. Did you...?"

"Not really. I just saw something disappear from the screen. What were you doing?"

"Just seeing if I could make some sense of all this. Take control, you know? The one thing that has bugged me the most about this whole ridiculous situation is feeling like I have no control over my own destiny at all. But, that could be changing."

"How so?" He sounded doubtful. I never did think he bought in to the whole idea of me being some kind of savior. Even when he told me all about that first day he said I was 'their' fairy-story, not his.

"Well. I managed to replicate some of the stuff Sutcliffe made me do without the need for crazy rage so that is good. I figured if I could replicate the powers without the need for extreme circumstance I must be in with a better chance." His eyes were on me and I felt more than a little exposed. I pulled the cardigan I was wearing close to my body and he looked away sheepishly.

"Makes sense."

"So..." Having sensed the need for a change of direction I tried to think of common ground as I still found myself in a weird no-man's land with Elias. He was so hot and cold. "Where is Ava? Why isn't she with us?"

"She doesn't know about all of this yet and I want to keep it that way if possible. She is with some friends, from The Collective, but they have assured me they will be discreet. She will be safe there until we figure out what we are doing." I felt sad for him. His eyes showed how much he missed her and I tried to imagine being so selfless. Well, I was for a bit but I managed a couple of days and was barely a person by the time I got back. While it was slightly different, their story combined all the weird complexities of sibling relationships; she seemed to be all he had so there was enough of a similarity for it to eat away at him.

"Makes sense." I pushed myself up and stepped away. I let my hand rest on his shoulder for a moment and I felt him exhale at the contact. "Elias?" He looked up at me through his fallen hair. "I do appreciate what you have done, are doing for me." He didn't reply. Instead, he rested his hand on top of mine and we stayed still together for a silent second. I turned away but I could feel the residual ache from him; the need or desire to say more and my head buzzed as one or both of us fought the urge to converse in secret, within the confines of our complex heads. I repeated the word 'don't' in my head. Over and over. I mistakenly looked back at him in spite of myself and those eyes were on mine but the message was received and he quickly turned away and slid down onto the sofa, his back arched as he rested his head. I left him there in the dark. He made an audible exclamation of his frustration from the room beyond and it tugged at something in me, some strange curiosity to see if I could ever really get him to open up properly. Though it was clear that Elias had so much in his head that even a therapist may struggle; I would almost definitely be biting off more than I could chew, than anyone could. The ongoing disaster that was our 'relationship' had started in chaos and continued ever since, punctuated by the briefest moments of normality and friendliness but largely just anger, the odd hint of resentment and some strange underlying tension since the kiss that never was. Despite all that, I still took some comfort in his presence and opened my mind as I thought "I'm glad he's here though" to myself with the knowledge he would likely hear it somehow.

I only made it halfway up the stairs before my sense of accomplishment and certainty of the world around me was predictably obliterated with a solitary flash of blinding light that I knew only existed in my mind. A searing pain ran the width of the space between my ears and brought me to my knees; my hand groped for the steadying reassurance of the wooden spindles that ran up the staircase but it wasn't enough to support my ailing limbs. I felt the intrusion of the wooden stair on the base of my back as I twisted and fell and at the exact moment of that contact my mind was enveloped with a thick haze. The gray swirling mass of intensity was screaming inaudible sounds, desperately morphing into half formed images. It was a message but the content and the sender remained a mystery. I tried with all the energy I could summon to decipher it, but I was weak from the pain and my earlier triumphs. My body was spent and in no shape for another experience and even my vain attempts were sucking the power I had left from me. I could feel my energy slipping through my fingers until there was nothing I could do to stop it. I felt Elias' arms beneath me and the weightlessness that followed.

When my eyes opened amidst the relentless throbbing in my head I was back in bed surrounded by the concerned faces of Jake and Elias while Pierre and Celeste stood in the doorway like children spying on their parents. Even the dim glow of the bedside lights was too much for my eyes and I shielded my vision with my hands. Jake gently rolled me toward him to give me some shade and I caught the flicker of a glare from Elias as I turned away.

"I think you need to leave us. Let her rest." I couldn't see it but I knew Jake's teeth were clenched shut; it altered the sound of his voice ever so subtly.

"I am not going anywhere until we know what happened." Elias was stubborn as ever and I could feel the tension building inside Jake. Poor Pierre and Celeste were looking sheepishly at the ground, contemplating their escape plan no doubt.

"She is here. With me. She can tell us about it in the morning. It's five a.m. She needs to sleep. Look at her, she's exhausted." They rose from the bed in unison; chests puffed out as an electric air of testosterone hummed between them like a static charge. Elias shot me a warning glance and made his thoughts perfectly clear. He was looking for a fight and nothing would have pleased him more than to coax Jake into that tussle that had been bubbling since the hostel.

"Stop it. Now. Both of you. I am fine. You should be used to weird crap happening by now. We don't need this ridiculous show of bravado or ego or whatever the hell it is every time something strange happens round here." They each took a step back and sighed with frustration. They were more similar than they would ever care to admit. "We won't make it if we can't all just be around each other. Look out for each other." Elias shook his head silently and walked towards the door. He shoved his way through the human blockade of Pierre and Celeste who promptly turned with sheepish awkwardness and headed back to bed.

I closed my eyes signaling my disinterest in going over any of it; and to make it clear that I was mad at him for being a jealous jerk-off. The message was received because the light went off without a word and he crept into bed behind me and held me tightly in an apology.

I felt his grip loosen as he drifted off to sleep, which made me mad as I was finding it impossible to put my overactive brain on standby. I took the opportunity to work my brain with minor, silent tasks like the careful opening and closing of the door to the bathroom, and the spinning of the light above the bed. Whether or not it was because I was angry or just because I was getting better I didn't care; I was doing it.

When I woke up it was gone nine and Jake's side of the bed was empty. The warmth of his skin lingered on the sheets and I rolled over to inhale him from the pillow. What sleep I had managed to get had washed away the residual tension from the night before and I was ready to stop being so angry. The smell of coffee led me to the kitchen where the rest of the group had assembled on mismatched chairs.

"Hey. You're up?!" Pierre was uncharacteristically bouncy. He turned away momentarily before sliding me a cup of black coffee and returning to the pan of eggs bubbling on the stove. Jake walked round the counter to me and kissed my forehead. "I'm sorry." He squeezed my hand and retreated back to his stool. I gave him a silent nod; just enough to make him think he still had work to do; I didn't want to be seen as a pushover. Though I remained hugely grateful he hadn't gone in for a kiss as my façade would have been ruined for sure.

Elias looked up from the paper he was flicking through. "So? You gonna tell us what the hell happened last night?" He folded the paper calmly and tossed it into the waiting trash. "Well?" Jake straightened up his shoulders ready to start again if Elias didn't back down and I warned him off with a look.

"OK. So everyone wants a show and tell." I stomped petulantly across the room's threshold and dragged one of the dining room chairs onto the linoleum in the kitchen. I slumped into it with a complete lack of grace and it made my point perfectly. They all looked like they were waiting for detention.

"I couldn't sleep. I came downstairs and decided that the silence and the peace might just be the perfect conditions for me to test out some of the crazy stuff I can apparently do now. And guess what? I can control them, the new powers. I moved a glass. With my mind. I projected an image from my mind onto the TV. It was pretty amazing." Pierre was still stirring the eggs like that was standard. Elias and Jake were taking it all in but Celeste looked like she had seen a ghost. "Celeste, are you OK?"

"Err. Yeah. I am just trying to work this all out. You can project images? Move objects? And you need a way to out these Venari freaks right?" We all nodded in unison apart from Elias whose attitude forced him to roll his eyes instead.

"Hang on a minute. Why have we just adopted her anyway?" Elias turned to Celeste who was already looking tense; her hands balled into trembling fists. "Who are you? I mean how do we know we can trust you?" He turned back to me. "We are just so willing to discuss all this crap in front of her, but we don't even know her. She could be on their side for all we know."

Celeste shook her head, her eyes down.

"Elias. Enough. She saved. My. Life. I trust her and right now, that is good enough. Keep your thoughts to yourself if you can't be constructive." Elias picked up his glass and threw it against the refrigerator. I thrust my arm out in anticipation as if I could stop the imminent explosion of glitter-like glass shards from showering the floor. A collective flinch drew our shoulders up to our necks as we waited for impact, all within a split second. My eyes were still clenched shut when the gasps broke my waiting concentration. I looked up at their faces, white with shock and realized immediately that the sound I had been waiting for, the shattering of glass had never come. My eyes followed the path of my outstretched arm and where the glass should have hit the refrigerator, it hung there, suspended in mid-air and moving with just the tiniest of vibrations. Replicating their shock I withdrew my arm and instinctively brought my hand to my mouth to silence the sounds of surprise. The second I moved my arm the glass followed its predetermined path and hit the door with a sound that was amplified by the stunned silence in that room.

"Erm. Okaaay." Pierre looked at me with a 'what the hell?' kind of expression and the others remained perfectly quiet. Elias looked like he was kind of angry his tantrum had been interrupted. I wanted to just diffuse the situation and pretend that it hadn't even happened, but I was riled by his expression and frustrated at the 'lab rat' sensation I was experiencing again. Without thinking, I found myself on my feet and with no regard for the blades of glass littering the floor, my hand slapped his face so hard the force turned his head as far as it could go. Pierre stepped back and Jake rose to his feet. "Elias. I think you need to leave. Get some air or something. Go." I was impressed with his reserved approach; my warnings had obviously sunk in. Elias tensed his jaw and took shelter behind his hair as he vacated the room and disappeared into the hall. The door slammed with a bang that reverberated through the house and Pierre smiled at me apologetically on Elias' behalf. A pang of guilt washed over me; I hadn't meant to take it all out on him. Elias had probably a little undeservedly taken the brunt of my pent up rage about basically everything. So much of what bothered me was before I even met him, so that really was unfair, but my subconscious bargained with me; he had been a serious ass recently and that was worthy of a slap if nothing else.

"I am so sorry about him Celeste. Ignore him. He gets pretty wound up. What were you getting at before?" The events that had just unfolded had turned her face ashen white and she had been made to feel inexcusably uncomfortable. "Please. Go on."

"Hang on. Are we all just pretending that this didn't just happen?" I looked up with a sigh, aware that I wouldn't get to move along without acknowledging that apparently I can also stop things mid-air. "You just stopped that glass. Literally, it was about to hit the door and you stopped it. This is crazy. I can't believe that I just watched that. Seriously."

"Yeah, that was new. I errm, haven't done that one before." Jake was still quiet but he didn't look perplexed. If I was taking a stab at what he was feeling I would have gone with pride. "I am not being rude, but can we just, you know...focus?" Her face fell and she nodded silently but I knew that conversation wasn't over.

"Well. I was just going to say that if you can do the projection thing there must be some way we can, you know, use the media. The Internet. Stop looking for answers from the top down. If we can't trust anyone at the top. Spread the word from the bottom up?" Jake looked at me with a glimmer of hope in his eyes that I hadn't seen for some time; as if the idea were falling into place in his head like the pieces of a jigsaw.

"Spell it out for me Celeste. My brain is pretty crowded right now and I am having trouble processing." She placed her hand on mine the way I had to her more than once. Like it was her turn to help.

"Did you guys ever see that viral film? The one about challenging human rights laws? It made the news. Was watched over two billion times or something stupid?" Pierre was nodding and trying to hurry up the process of chewing his eggs so he could partake in the conversation. A look of urgency spread across his face.

"Are you talking about All Change Now?" He looked truly excited. "I saw that everywhere. They were talking about it in forums. It made every paper. It was incredible." Celeste was smiling now too; infected with his boundless enthusiasm. It rang a bell. Then I remembered. I had watched a news special on how this public movement, a grass roots approach had altered an integral part of the approach to human rights laws in more than fifty countries.

"Yes. That's it." She bit her lip and we were all on tenterhooks. "Well. The leader of the movement, the person who created and managed the viral campaign? He is my brother." Pierre was open-mouthed. Jake and I looked at each other with excitement. This was what we needed, someone with connections.

"Your brother is Jean Frances Guillame?"

"Uh huh. But he doesn't use that now. Says it is the old him. Now people call him John Piper. He was...errrmm, how would you describe? Feeling famous, so he picked himself a name that the papers would get right, you know. To soak up the glory. Anyway…"

"So how do you think he can help us?" I was becoming an expert conversation interrupter; it was not a skill I was proud of, but I was greedy to hear how this might help.

"Well… I was thinking maybe there is some way you can project things you've seen and things you know. Show the proof to the world… we can kind of start our own movement. They cannot win if everyone knows. Right?" I looked at Jake, who obviously hadn't dismissed the idea out of hand. Pierre was practically bouncing with glee at the very notion of it.

"I think that is an awesome idea. In theory. Do you think you can Scarlett? Project I mean?" Pierre was all lit up with anticipation.

"I… I don't know. Maybe. I need time to practice. A lot of time. It is too raw right now and the scale I have tried it on is negligible in comparison to what you are talking about. Plus just throwing the idea of projection around is not, in itself, an actual plan." Celeste rose to her feet, coffee in hand.

"How much time do you need… are we talking days? Weeks? Months?" She was already calculating in her head as she produced her phone from her pocket.

Jake reached over and grabbed my hand. "Scarlett. Think about this carefully. If we are really talking about showing everyone everything, this is a big deal and it has to be spot on. We can't mess around with it. Whatever we do has to remove all doubt and show them for what they are. Are you ready for that? Are any of us ready for that? I don't want you getting caught up by them again to win this." His eyes were heavy with fear. "I've just got you back." It was so feint and under his breath that Celeste and Pierre, not knowing him like I did, didn't even register it. I squeezed his hand.

"I think there's a chance it could work. So long as I get the chance to map it all out. Really get hold of it. But I'll need time and practice and I don't know how much time we can afford. Without a vision I am relying on the chance to tune into something which is still pretty challenging, except with…" And at that moment, as if he were answering my thoughts, Elias appeared in the doorway. None of us had heard him come back in.

"You think some freaky mind movie is going to make people believe? Don't you think there is a chance that people will just think it is some sick viral joke? Would you have believed it if you hadn't lived it? Besides..." He strode back across the kitchen; glass crunching below his sneakers. "Who's to say you can show them enough anyway?" I placed a gentle hand on Jake's knee; willing silently for him to let me handle it.

"Well. Thanks for the vote of confidence Elias. But, last I checked you sure as hell didn't have any better ideas. We need something and right now; I don't have anything else. Do you?"

He dragged his hands through his hair in exasperation. I

marched to where he stood and held eye contact. He didn't speak. "Didn't think so." My back turned I looked to Celeste for the next step.

"Shall I call my brother? He will find somewhere safe for us to stay so you can experiment, practice. Whatever."

Jake took the lead amidst the silence. "Yes. Thank you Celeste. That would be great. Where does he live?"

"Amsterdam. Which, I know, is not without its problems for us. But if we can get there we will be a safe enough distance apart from them right?" Her face was electrifyingly positive. It was clear she was finally feeling like she could play a role in this macabre show and she was the only one who was happy to be involved. I nodded. Distance was good. I just hoped her brother was as good as they seemed to think.

Celeste left and ran up the stairs to make some progress, leaving the three of us staring each other out; trying to rationalize.

"Passports." I had a sudden and concerning thought. "Do we all have them?" Pierre and Jake nodded. Elias was still pouting. "Well, Elias?"

"Yes. I have it with me."

"You can stay you know. You did your duty. Call it time served. No one is making you come. So if you want to stay, go back to the city and we will go without you. I could do without you whining like a bitch the whole time. We are all scared Elias. But that is no excuse to treat people like dirt. So, decide."

He flicked his hair from his eyes, which were glassy with tears he was desperately trying to hold on to. "I'm sorry. I just. Well I suppose I was naïve. I didn't realize how deep this was going to get and I am worried for my friends, my family."

"Don't you think we all are? Me? I have the whole Collective waiting on me for a miracle and family and friends that I love who are in grave danger because of things I didn't even know I could do this time last year. I have never been so scared in all my life. I didn't even realize it was possible. But we are here and for whatever reason we are in it together." I approached him and felt him recoil. I extended my arms and pulled him into me. "I know how much you have put at stake for me. I will never be able to articulate how grateful I am. And for keeping Jake safe." Jake sighed incredulously. "But please. Think carefully about what you want to do. If you decide to come with us, great. If not that's OK too but you can't keep getting all aggressive and pouty. You are better than that and it isn't helping anyone." I looked through the stupid bravado and gave in to a rare request to open my mind. I begged for him to let go of all the crap and just be normal, as much as we could. His eyes glazed and then averted, the walls went back up.

I was about to walk away when he buried his face in my shoulder and without saying a word answered all my questions. He was in for the long haul and we would just have to be mindful of how delicate he was. The dark and moody exterior was a thin veil protecting a terrified, lonely boy.

"I will go and make a couple of calls. Let them know we may be moving on in a day or so. What do you want me to do about getting some guys out here for tutorial purposes?" Pierre looked to me.

"I think it seems we won't have the luxury of time for that. Leave it for now. I will get to work on my own for starters and evaluate later." He headed out of the kitchen and left the three of us. The air of tension had lifted and Jake stood and offered Elias his hand. Elias shook it and the two of them engaged in a weird guy nod appreciation thing but it signaled at least a temporary peace agreement and that was what I needed.

Celeste bounded back down the stairs and sat back down alongside me. "OK. I didn't go into all the details with him. I thought it better not to at this stage. But, he says he knows of a safe place we can hide out and he says in terms of getting a message out he has everything we need. We can go as soon as we like." She pulled her phone out and started scrolling up and down on its screen. "There are night trains from Paris and it will only take us three to four hours. We just need to pay; they aren't so cheap."

"I can drive us. It is better than public transport. We are more likely to be seen that way. I'll plan a route." Elias disappeared again but not before I could mouth a thank you at him.

In less than twenty-four hours we had mobilized an entire plan. The route was sorted; we would take a slightly longer path round Antwerp but Elias reckoned we could do it in around six hours. The bags were packed and the van loaded.

Pierre locked up the house and hid the key at the base of the gatepost as we left. Another new place and more running. The sense of victory I had felt when I had harnessed the powers was fleeting and had evaporated now as I watched the house move out of view bathed in the evening sun. I knew this was the last sign of anything idyllic for some time.

I knew I was dreaming but I couldn't wake myself. I could even feel the rumble of the van's tires on the asphalt below me but it wasn't enough to release my mind from being so tightly bound. I could feel the pain; the same as the one on the stairs at the house; it increased in intensity and my mouth let out a silent cry. There was no sound in this weird dream state.

I was in another dark room, apart from a solitary wooden chair. It was empty and there were no signs of life. I watched it, studied the scene in case I was missing something but I couldn't figure out what the message could possibly be here.

Lights started to flicker and twinkle in my periphery before a flood of luminescent shapes merged over the chair and formed a shape. A woman. Her head was hung low; her arms were restrained behind her. She had brown blotches of old blood and dirt smeared over her skin. Her chest heaved; it rose and fell with weary, fought for breaths. She looked close to death. It definitely wasn't me. She was older, much older. Her gray hair hung dank and greasy by her face down to her knees and as the light dimmed she formed as a full, clear picture.

I shouted from within the dream, pleaded with her to tell me who she was. She remained motionless for what felt like an age. When I thought I had to surrender hope that she would not communicate with me, she lifted her head. Her eyes were shrouded in darkness. She was urging me to understand something. She knew me and I her somehow; though I had never seen that face before and my senses were alight with recognition. There was an unspoken longing for me to understand something but I couldn't make it out.

A sudden stop brought my dream to an abrupt end and I opened my eyes to see Jake looking down at me where my head lay on his lap. "Everything OK?" He was so used to me acting weird there wasn't even a hint of panic in his voice. I nodded, still lost in the dream. Who was she?

"Where are we?" I looked to the seats behind; Pierre and Celeste were still asleep against their respective windows.

"Just stopping for gas." Elias hopped out and his shadow passed my window. I pushed myself back up to let Jake out of the van and accidentally kicked the bag at my feet. It was hard. It was filled with the books I had brought away from Jacques' house, still untouched thanks to all the running away we had been doing on a near constant basis.

I heaved the bag onto my lap and opened it. I was searching for answers as usual. I pulled out a book at random, another leather bound journal that smelt of history and secrets.

I yanked it out of the pile and a small square of card fell to the floor. There were words penciled on its back.

Simply, *Me and A.*

I turned it over to see a smiling Jacques with his arm round a woman. They were smiling broadly though the picture was slightly obscured by his forearm as he had clearly taken the picture himself holding the camera as far away as possible. The face; barely recognizable, the hair was a stark contrast to what I had seen. In the picture it was graying but alive with curls and the eyes were brighter; not without weariness, but not so shallow and devoid of light. It was Alice.

A montage of realizations flickered through my mind. The dream. The attempted contact. The way the Venari always knew how to find me.

She was still alive.

How could I have missed this? It made perfect sense and I was so infuriated at how slow I had been. Alice was alive.

Jake bounded back into the van with a huge bag full of candies and potato chips. A liquorice bootlace hung goofily from his lips. "You OK? You look like you've seen a ghost." I had. I stuffed the photo back into the book and shoved them both back into the bottom of the open bag.

"No. No. I'm fine," I lied.

Elias hopped in and the van started to move. We were on our way to Amsterdam to start the unveiling of the truth, but now I knew. They would know where I was because Alice would lead them right to me. While I was confident she would buy me time – her past behavior had led me only to believe she was on my side – her face in that dream made it clear. She was broken and suffering and they would make her talk by all means necessary. Now, more than ever they would go to all lengths to find me. All this time I had been so blind to what was the most obvious plan; for them to capture and use the one person who seemed, for reasons unknown, to have this connection to me and my future. She was the next best thing and they were sucking the life from her in order to take control of mine. I felt sick again; Alice had been presumed dead for years but they had been torturing her this entire time. The realization that almost nothing was left to chance struck me. If they hadn't got me in Salem when they did, it would only have been a matter of time. I may have hurried things up with my visions and the digging for information, but clearly this went deeper and they were always coming for me.

I looked around at my fellow passengers, my friends and the boy I loved. A deep-rooted fire burnt within me, a fierce need to protect them. I would stop this. I had to.